Bluebonnet Bride

MOLLY NOBLE BULL

Scrivenings
PRESS
Quench your thirst for story.
www.ScriveningsPress.com

Published by Scrivenings Press LLC
15 Lucky Lane
Morrilton, Arkansas 72110
https://ScriveningsPress.com

Edited by Kathi Macias.

Printed in the United States of America.

Paperback ISBN 978-1-64917-088-0

eBook ISBN 978-1-64917-089-7

Library of Congress Control Number: 2020949284

Cover by www.bookmarketinggraphics.com.

All scriptures are taken from the KING JAMES VERSION (KJV): KING JAMES VERSION, public domain.

All characters are fictional, and any resemblance to real people, either factional or historical, is purely coincidental.

Published in association with Joyce Hart, agent, Hartline Literary Agency

I loved *Bluebonnet Bride* by Molly Noble Bull. I've loved all her books I've read. This novel is set in two states, and Molly painted the setting with broad strokes of authenticity. And her characters drew me into their lives, making me love them through the end of the story. The story had enough twists and turns to keep me turning pages. You won't want to miss this wonderful contemporary tale.

— LENA NELSON DOOLEY - AWARD-WINNING, BESTSELLING AUTHOR OF *FOUR SEASONS OF LOVE*

This book is dedicated to Charlie, Bret, Burt, Bren,
Jana, Linda, Angela,
Bethanny, Dillard, Hailey, Bryson, Grant, Grace,
Kathryn, and Jeanette

But to God give the glory.

SCRIPTURE

If you forgive others the wrongs they have done you,
your Father in Heaven will forgive you.
But if you do not forgive others,
then your Father will not forgive the wrongs you have done.

— MATTHEW 6:14-15, KJV

ACKNOWLEDGMENTS

I would like to thank Jeanette Pierce, Katherine King Brocato,
Mona Christensen,
and
Bethanny Bull
For their help during the writing of this novel.

1

She'd had another of those horrible flashbacks straight from her teenage years.

Gina Hollister sucked in her breath, releasing it slowly. The words, *You're incredibly stupid*, continued to play in her mind. Incredible. She hadn't known the meaning of the word when she heard it for the first time. But she knew *stupid*—even back then.

She stepped out of her car and stood there for a moment with her purse on the top of her ten-year-old white Buick. Why did this happen now? It was Friday morning, and she had an important meeting with the father of one of her students, a man she'd never met. Would the flashbacks ever end?

Her purse strap slid toward her, with the brown loop hanging over the car window. She reached for it—one second too late. Her handbag turned upside down, landing on the concrete parking lot. She'd forgotten to zip it up—again. Everything inside spilled out with a cacophony of tinkling and jingling.

Gina counted to ten. She was a PhD now and an intelligent person, not an accident-prone airhead. She merely had a problem with depth perception and dyslexia. *Merely?*

Dyslexia had colored her entire life with a black marker.

She'd studied hard for years. Would she ever be normal? Was there such a thing?

Lord, she prayed, *make me like everyone else.*

Her tube of lipstick rolled beneath her car. *Oh, no!* Her jaw and both fists tightened simultaneously. She leaned forward and bent down, careful to keep the hem of her long white dress from brushing the pavement. Slowly she gathered every item she'd dropped.

Except the lipstick.

It rolled beyond her reach. If she wanted it, she must kneel on her hands and knees. Her dress could become a disaster.

She wanted it. The lipstick was the last tube in existence in her favorite shade of peach. She set her handbag on the pavement beside her, folded her skirt up, and bent forward. Derriere elevated, she reached for the tube. Her fingers touched its smooth, slick surface; gripping the lipstick, she rocked back on her heels, preparing to rise.

"What have we here?" somebody said from behind her.

She recognized the man's voice. She'd heard it the previous night when she listened to messages left on her cell phone.

"Need any help?" he asked.

Gina looked up, and her breath froze in her throat. Steve Bryson looked down at her. She'd never seen him until that instant but knew him immediately. That low, slightly raspy voice couldn't belong to anyone else. Yet there was something besides his voice that seemed familiar. She frowned. What could it be?

He reached out as if to help her up. She took his hand, and a tingle shot through her. *Wow!* Gina stood up beside him. She'd expected him to be handsome, but nobody told her he was so tall, so young-looking, so electrifying. Like his daughter, Steve had thick, dark-brown hair and brown eyes. But that didn't begin to describe him.

He would have no difficulty describing her, she realized. She probably looked like an extra on the set of a historical western movie. If the laughter she heard in his voice and saw in his eyes were any indication, he'd been watching her for a while.

In a white ankle-length gown and matching cowboy boots, Gina was dressed as a character in a western novel, set in 1881 Texas, for the end of the school year costume party. Should she try to explain why she was wearing a costume to their first meeting? Or would a billionaire like Steve Bryson even be able to comprehend a situation like hers?

The party was originally scheduled for next week. Gina was about to walk out the door of her apartment when she remembered. Nicole had changed the date of the event to later this morning, and she expected Gina to help with the party decorations. No time for that now.

At the last possible moment, Gina had changed from her navy-blue business suit to this outfit. She must look out of place, to say the least. If only she could climb into her car and vanish before Mr. Bryson learned the identity of the lady he'd helped to her feet.

A man as rich and sophisticated as Mr. Bryson would expect a PhD to dress in keeping with her position at the university, not to mention the fact she hadn't answered any of his questions. *In the words of my grandmother, I must seem as strange as what Grandma would call a mad scientist.* She forced a smile.

He returned her smile, studying her carefully.

She ran her fingers across the embroidered design in blue wool thread on the front of her dress. Why did she keep feeling they met a long time ago? *He reminds me of someone. But who?* If only she could remember how she knew this guy, if in fact she did.

"Are you Sacagawea?" he asked, a teasing glint in his deep, dark eyes. "The historical Native-American girl we read about?"

Sacagawea? "I'm Cheyenne," she said, dragging out each syllable. "But how could you possibly know my family history?"

His grin highlighted dimples, one on each cheek. "Glad to meet you, *shy Ann.* I'm *shy Steve.*"

Bold Steve suited him better.

"What brings you to Austin, Texas?" he asked.

"I live here, and I'm wearing a costume, sir, taken from a character in a story. This dress has nothing to do with Native-Americans. However my great-grandmother *was* Cheyenne."

Why was she revealing information to a man she barely knew? She should relax, calm down.

Steve pressed his lips together. His mouth turned up at the edges. "May I direct you somewhere, ma'am?"

"As a matter of fact, I'm on my way to your office. I'm Dr. Gina Hollister."

He blinked, a look of astonishment on his face. "You? I would never have guessed." A glint of humor danced in his eyes before he peered down at his watch. "As pleasant as it is out here in the sunshine, we might be more comfortable in my office."

His office would be cool and, perhaps, luxurious. She decided her explanation could wait, at least until they went inside.

Steve set the palm of his hand against the small of Gina's back, guiding her across the parking lot as if he thought she couldn't find the way on her own. Well, she knew where his office was and didn't need any help getting there, but she had no intention of pulling away and drawing more attention to herself.

They strolled toward the modern high-rise, then entered Steve's glass-and-brick reception area on the third floor. Gina waited while he opened the door to his private office.

As soon as she stepped onto the marble tile floor, she sensed Steve's presence all around her. She watched him go over and stand behind a large oak desk.

"Please sit down." He motioned toward an empty chair.

"If you don't mind, I'd rather stand." Gina wore a costume, while he wore a navy suit and a royal blue tie. Her hands shook.

What might she feel if she sat down and attempted to answer more of his questions? She had to pull herself together.

She took a big breath of air, then released it slowly. "And again, Mr. Bryson, excuse the way I'm dressed. I'm on my way to a party my business partner and I are giving for our students later this morning." She shrugged because she couldn't think of anything else to do. "I promised the children I'd wear a costume."

"No explanation necessary. You look great."

"As I said earlier, some of my ancestors were Native-Americans."

"I thought most Native-Americans had dark hair," he said, "not long auburn hair like yours. And your eyes are blue."

"I'm only one-eighth Native-American. But my mother was one-fourth. Mom came from Oklahoma originally. That's significant up there."

"So I've heard."

I sound pathetic, telling him my family history. Annoyed with herself and still trembling inside, she knew she was talking too fast. Her heart raced as if it were about to jump out of her chest, and her forehead and the palms of her hands were moist.

"You look a little overheated," Steve said. "Would you care for something cool to drink? We have iced tea, or I might be able to come up with a soda or two."

"Nothing for me, thanks."

Gina dropped down onto the cushioned armchair he offered her earlier because she no longer trusted her shaky knees to support her. He settled into the oversized armchair across the desk from hers.

Every movement Steve made from the moment she first saw him was executed with the grace of a professional athlete. She'd always admired people who handled their bodies well, wondering what he thought of her little fiasco in the parking lot. A professional attitude was required if she hoped to keep his daughter as a tutoring student until Amanda and her father left for Colorado. Presently such a goal appeared to be drifting from her grasp.

Without taking his eyes from hers, he picked up a yellow pencil and tapped it lightly on the desk. His penetrating appraisal made her self-conscious. Still she met his gaze head-on.

"My assistant has been coaxing you to take the job I'm offering," he said. "I want to thank you for agreeing to discuss it with me."

"I'm doing it for Amanda, Mr. Bryson."

"I gathered that. I know my daughter is grateful. You see, I need your help, Doctor."

Despite his self-assured persona, he sounded a bit desperate, and sort of kind as well. "I appreciate your show of respect, sir, but you don't have to call me Doctor. It's not as if I'm a medical doctor."

"Thanks for the clarification, *Doctor*." He grinned. "But I must go to Colorado this summer on business. I own a home there about thirty miles from Durango, and I plan to take my daughter with me."

"Yes, I know, and a rather large home I understand."

"Then you might also know my mother-in-law thinks Amanda must continue her tutoring sessions this summer or risk slipping farther behind in her studies next fall."

"That was my recommendation."

"Could you find it in your heart to go to Colorado this summer and tutor her?" His voice held a sense of urgency, tempting her to give in.

"I'm sorry," she said, gathering her thoughts. "You're wasting your time if you're trying to persuade me to change my mind. But I'd be glad to provide you with the names of several people with the same credentials as mine."

"I thought of that, but Amanda wants you." Steve grew silent for a moment. "I'm sure you're aware of Amanda's reading and spelling problems."

"I've been her private tutor since before I entered graduate school."

"Amanda's only fourteen, Doctor. I believe she's smart as well as beautiful. I would think her so-called problem would be hard to deal with."

Gina's blink ended in a nod.

He hesitated. "In your opinion wouldn't Amanda's so-called problem be especially difficult for someone at her age?"

"Reading and spelling problems are always difficult to deal with regardless of I.Q., physical appearance, or age."

"I suppose that's true." He cleared his throat. "As you must know, Amanda lost her mother recently in a boating accident." His eyes held a trace of sorrow. "I always knew Myra wasn't much of a sailor, but ..."

"I thought a lot of Mrs. Bryson, sir, and it was tragic she had to die so young."

"Amanda knows you liked her mother." He paused again.

Gina drummed her fingers on the arm of her chair, waiting for him to continue. His pause seemed to last forever.

"Myra was my ex-wife before she was my late wife," he said at last. "I'm Amanda's only parent now. Myra and I divorced when she was seven, so Amanda doesn't know me very well. Myra and her mother wanted it that way, and I didn't want my only child to go through a custody fight."

Mr. Bryson sounded gentle, kind, and nothing like the horrible womanizer Myra had described. Gina wanted to believe him, but it was out of the question. Myra had made it clear. Steve Bryson was good at pretending to be one person, while being another.

He has to be lying.

STEVE WATCHED HER FOR A MOMENT. "You've helped Amanda with her studies—a lot. You've helped her cope with the death of her mother, too, and all the other changes in her life. For that I thank you. Again, I sure hope you change your mind and take the job."

Gina opened her mouth to reply.

"I'd also like you to help my daughter and me bridge the gap at this critical time in her life."

"Perhaps you should have tried bridging the gap a long time ago, Mr. Bryson."

"I wanted to," he admitted. "Believe me. I won't go into all the reasons, but until recently seeing my daughter was almost impossible."

Impossible? According to Myra Bryson, Steve rarely tried to see Amanda after the divorce.

"I'll have to be gone at least part of the time while we're in Colorado," he said. "So of course Amanda will need to be with someone I can trust."

"Are you saying you want to hire me as Amanda's nanny?"

"Not at all. I know you have a doctorate in educational psychology. I'm willing to pay you well for your services during the time you're working for me. More in fact than you'd make teaching at the university."

"As I told your assistant and your lawyer, my partner and I are planning to start a business this summer near Hill River, Texas, so I can't very well do that and tutor Amanda in Colorado at the same time."

He lifted his eyebrows. "Sounds interesting. What kind of business are we talking about?"

"We plan to build a center for children with learning problems as soon as our loan goes through."

"If you don't mind me asking, has financing been a problem?"

"I do mind you asking."

"Sorry. But I might be able to help you in that area."

"Oh?"

"I sometimes buy property for my employees and allow them

to pay me back slowly, without any kind of down payment and at a fair interest rate."

"You mean a sort of rent-to-own agreement?"

"Exactly."

Her partner, Nicole Danton, didn't know it yet, but their loan application had been turned down by yet another local bank. The loan officer Gina visited on Wednesday said neither of them had established enough credit to make such a loan feasible. Nicole would be shattered by the news. Now all Gina had to do was find the right time to tell her.

They were counting on building the center. When the dream seemed beyond their reach, here was Steve Bryson, offering them risk-free credit.

Well, almost.

Steve was watching her from his side of the oak desk. He'd done a great sales job on her; she was beginning to weaken. Could he possibly know she was considering his offer seriously?

The rent-to-own agreement appeared to be the only real chance she and Nicole had. Nevertheless the two should probably discuss the matter before Gina accepted a whole summer of work. On the other hand it would be nice to have the issue settled before informing Nicole they had a serious problem. But Steve's daughter was the main cause of her concern. For Amanda's sake, maybe she should go on and accept his offer.

Amanda was motherless now. Soon she would be moving in with a father she barely knew. The young teenager would need to be with someone she could trust as she struggled with all the problems her new life was sure to bring. Amanda needed a stabilizing influence in her life, now more than ever.

For weeks Amanda had begged Gina to accept the employment opportunity her father offered. The teenager would be pleased if Gina accepted.

If the sudden look of excitement on Steve's face reflected his thoughts and feelings, he must sense Gina was seriously considering his offer after all. As the head of a multibillion-dollar corporation like Bricot, he was probably accustomed to having his own way in business as well as with women. But it would be a snowy day in Austin before Gina fell under his spell.

"You're taking the job," he said, cutting into her thoughts, "aren't you?"

"I think so."

His smile lit up his handsome face. "Welcome aboard." His dimpled grin became a heartfelt chuckle.

In spite of her misgivings about Steve, Gina found the rich, unrestrained sound of his laughter almost as comforting as his voice. "I'll want some ground rules," she said, "before I sign a contract to go to Colorado with you and Amanda."

"What kind of ground rules?"

"I don't know yet. I know what I want to say, but I haven't written anything down. When I do I'll let you know."

He appeared to hold in a smile or maybe a belly-stretching laugh. His eyes twinkled as if he found her amusing. "I can hardly wait to see those rules of yours, Dr. Hollister."

2

hy did Steve grow silent all at once? What was going on?

"Oh, and I'll want you to stay the entire two months," he finally added. "I'll have to check to see when my lawyer has some free time to sign the legal agreements."

At first Gina didn't answer. Everything was happening too fast. She hardly had time to catch her breath, much less say anything. "Speaking of checking," she said after long pause, "I'll need to speak with my business partner, Nicole Danton. I want to make sure she's okay with all this."

Steve looked pleased with himself as he straightened some papers on his desk. "Of course."

He was captivating, but Gina had not forgotten her reasons for mistrusting him. "Would it be possible for me to receive a pay advance?" she asked, knowing she was stretching the boundaries a bit. "I'd like to have it today, if possible."

"No problem."

He opened a desk drawer, pulled out a checkbook, and filled it out. Then he reached across his desk and handed her the check. Steve leaned back in his chair, put his hands together behind his head, and stretched.

He certainly seemed relaxed. She sure wasn't. His cute-guy image would be hard to miss, not to mention the high cheekbones, perfectly formed nose, and those dark, wide-set eyes. Yet Gina kept remembering everything Myra had said about him. If he were an honorable man, she'd be trying to figure out how to attract his interest on a more personal level. As it was, Gina wanted to close the business deal and leave his office as soon as possible. She glanced toward the door.

"There's something else I'd like to mention before you leave," he said.

She forced a calm response. "What might that be?"

"I'd like to see the property I'll be financing, and I'd like you to drive out to the building site with me. I've heard of the little town of Hill River for years, and I'm looking forward to seeing it for the first time."

A thought came to her. Myra Bryson had said Steve was a womanizer. If he was she might be getting sucked into an uncomfortable situation. "You want me to drive to Hill River with you, sir? Why?"

"It's a formality." Steve sent her a long appraisal. "I believe I can visualize the project better if I see it through your eyes."

Obviously he found her entertaining. Why else would his mouth curve upward every time she said or did something?

"I'll admit I don't usually do this. In your case I thought it might be a good idea." He cocked his head to one side; his smile widened. "We'll be working together closely for the next few months. I thought it would give us a chance to become better acquainted and make plans for the trip."

"All right," she said. "You're my future boss. Making plans for the trip does make sense. When would you like to leave?"

"Let's see." He glanced down at a paper on his desk. "Today is Friday. I'll pick you up tomorrow afternoon around two. And wear something casual. We'll be having a picnic before driving home." A dash of amusement warmed his smile. "I'll be bringing my swimsuit. Feel free to bring yours too, if you're so inclined."

Gina stiffened. A fast comeback flooded her, conceived in her mind to make Steve as uncomfortable as he'd made her and filled to the brim with sarcasm. Her moral code stopped her. Instead of hitting back she'd turn the other cheek. For Gina to retaliate meant being hit twice, once by the offensive comment and again when her own harsh comeback crushed her heart.

Phil Arnold's face formed in her mind. She hardly knew Steve Bryson, yet he somehow reminded her of her former fiancé. How strange was that? Not only did both men like to get a rise out of her, they used some of the same tactics. Steve called her Shy Ann. Phil had called her Teach. She might have thought Phil and Steve were twins separated at birth. But Steve had olive skin, while Phil was a blue-eyed blond like Gina's handsome father.

She lifted her chin a notch, focusing her gaze on the ceiling not far above his head. "It's late, sir. I must go. I want to thank you for taking time out from your busy schedule to talk to me and for your offer of help. I'll see you Saturday afternoon at two."

And she wouldn't be bringing a swimsuit.

Gina turned toward the door, praying she'd be given the poise and strength to leave Steve's office without bumping into something or otherwise embarrassing herself. In the hall outside his office, she sent up another prayer, thanking the Lord for making it through the interview with Steve.

STEVE BRYSON GAZED out his floor-to-ceiling window on the third floor, watching Gina stalk across the parking lot in the direction of her car. He grinned. How many other executives were standing at their windows, doing the same thing? He'd expected Amanda's tutor to be professional; it never entered his head she'd be so beautiful.

He continued to watch until Gina's white Buick disappeared from view. She'd said she was going to a party for her students, and his daughter would be there. Amanda liked ginger cookies as much as Steve did. He'd have his secretary order some, cut in the shape of the Gingerbread Man, and sent to the party as soon as possible.

Gina might like him a little more for sending them, and Steve did want her to like him. *Gina*. Was he trying to impress the good doctor? And so what if he was?

Funny, the name Gina didn't fit her somehow. He reached for his cell phone, touching in his lawyer's number. After a moment the lawyer picked up.

"Mr. Bryson, hello."

"Hi, Joe. Got a minute?"

"For you? Sure."

"Remember the investigation I had you do on Dr. Gina Hollister?"

"The one I hired a private investigator to run?"

"Yeah. Well, I never read the report. You read the main points over the phone. I'd like to read the whole thing. Mind sending a scan or faxing me a copy?"

"Glad to. I'll get right on it."

"Thanks, Joe. And I hope you have a great day."

Ten minutes later Steve's secretary came into his office with a smile on her face. "Here's the fax you wanted, sir."

"Thanks, Josie. You're a peach."

She blushed and left the room.

He read the fax quickly, finding it a little dry. The facts were there, but he wanted more. He would have his assistant, Drake Rather, see what else he could dig up. Steve found Dr. Hollister extremely exciting and wanted to learn all he could about her.

BESIDES MYSTERIES AND BIBLE PROPHECY, Gina's reading interests consisted of sweet historical romance novels and westerns. An old-fashioned girl, she preferred rural areas and small towns to city lights and heavy traffic. She'd mapped out a route from Steve's office to the party, keeping her off the freeway. Now seated behind the wheel and waiting for the traffic light to change, Steve's words came back to haunt her.

His meaning was clear. Steve was talking about more than a swimsuit when he said, "Feel free to bring yours too, if you're so inclined."

Well, Gina was not "so inclined." The entire scene in the parking lot and in his office played in her mind as if it were happening now. She needed to focus her eyes and mind on the road ahead and keep driving.

She drove on, glancing out a side window, recalling the way this part of the city had looked when she was a child. It was a farming area then. Now the entire area was dotted with lovely homes for families. Amanda Bryson's grandmother, Mrs. Lola Ford, lived in one of them—a white colonial behind a guarded gate.

Mrs. Ford's two-story house was one of the largest and most elegant homes in Austin. Everybody said so. Gina also admired the lovely "summer house" directly behind it.

More names from her past she didn't want to remember appeared on her mental screen. Stella and Trudy were bullies from Gina's high school days. She might never forget the hateful things they said and did, and they lived in this neighborhood.

The light changed from green to yellow. Almost immediately, it turned red. Her foot touched the break pedal. If only something as simple as stepping on the break would remove unwelcome thoughts and memories from her mind.

Did Steve know Gina was a Bible believer? The thought had just popped into her head, but surely he knew. Someone would have told him. She dismissed the question.

She hadn't known how to respond to Steve's teasing without sounding sarcastic. Now she'd left his office, and dozens of snappy comebacks she would never use but would have put him in his place dominated her thoughts.

To be fair Steve would probably agree to every item in the agreement she wanted him to sign. The joking around could be his way of making her feel at ease.

Gina supposed she should give him the opportunity to prove himself. But why was Steve Bryson suddenly in her life? They had nothing in common except love for Amanda, and she didn't think he was a churchgoer. It wouldn't be easy, but maybe she should take what she learned in church as a child to heart and help him in some way.

THE COSTUME PARTY was in an old public building. By the time Gina arrived, the younger children had gathered around the refreshment table, wearing masks and colorful costumes. The older students in white aprons were standing around too, attempting to look busy. But where was Amanda?

A little boy dressed as Superman stood right in front of her. Gina smiled. "Do you know where Amanda Bryson is?"

He shook his head. "I'm with Miss Danton's group, and I'm new. I don't know anybody."

"Thanks, Superman."

Gina searched for Amanda. She didn't find her, but when Nicole Danton waved from across the room, she waved back. Always full of surprises Nicole looked hilarious. Gina couldn't be sure, but her business partner must be the Big Bad Wolf.

The headpiece alone made Gina want to laugh out loud, with those pointed wooly ears and outrageous red tongue dangling over Nicole's right shoulder. Gina wondered how a petite person like Nicole could hold up such a heavy mask.

Nobody fit the image of the Big Bad Wolf better than Steve Bryson, she mused. He probably wouldn't consider attending a party for children, much less wear a costume.

RED, blue, and yellow balloons floated in the air, attached to gold strings. They were taped around doors, windows, and on every wall. She couldn't have been more surprised to see how cheerful her partner had made the normally drab hall. *Good job!* Nicole had managed without her help.

But where was Amanda? And where did the photograph on the wall come from?

Gina went and stood in front of a blown-up photograph of a castle. As a child she'd loved stories about castles and knights in shining armor. She read the inscription under the picture:

"Travelers love German castles. Neuschwanstein Castle was built by King Ludwig II of Bavaria. Some call him the 'Fairytale King.'" Too bad she couldn't afford trips to Europe, so she could visit interesting locations.

She joined a line of children at the refreshment table. "Have any of you seen Amanda Bryson around here this morning?"

Everybody shrugged. Then a little girl wearing a red hood pointed to a door on the other side of the room. "I know who Amanda is, and I saw when she went to the kitchen."

"Thanks, Little Red Riding Hood." Gina smiled. "It's not every day I get to meet a celebrity like you."

The child looked down at her costume, grinning from ear to ear.

So Amanda was in the kitchen. Gina could go right in and talk to her. Instead she'd give Amanda a few minutes. She placed a tiny sandwich and a cup of ice cream on her plate, then glanced over at Nicole.

The children were eating ice cream and drinking red punch. Nicole had removed her mask and was also drinking punch while having a conversation with some of her students. Gina didn't want to interrupt.

She went and stood in one corner of the room. An opened newspaper lay on the table next to her. She glanced down at the headlines: "World Famous Scientist Makes Incredible Discovery." The name Ward Dremont was written in smaller print. Wasn't he the horrible scientist she and her grandma read about, the one hoping to turn humans into super-humans or maybe super-animals?

Gina had first heard of him on television. Then the conversation with Grandma sparked her interest, and they'd agreed. Mad Scientist was the only name that fit a scientific genius like Ward Dremont, who reminded her of someone.

She was about to reach for the newspaper for a better look when Nicole started toward her from the other side of the room, carrying her refreshment plate with her. She still wasn't wearing her mask.

Nicole grinned. "Hi."

Gina nodded, smiling right back at her friend. "Hi, yourself."

Nicole's infectious grin started in her eyes, and from the animated expression on her face, she had something on her mind she was dying to share. *Cute* described Nicole perfectly. Her short black hair curled softly around her pixy face as it always did. Gina still wanted to read the newspaper but might have to wait until she got home and read her own copy.

"Sorry I couldn't be here any sooner." Gina motioned toward the poster of the castle on the other side of the room. "Where did the picture of the castle come from?"

"It was there when I arrived. Apparently a travel convention was held here recently. Guess they forgot to take that one down. So ..." Nicole giggled girlishly. "Out with it. I know you have something you want to tell me about your conversation with Steve Bryson. I can hardly wait to hear it."

"The meeting went well." For now Gina hoped to leave out the part about accepting the job offer.

Nicole shook her head. Ebony curls trembled. "I don't think I've heard all you have to tell. Come on, Gina. I'm asking for details. Is Amanda's father as big a flirt as we've always heard?"

Gina shrugged because she didn't want to talk about Steve Bryson. "As I said, the interview went well." She glanced toward one of the yellow balloons. "By the way, the decorations are great. Sorry I couldn't help."

"No problem. The older children filled in. You can do the decorations next time."

Nicole put her plate on the table next to the newspaper and attempted to consume an especially runny ice cream cone. A drop of strawberry ice cream dripped down the front of her brown velvet wolf costume.

"Lick around the edges," Gina suggested.

"I'm trying."

Gina knew better than to tackle something as potentially messy as an ice cream cone and instead dipped a plastic spoon into her cardboard cup. The cold sweet taste of vanilla soon filled her mouth.

Nicole appeared to be holding up rather well if, as Gina thought, her boyfriend was on the verge of breaking up with her. Nicole and Robert went out on the previous night. Gina was eager to hear how things turned out, but it was up to her friend to choose the time and place to answer those kinds of questions.

"You've stalled long enough." Nicole sent her a heart-to-heart appraisal. "I want to know what happened during the interview with Steve Bryson."

"I'm not stalling. Mr. Bryson is merely the father of one of my students. Amanda lived with her mother until Myra's untimely death in the boating accident. All I wanted to do was meet her father, since Amanda will be living with him now."

"Are you sure something isn't going on between you two? I saw a certain look in your eyes when I mentioned him. I haven't seen you smile like that in ages."

Gina hesitated, searching for a comeback to end the war before it got started. Then one of Nicole's students came into view.

Dressed as a fairy princess, she came right up to them. Her shimmering pink costume brushed against Nicole's velvety one. The little girl stood on tiptoes, whispering something in Nicole's ear. Glitter-dust, like pink snowflakes, fell around their feet. Then Nicole nodded and smiled, patting the child on the shoulder, and the fairy princess went to join the other children. But would Nicole still smile when she learned Gina accepted the job Mr. Bryson offered?

After another long moment, Gina broke down and told Nicole about the new job.

"Why would you consider taking a job like that?" Nicole demanded.

She'd sounded angry. However, Gina knew Nicole well enough to know it was an act, designed to ruffle Gina's feathers a little.

"You know we're planning to build a learning center this summer," Nicole went on. "Do you expect me to supervise the work all by myself?"

"The bank loan didn't go through." The edges of Gina's mouth turned up, hoping to put a positive stamp on the news. However, she knew from experience her smile probably looked forced. "Mr. Swain at the bank said we didn't qualify, but ..."

"But?" Nicole looked as if she'd lost her last friend.

"I'm sorry. If I go to Colorado and tutor Amanda, Mr. Bryson promised to make us a rent-to-own loan so we can build the center. I think we're lucky to have gotten a deal like that."

"I can't believe this guy," Nicole fumed. "Getting you to accept his employment offer the way he did was bad enough. Offering to give us a personal loan to sweeten the deal? Well, I have to ask why, Gina? What does Bryson get out of all this? You?"

3

Gina shook her head. "If you think Steve Bryson gets me, you're wrong. His ex-wife died a month or so ago, and—"

"I know all that."

"You couldn't know he wants a father-daughter relationship with Amanda now. I just found out myself, and Amanda's indifferent to him."

"I don't blame her after what you told me."

"Besides helping Amanda with her studies," Gina went on, "all he wants me to do is help him communicate with his daughter."

"What could you do? Hold his hand?"

"Nicole."

Nicole shook her head. "Frankly I don't trust the man. I can't believe the way Bryson forced you into this."

"He didn't exactly force me. I could have refused."

"You can't mean you really intend to go to Colorado."

"I told him I would. It was the only possible answer to our problem."

"I can think of a few others."

Gina laughed at her peace-loving friend. "Put down those tiny fists. You look ridiculous."

"Not a chance. I'm not the Big Bad Wolf for nothing." Nicole punched the air to make her point.

Nicole's heavy gold college ring with its blue stone captured the sunlight coming from one of the east windows. The third finger of her left hand was still naked.

Gina empathized with her friend. Nicole had hoped Robert would give her an engagement ring. Gina had once hoped she'd be able to keep hers.

"Why Colorado?" Nicole asked, bringing Gina back to the present.

"I was told Mr. Bryson has business interests there."

"There and everywhere else around the world," Nicole mumbled. "Men like Steve Bryson will go anywhere as long as there are plenty of women around."

"Mr. Bryson couldn't be as bad as we heard he was. Nobody could. Spending the summer in Colorado sounds like fun. His lawyer said we'll be staying in a very large house in the style of old Germany. I suppose they use it as a ski lodge. Doesn't that sound exciting?"

"I'd say it sounds convenient—for a man like Steve. Has he also employed a hundred violinists to play sweet music under your window every night? Or does he plan to hold you captive in the tower of a German-style castle somewhere?"

"Be reasonable, Nicole. Unless I do this we can forget about our plans to build a learning center in the Texas Hill Country."

"The loan would have gone through."

Gina shook her head. "No, it wouldn't have. Now it will." She placed her hand on her friend's shoulder. "This is an answer to our prayers."

"It's sure not an answer to mine."

Out of the corner of her eye, Gina saw Amanda Bryson start across the room in their direction. "Amanda's heading this way," she whispered. "Let me be the one to tell her I've decided to accept the job."

As they watched Amanda stumbled, possibly on a crack in the rough concrete floor. She caught herself and looked around to see if anyone was watching.

Gina looked down but not soon enough. Her eyes merged with Amanda's dark gaze. A narrow streak of red punch stained the front of Amanda's blue dress and a corner of her white apron.

Sympathy flowed to Amanda because Gina knew exactly how the teenager felt. From experience she also knew that to say anything about it would only make matters worse.

"How are things going back in the kitchen?" Gina asked casually as Amanda stopped in front of them.

"I spilled some punch on the floor and a few other places." She tried to cover the stain on her apron with her right hand. "Other than that everything's fine."

"Did you mop up the mess?"

"More or less."

"I'll go in and check," Nicole put in. She turned to a teenage boy standing nearby. "Come on, Freddie. Get over here. Make yourself useful."

The look on Freddie's face as he and Nicole walked off reminded Gina of a dog caught in a canine catcher's net.

Gina grinned then sniffed the air. "Do I smell gingerbread?"

"You mean this?" Amanda reached in the pocket of her apron and pulled out a cookie cut in the shape of a gingerbread man. "Daddy had two dozen of these sent over. They arrived a few minutes ago. Guess he thinks I'm still five years old."

"Sending cookies to the party was a nice gesture on your father's part, Amanda. They're perfect for the younger children."

Amanda went over to the trash can in the corner, discarded her cookie, and glanced back at Gina. "Last night Daddy called again. He still wants me to go to Colorado this summer."

"I know."

"Know? You talked to him?"

"Before I came in here. I told him I'd go to Colorado after all."

Amanda's dark eyes sparkled. "You did?"

"Yes."

"Oh, Dr. Hollister, I've been praying you'd say that. I'd about given up hope. I mean you and Dr. Danton are still planning to build the center, aren't you?"

"Yes but it wouldn't have been completed in time for the fall term anyway. So I got to thinking. What's the rush? We'll start building in September."

Nicole came out of the kitchen, a dishcloth in each hand, and started toward them. Gina knew Nicole didn't want her to go to Colorado, and she'd do all she could to stop her. Gina hoped that by the time she left, Nicole would accept her decision.

Besides hoping, Gina also prayed that taking the job Steve offered was the right thing to do and not some scheme cooked up by her overly active imagination. Steve reminded her of someone, but she still couldn't figure out who. Was her imagination working overtime?

ON THE DRIVE back to her apartment, Gina switched from thinking about Nicole's opinion of Steve Bryson to the article on Ward Dremont, then back to Steve again. Did Steve have ungentlemanly designs on her as Nicole implied? If so he'd be greatly disappointed. She wasn't interested in Steve Bryson—at least, she hoped she wasn't. And she planned to read the entire article about the mad scientist as soon as she got home.

Then she remembered she'd forgotten to renew her subscription to the local newspaper. Maybe she could learn something on the subject via one of the 24-hour television news channels.

Antique furniture and a feeling of safety and acceptance greeted her as soon as she walked in the door. Gina clicked on the television, listening as she changed out of her costume. She'd convinced herself that Ward Dremont's new discovery would be the biggest story of the day, but she was wrong. Gina had to wait over half an hour to hear one of the shortest news reports in the history of journalism: "Dr. Ward Dremont, head scientist working on what he is calling Project Humanity 205, will be getting financial backing from an unnamed billionaire. Updates at 6 and 10. Stay tuned for the weather."

Steve Bryson was super rich. Was he the one financing Dremont? She shook her head. No, that would be too ironic.

Why did her every thought now begin and end with Steve Bryson? And why would Steve finance someone like Ward Dremont? Gina bit her lower lip. Maybe she was just tired. *Not too tired to go to my computer and search the Internet for Ward Dremont and see what I can find out.*

She was about to enter her tiny office when she heard a knock at her door.

"Gina," her mother called from the hallway outside, "are you home?"

"Yes, Mama." Gina smiled and opened the door.

Her mother entered her apartment, holding a covered dish in both hands. Gina's parents divorced years ago, yet her mother still went by her married name, Mrs. Lucille Hollister. Since Gina's father walked out on the marriage, the sadness in Mom's gray eyes was obvious to anyone who knew her. On that particular day, however, Gina saw joy in her mother's eyes when invited to come inside.

Her mother handed Gina the metal pan covered in aluminum foil. "I brought your supper. I know how busy you are."

"How sweet, Mom. Smells good, too. Thanks. What is it?"

"Soupy pinto beans and cornbread mashed and all mixed together the way you like it."

She could taste it already. "You shouldn't have gone to so much trouble, but I sure am glad you did."

She took the covered dish into the kitchen, placing it on the cabinet next to the stove top while digesting all her mother had said—and what she hadn't. If she knew her mother as well as she thought she did, Mom was hiding something. Was it a man? Was Mom dating someone? If so it was about time! If her mother's bubbly voice wasn't enough of a clue, Mom was wearing an intoxicating new perfume, the kind most men found irresistible.

Gina breathed in a whiff of perfumed air. "What's up, Mom? And don't say 'nothing.' It's written all over you."

Mom laughed softly. "Whatever do you mean?"

"You're dating someone," Gina exclaimed. "Aren't you?" Gina grabbed her mother's hand and led her over to the couch. "I want to hear everything, absolutely everything. And when's the wedding?"

"Wedding? Well, I know you've been wanting me to start dating again, but—"

"You're going to marry the guy, aren't you?"

Her cheeks flushed. "I think it's premature to discuss something like that."

"But you *are* seeing someone?"

"Yes." Mom ducked her head. "In fact he's taking me to a dinner party next Friday night."

"He must be fabulous, or you wouldn't have found him interesting. So what's keeping you and Mr. Wonderful apart?"

Lucille Hollister fingered the strap of her white leather purse.

"Well, out with it, Mom."

She moistened her lips and took a deep breath. "He doesn't think his daughter would approve. His daughter was hurt by her parents' divorce and hasn't recovered from it yet."

"Doesn't she love her father?" Gina asked. "For heaven's sake, doesn't she want him to be happy?"

"Of course she wants him to be happy. I think she loves her father very much."

"Then why ...?"

Lucille lifted one hand in the same halting gesture she'd used to hush Gina as a child. "You don't know all the facts yet, Gina, so you're not in a position to know what should or shouldn't be done." She glanced down at her watch. "I stopped by to say hi, but I have an appointment in thirty minutes. I'll be late unless I leave immediately."

Gina wasn't through pumping her mother for information. "Is your appointment with *him*?"

"Yes." Her mother rose from the couch. "I'm not answering so much as one more of your questions."

"I'll be wondering about your date." Gina followed her mother out her front door and into the hall. "You will call me and fill me in on all the details, won't you?

Her mother smiled and stepped into the elevator.

The doors closed. Gina wanted to call her back, but it was too late. She didn't know her future stepfather's name, and she forgot to tell Mom about Colorado. Oh well, there'd be plenty of time for that. They wouldn't be leaving until the last week in June.

Memories of her parents' divorce returned like a hard slap in the face. The recollections continued as the beans and cornbread warmed in the oven. Gina's father walked out on her mother, not the other way around. Then he demanded a divorce and ran off with a younger woman. Her mother had always said she'd never marry again, but after so much heartbreak, Mom had earned the right to find happiness.

Gina turned on her computer, typed in the name Ward Dremont in the search slot, and touched the enter key. Several sites came up, each telling about this famous scientist. She was in a hurry, clicking on the site at the top of the list.

An error message flashed on the screen. *Rats.* The Internet was down again. It was obvious she wasn't going to find out more about the mad scientist or the identity of the billionaire backing him, at least not immediately—and she did like *immediately*. Gina turned off her computer.

After eating a generous serving of pinto beans and cornbread for supper, she wasn't hungry anymore. She tried again to get on the Internet but without success. If that wasn't enough, her cell phone needed to be recharged.

The taste of cold, sugary chocolate ice cream drew her to the kitchen. As a child her mother had often offered her sweet desserts to cheer her up when her day went wrong or was particularly stressful. This was one of those days.

AN HOUR later someone knocked at her door. She peered through the small glass window to see a man wearing a delivery company uniform standing in the hallway, holding something in his arms. What was he doing here? She didn't order anything. Puzzled she opened the door.

"Are you Dr. Gina Hollister?"

"Yes."

"Then these are for you." He pulled out a receipt pad. "Sign here."

She squinted trying to make out the return address on the receipt, but it was impossible to read from that distance. The delivery man tapped his forefinger on the top of the white box, waiting as she dug in her purse for a tip. When he finally handed her the box and left, an air of anticipation engulfed her. The box smelled like roses.

Who would be sending her flowers? Gina untied the ribbon with eager fingers and opened the box. Inside she found eighteen yellow roses. She searched for a card but couldn't find one.

Gina put the flowers in a milk-white vase, filled the vase with water, and set it in the middle of her small dining room table.

She was about to dump the empty box in the trashcan when she noticed a rather lengthy note hidden behind a sheet of silver paper.

"Dear Dr. Hollister," she read. "Steve Bryson here."

Mr. Bryson? What's he up to, sending me flowers? Gina continued reading.

"I might have upset you today, ma'am, and I want to apologize. Sometimes I tend to forget a stranger wouldn't know I have a habit of teasing people I like. In the future, I'll try to tone down my remarks.

"After you left my office, my aunt phoned from her home in Houston. She reminded me that besides being part English, Italian, German, and who knows what else, I'm also part Native-American on my father's side. Primarily, though, I'm plain old American, and I like a relaxed atmosphere when dealing with my employees.

"On the chance we might not get along in the future, maybe we should come up with a plan. My aunt reminded me that according to the history books, some Native-Americans smoked peace pipes. Maybe we should consider something similar. Peace in the workplace is always important. In any case I'm truly sorry if I upset you in any way and hope these flowers will express how much.

Sincerely,

Steven Edmond Bryson, III"

The thoughtful gesture pleased her, but she doubted Steve purchased the flowers himself. He would have one of his secretaries do chores like that. At least he signed the card.

Memories flooded her mind of another box of flowers and an engagement ring she had returned. Phil had his secretary send her flowers, and then he ran away with the secretary.

Steve did claim to be sorry for making her feel uncomfortable. Perhaps he was. It was thoughtful of him to send flowers, but as Nicole would say, what did he hope to gain?

4

Gina watched the ten o'clock news. Any new facts on the mad scientist were missing or unavailable, as well as the name of the mysterious billionaire financing the project.

On Saturday morning Gina got up early. She had a lot to do and not much time to do it. After breakfast she started packing. She already had a few boxes left over from the move to her current apartment, but she would need more. She planned to pack until noon, eat a quick lunch, and get ready for her meeting with Steve.

About ten she sat down at the kitchen table to catch her breath and think. She'd only be taking her clothes, her personal items, a small television, and her computer to Mother's. She'd rent a storage building and keep her furniture and the rest of her belongings there until she returned from Colorado.

The phone rang. She picked up.

"Hi Gina. This is Dad."

Her father, better known as Tip Hollister, was always full of surprises. His phone calls often pulled up the very memories Gina wanted to forget, forcing her to hang up on him several times. Perhaps it would be best to end the conversation before her temper erupted again.

"I'm busy, Daddy. Would you please call back another time?"

"Wouldn't you be busy then too?" he asked pointedly.

Gina stiffened. She'd tried, but she couldn't forgive her father for having an affair and hurting her mother the way he did. In her mind her father and Steve Bryson were two of a kind.

"I'm here in Austin on business and wanted to speak to my little girl. That's all."

His tender words melted her, but she couldn't let them blind her to the truth about her father. "Did you bring that cute young thing with you?" she blurted out.

"I haven't seen Jennifer in over a year."

"Then who are you dating now, her younger sister?"

"Who I'm seeing or not seeing is none of your business, young lady."

"You're absolutely right," Gina said. "But I take it you're dating someone. Her name doesn't matter."

"You matter, Gina," he said. "At least to me."

Gina bit her lower lip. *You matter to me, too, Daddy.*

Honor thy father and thy mother, she reminded herself as the scripture verse flashed into her mind. Yet sarcasm had spewed out of her mouth like a waterfall, all aimed at her father.

Bitter, cutting statements were so unlike her. Or was she deceived in thinking she was a better person than she truly was? She needed to apologize, but all cleansing words of restoration appeared to be lodged in her throat.

Nicole had said she needed to learn to deal with her father, but dealing with Tip Hollister would mean establishing some kind of relationship with him. She couldn't handle that now.

"I have to go," she said after a long pause. "A friend is coming to pick me up. You do understand, don't you?"

"Of course, honey. May I call you again?"

"We'll see. I have to go."

"Goodbye, Sweetheart."

"Goodbye, Daddy." Tears welled at the edges of her eyes as she put down the receiver. She'd called him Daddy, not once but twice. She hadn't acknowledged him as her father for a long time, and she should have apologized. At least she didn't hang up on him.

By noon Gina's living room looked like a disaster zone with half-filled boxes stacked on the couch, chairs, and floor. She'd tried to get on the internet several times without success. Steve Bryson was expected to arrive in less than two hours for their trip to Hill River, and she'd spent most of the morning packing. Housecleaning was not on her list. However, she planned to light an apple pie-scented candle to refresh the air before he arrived.

AT FIVE MINUTES AFTER TWO, Steve arrived, and Gina ushered him inside. She shrugged. "Sorry I can't offer you a chair."

Briefly he studied her cluttered living room and grinned. "No problem."

"By the way, have you been able to get on the Internet lately?" she asked.

"No, I think it's down. It's been going on and off a lot lately. You have to catch it at the right time."

"Sounds fishy to me."

His grin became a muffled laugh. "It could be part of a deep-state conspiracy, if you're into such things."

Gina refused to meet his eyes. Was he putting her down again? Not only did she wonder if perhaps Steve was connected to Ward Dremont in some way, but some of his facial expressions and mannerisms reminded her of her father.

She longed to share her misgivings regarding Daddy, but could a business tycoon like Steve understand how the negative phone conversations with her father affected her? She might never understand why her daddy betrayed her mother. If only she could accept things as they were instead of as she wished them to be.

Steve sucked in his breath then released it. The sound of it was loud enough to be heard in China. "The apple pie you're cooking smells delicious."

"It's not pie," she said with a smile. "It's a scented candle." Gina crossed the room and blew out the candle. The flame became a fleeting puff of smoke.

Steve gave the clutter in her living room another lighthearted appraisal. From the look of amusement in his eyes, Gina thought she knew exactly what he was thinking.

"Sorry everything's such a mess," she said. "I've been packing for the move and haven't had time for housecleaning."

"No problem." He grinned boyishly, propping one hand on a marble-topped table. "Nice furniture you've got here."

"Thanks."

He removed his hand from the table, and she saw a thin layer of dust coating his right palm. He wiped off the dust on the leg of his jeans and glanced back at the table. "Antique?" he asked.

"Yes, but the dust is fairly new."

Steve's deep laugh echoed around her as if he thoroughly enjoyed her company. Then he went over and stood in front of a blown-up photograph. She followed him but not too close.

"I like this photograph." He cocked his head at an angle. "Three little girls picking wildflowers." He glanced back at Gina. "Do you know who the girls are?"

"The one with the long black pigtails is my great-grandmother. The other two are neighbors. I was told my great-great-grandmother took the shot with a Brownie Camera."

"I've heard of those. A box camera from Eastman Kodak, isn't it? Very popular back in the nineteen-thirties. They say you could blow up a picture with a Brownie. You'd take a shot with a newspaper in the background and be able to read the date when the newspaper came out."

"I've heard that, too," she said. "The photo was taken in Oklahoma."

"I spent my undergraduate years at a small college in Oklahoma. Saw a lot of wildflowers there, too."

Gina was standing a foot or so behind him. She moved forward and stood beside him. "The girls are standing in a field of bluebonnets, the Texas state flower. I wish the picture was in color."

"Had you considered having the photo tinted? I'm told photographers can do wonders with color these days."

"No." She shook her head to confirm it. "I like to keep things the way they were originally." *Including marriage*, she thought, thinking again of her parents' divorce.

"I like your sense of history and family. There are a lot of antiques here. May I conclude you're an old-fashioned girl?"

"You could say that." She shrugged offhandedly. "As you know I plan to open a business in a small town."

"And let's not forget those religious values of yours," he reminded her.

"I'm glad you're aware of them." She manufactured a smile. "God is very important to me, if that's what you mean by old-fashioned. Am I right in assuming you're more of the city type?"

"I have to be," he said. "My businesses take me to cities all over the world."

He watched her as if he knew her secret thoughts and feelings. She felt an attack of embarrassment coming on and gnawed her bottom lip. A flash of humor softened his handsome face, and his gaze moved to the roses on her dining table.

"So," he said, "the flowers came."

"Yes, and they're lovely. Thank you. I sent a thank-you message your way. Hope you got it."

"Oh," he said, "I haven't read it yet. But I will sooner or later."

He pushed his hands deep into the pockets of his jeans as if searching for his keys. Was he having second thoughts about their day together? She knew she was.

"Shall we go?" He tilted his head toward the door.

"I'll get my purse."

STEVE WEAVED his way through Austin traffic with Gina beside him, conscious of her presence. At the edge of town, he turned south onto the interstate. From Loop 410 in San Antonio, they traveled west to the small town of Hill River. At last they arrived.

"So this is Hill River, Texas." He wheeled the car into a parking space. "Nice. I know it must be special to you. I'd love to know why, if you'd care to share with me."

"My family vacations in Hill River, has for years. It's a tradition in the Hollister family. Hollister brides marry here in the spring when the bluebonnets are in bloom."

"I envy you." He helped her out of the car, his emotions on high alert as he took her hand. "There are no traditions in the Bryson family that I know of, other than making a lot of money."

They started walking. Her reply was a smile, and she looked fantastic. She wore a white blouse, a flowered skirt hugging her tiny waist, and she was probably photogenic. But he knew there was more to Gina than a perfect face and body. He'd already seen she had a sense of humor and seemed totally devoted to his daughter. He removed his camera from its case, thinking how he could hardly wait to take her picture. "I think I'll take a couple of shots right here."

"I take pictures with my cell phone," she said. "You use a camera."

"Yes. But sometimes I take pictures with my cell. It all depends on the situation." He'd glanced away, but he turned to Gina again. "Is this where you plan to build the center?"

She nodded. "Yes. My business partner and I call it Bluebonnet Hill."

"Bluebonnet Hill. Sounds like the title of a song."

"You must be thinking of 'Blueberry Hill.' It's an oldie from my grandmother's day." She hesitated. "Actually, she's my great-aunt."

"Your grandmother is also your great-aunt? Interesting." After a moment when she hadn't responded, he said, "You know a lot about old songs, Doctor."

"My great-aunt from California reared my father. I think of her as my grandmother and call her Grandma. And Grandma collects old everything, including recordings."

Steve was puzzled. Why did Gina keep telling him things only close friends knew? She was a strange and a very beautiful lady, and it was time to change the subject. But before he could open his mouth, she looked up at him and smiled. Again.

"It's so beautiful here," she said. "Wish we'd come in the spring instead of summer, though. I love wildflowers, and bluebonnets would be in bloom then."

She motioned for him to follow, and they headed for the top of the hill.

"The rocky soil here isn't kind to plants, including the Texas bluebonnet," she continued. "They have to squeeze between the rocks and try hard to reach the sunshine." She glanced down at the valley below. "Their struggle to reach the surface reminds me of some of my students with dyslexia, always trying harder and harder to fit in, to be like everyone else."

"You're talking about Amanda, aren't you?" he asked.

"I'm talking about everybody."

Steve had moved ahead of her. He waited for Gina to catch up, watching her closely. The deep blue color of her eyes reminded him of the bluebonnets she mentioned, and her long hair fell across one shoulder. She flipped it back, grabbing a strand of hair and twirling it around her forefinger.

Steve snapped another picture, but she didn't look up, so he figured she didn't notice. Rather than take pictures of her, he reminded himself he should be memorizing the list of rules she'd made him promise to sign.

Now what was on the list, the one she finally gave him on the way here? Something about no physical contact. He'd already held her hand. If he blew it, broke any more of her rules, Gina could run so fast and so far he'd never see her again.

"Gina."

She was looking in another direction, but she turned toward him.

"Doesn't this area of Texas look a lot like southern Germany with the river and those green hills?"

"I wouldn't know," she said. "I've never been to Europe."

"Surely you've been to Colorado."

"No." A strand of hair fell across her forehead. She pushed it back and tucked it behind her ear. "My family never took trips when I was growing up. In the summer we spent our vacation time here visiting relatives."

"Then you're in for a treat."

"Treats are nice, but I prefer work."

"There'll be plenty of time for work, too." He snapped another picture, hoping she wouldn't object.

"Have you taken a picture of the river?" she asked.

"Not yet."

"The view is spectacular. You should take a shot from up here."

"I'll do a river shot later. First I want a close-up picture of you with the hills in the background." He cocked his head in the direction of a profusion of trees and bushes. "Would you mind sitting down under that big tree?"

"Why? I don't need to be in the picture."

"I'd still like you in it," he said.

"I thought you were taking snapshots to familiarize yourself with the area for the loan."

"Who says loan portfolios can't be interesting? Now hold still."

Gina sat down. He lifted his camera for a close-up of her face. She stuck out her tongue.

"Hey," he said with a chuckle, "can't you cooperate a little?" He took another picture. "Now that one's going to be great." He didn't add that he liked the funny one, too.

5

Gina took in a deep breath of country air. She always felt at peace among the hills and loved having someone share the beauty of her surroundings with her. But all Steve seemed interested in was taking pictures. She shut her eyes as childhood memories returned to her mind. She remembered how great it was spending a week at Hill River every summer, attending family reunions, staying in cabins owned by relatives, and connecting with Hollister cousins who arrived from Texas to California.

The quiet wonder of the entire area had always impressed her. Years later she managed to talk Nicole into selecting Hill River as the site of the learning center.

A small ant made its way across the hem of her skirt. Without thinking Gina brushed it away. As an afterthought she checked the condition of her white lace blouse.

The afternoon was hot even for southern Texas in early June. Her hair felt damp underneath. If she hadn't moved over into the shade, perspiration would be trickling down the back of her neck. Gina glanced at a group of trees nearer the river. She studied an ancient oak that towered above all the others.

Gina had always called the big oak "her tree." Patches of

sunshine filtered between the branches. She never shared her private thoughts with anyone but God, often while under the tree, and it always looked cool and inviting. Now she also longed to share her secrets with Steve. But she wouldn't. No! She'd keep them all to herself. With renewed determination, she trekked to the big oak in the clearing.

A mixture of tall grass and weeds brushed her bare legs. Gina sat down under her tree, spread out her pink flowered skirt, placed her carryall bag at her side, then leaned her back against the tree's trunk.

Steve had taken some of the shots with his cell. Then he'd pulled out his big camera again. She imagined him peering at her through the telescopic lens, and even that didn't upset the restful feeling growing inside her. But she always felt better on Bluebonnet Hill.

"Looking at you sitting there," he said, "nobody would guess how smart you are."

Gina tensed. Unpleasant childhood memories of a time when her peers thought Gina was anything but smart shot through her mind with unsettling results. Steve appeared to be unaware of her sudden discomfort, clicking pictures of her from every possible angle.

How smart you are, he'd said.

She knew how easy it would be to change those words to, *How dumb you are*. Or, *Gina, you sure are stupid*.

"You sure are stupid" were Timmy Martin's exact words when, in the sixth grade, Gina was unable to answer a question in class. She and her mother had moved back to Texas by then, but her intolerable relationship with her fellow students hadn't change.

Stupid.

Gina blinked as the unspeakable word bounced around inside her head. She glanced again at Steve, who slung the leather strap of his camera case over his shoulder. She figured he'd taken all the snapshots he intended to take, at least for now. He ambled down the rock steps, straight toward her.

Gina looked off in the direction of the river, hoping Steve hadn't noticed how detached she'd become and how helpless she sometimes felt to change things. He sat down beside her. In spite of everything, his constant attention and scrutiny made her feel extremely attractive. She forced herself to forget the past and to concentrate on the purpose of their meeting.

"I'd like to discuss your daughter a little more." Gina cleared her throat before continuing. "Amanda doesn't want to live with you, Mr. Bryson."

His handsome face clouded over. "You think I don't know that? She thinks she wants to live with her maternal grandmother, so she can continue to go out to the stable and ride her horse every afternoon. And please, call me Steve."

Steve? I don't think so. "Mr. Bryson." She looked him squarely in the eyes. "It might make it easier on Amanda if you moved in with her grandmother there in Austin for a while, instead of moving her so far away."

"Move in with my mother-in-law?" He laughed halfheartedly. "No thank you."

"Couldn't you stand Lola Ford for a little while?"

He moaned.

"It might help," she insisted. "Compromise is always a good tactic when trying to get along with others. Don't you think?"

"You don't know my mother-in-law. She'd move out before I had time to unpack. Besides, a good businessman never compromises. It's not part of our vocabulary."

"Maybe it should be."

He hesitated, gazing at her intently. "You care about your students, don't you?"

"I do."

"That's refreshing. It's obvious to me you're a very kind, compassionate person. I was lucky to have hired you."

He seemed to have a knack for making her feel special and

confused at the same time. Hadn't Myra warned her? Gina remembered her saying, "Steve's captivating charm never goes deeper than his golden tan."

Gina still sat with her back against the trunk of the tree and her legs outstretched in front of her. She sat up straight then, crossing her legs.

"Amanda could run away to spite you. It happened before."

"Myra must have told you about that," he said. "The other time it was partly her fault."

"You're talking about Mrs. Bryson?"

"Yes." He hesitated. "I don't mean to criticize my late wife, but you're my daughter's teacher, so you need to know certain facts."

"Anything you can tell me would be helpful."

He closed his eyes. "After spoiling the daylights out of Amanda from the day she was born, Myra suddenly put on the brakes—tried to discipline our daughter for the first time in her life. Of course it didn't work."

"This was after the divorce?"

"Years after." Silence stretched between them. "Let's go down to the water, Doctor. I want to see the river now."

GINA AND STEVE sat on a wooden bench at the river's edge. She sensed there was more he wanted to say. If only he would open his mouth and say it.

He reached down and grabbed a small river rock. "Amanda spent the weekend with me shortly after her thirteenth birthday," he said. "I hadn't seen her in a long time, didn't know about my ex-wife's new rules with regard to Amanda, and ..."

"What rules?"

"Oh, you know." He shrugged. "Out of the blue Myra would tell Amanda to stop doing something she'd allowed her to do all along without bothering to explain why."

"Do you think it caused Amanda to rebel and run away?"

"I wish I knew."

"Will you be better at handling your daughter than her mother was?" Gina asked.

"Yes, I believe I will because I'll let Amanda know my rules before I try to enforce them."

"That's always best of course, but I saw a lot of resentment in Amanda just waiting to come out. And there's also a boy who works at a stable in Austin she says she likes."

"If she's like her mother, she'll want a lot of boys in her life," he said, a hint of bitterness in his voice. "But Amanda's still a baby."

"I disagree." Gina recalled the ginger cookies he sent his daughter on the day of the party. If possible she needed to think of a tactful way to let him know his daughter was growing up. "Mr. Bryson," she continued, "I'm sure you know Amanda will celebrate her fifteenth birthday in late October."

"Of course I know. I've sent her an expensive doll on every birthday since she was born."

"At her age clothes might be a more suitable gift, don't you think? Girls love to dress up and impress boys."

He looked out at the rushing river. "You may be right about the clothes idea, but as I said, Amanda's still a baby." He tossed the rock he was holding in the direction of the river and reached down for another one. The first rock rolled down the slope but never quite reached the water. He drew back his arm and aimed again. The second rock sailed through the air faster and harder than the first, landing in the river.

Steve leaned forward, dangling his hands between his knees. "And as for boys," he added finally, "I've had plenty of experience with females who have boyfriends."

There were several other Amanda-related issues Gina wanted to discuss with him, but he seemed lost in thought. She sensed he wanted all serious talk to end, so she waited silently.

When he turned back to Gina, a hint of warmth had

returned to his eyes. "I plan to send my housekeeper and her daughter on ahead to get the house ready. I believe I told you my land is about thirty miles from Durango, and I think you'll like Gretel and Netty. Gretel is German. Sometimes I call her Gret. Gretel married an African-American soldier stationed in Germany after the Vietnam War, and they moved to the states and had a daughter. After their marriage broke up, Gret went to work for my grandparents and brought Netty with her. Now they work for me, and what a comfort they are."

"How ironic." Gina couldn't help smiling. "Nicole, my business partner, tells a similar story. Her father was also an African-American soldier stationed abroad when her parents met. But her parents still love each other, according to Nicole, and are still married."

"That's good," he said.

"Yes it is."

She wanted the conversation to continue, hoping to hear more about Gretel and her daughter, but his eyes proved his thoughts were elsewhere. After a long and silent moment, Gina decided he was either asleep or daydreaming, so she got up and moved away from him.

Gina edged toward the river. A cool breeze coming off the water sent her curls flying. The water would be cold, refreshing. *What would he think if I took off my sandals and waded? Would he notice, and why does it matter if he does?*

Steve dated models, movie actresses, and beautiful women who traveled the world as often as he did. Gina didn't fall into any of those groups. She knew of no other place on earth she'd rather live than Hill River, Texas.

Like Gina the river was a contradiction. Calm most of the time, the flow increased when it hit protruding stones and rocks. She picked up a small round rock and threw it into the shallow water near the river's edge, anticipating the *plop* it would make when the rock hit the water. The ripples disappeared; the water cleared. She could see all the way to the bottom.

The crunch of footsteps on the rocky path mingled with the gentle rush of moving water. She turned. Steve stood right behind her, looking far above her. Gina shaded her eyes from the blinding sun with both hands and looked up, too.

A silver flash followed, alerting her to a jet plane flying low overhead. Was Steve wishing he was flying off to some far away destination instead of standing by a river with her?

Gina picked up another rock. "Catch." She threw it his way.

Steve caught the rock and tossed it in the river. Like the intimate moment she thought they'd shared earlier, the rock sank to the bottom. She knew he was ready to leave their current location when he searched for his car keys.

GINA KNEW Steve had picked up sandwiches and corn chips in Austin before dropping by to pick her up. They would go on a picnic on the grounds where her family held reunions.

"Gina ...I mean, Doctor," Steve said, removing the food from the picnic basket, "how long has your family had reunions here?"

"For as long as I can remember. Reunions in our family take place annually," Gina explained. "I think I mentioned that in our family, weddings are held here when the bluebonnets bloom. Does your family have traditions?"

"My family is small," he said. "I've never been to a family reunion. It must be fun."

She nodded. "It is."

Was Steve playing games with her? Or was she seeing a different side of him? He seemed truly interested in her and her family. But was he? Really?

After they finished eating, Steve drove to a camping area a few miles down the road where swimmers gathered. He parked in front of a line of bathhouses.

"So this is the place," he said.

She nodded. "Yes. This is the bathhouse where swimmers and tubers go before getting in the water."

Steve's brows drew together. "Tubers, did you say? What's a tuber?"

"Someone who floats down the river in an inner tube. What else?" Gina shrugged. "Surely you didn't think I was talking about a class in botany."

He laughed. "I had a lot of science courses at the university when I was a student. Can't remember anything about the kind of tubers that float down rivers."

"All work and no play make ..."

He nodded. "I know."

When he laughed again, Gina surprised herself by laughing with him. She reached for her carryall bag. "I'll be going in the bathhouse now and changing into my river clothes. See you later."

He grinned. "You better."

GINA WENT INTO THE BATHHOUSE. She changed into a pair of faded jeans and a long-sleeved yellow print shirt, then realized she wasn't alone. Practically every female in the dressing room had dressed as she had.

"I wear swimsuits every once in a while to please my husband," a young woman remarked as they stood in front of a line of mirrors. "But jeans and a long shirt sure beat a bad sunburn."

"I can't disagree." Gina ran a comb through her hair. "And I can think of a couple more reasons besides."

After she finished dressing, Gina hiked back to the parking area to meet Steve, who was wearing only a pair of swimming trunks. She expected him to make a comment about her long-sleeved shirt, but he didn't say a thing. They walked down to the water.

Every woman at the river must have noticed Steve's trim, sleek body in the light-blue swimsuit he wore that afternoon. Obviously the man worked out.

Steve jumped into the river, but Gina lagged behind. He laughed and splashed water on her. Then he motioned for her to join him.

"Come on," he called. "Get in."

"The water's cold."

He laughed. "Yes, but it's great. Come on." He threw water on her again.

She giggled. "Stop that." She splashed him back but didn't attempt to join him.

"Don't tell me you're afraid of water. Or did you have your hair fixed at one of those beauty places my mom talks about?"

"No, silly. It's because I know how cold the water is. And for your information, I've known how to swim since I was six years old." She kicked at the edge of the water.

A spray of river water dotted his face. He laughed and rubbed his eyes. "I'll get you for this." Steve grabbed hold of her hand and pulled her into the river. Still laughing he held her close.

For Gina and perhaps for Steve, what had started as a sort of water game became something more. Gina decided it was time to change course. "I guess we should get started tubing down the river. Don't you think?"

"You're the boss." Steve released her.

"I thought you were the boss."

"Right now it's debatable."

He'd tied their inner tubes to an exposed root of one of the ancient cypress trees. Steve handed her a tube and untied the ropes, then they climbed into their inner tubes.

STEVE GRINNED, inside and out, as they floated down the river. He hadn't had so much fun since ... His smile fell away. Since he and Baylee went swimming, back in ancient history. He wouldn't think about her now, not when he was having such a wonderful time. It was bad enough she entered his mind earlier when he threw rocks in the river.

He turned to Gina and forced a grin she must have liked because she giggled. Then for several hours they laughed and joked and had water fights.

Gina looked exhausted by the time they arrived at the end of the line. Steve hired a cab to take them back to his car. Less fortunate tubers walked back to the parking area, carrying their tubes with them. It was a five-mile hike.

A group of teenagers were walking along the road near their cab.

"Hey," Steve called. "Need a ride?"

"Sure," one of the young men said.

"Then get in. There should be plenty of room if we double up."

The young man put his arm around an attractive young girl. "Come on, Cindy. Let's go double up."

The cab driver seemed willing to go along with the plan, and he tied their tubes to the top of the van. The young man climbed into the automobile before any of his friends, then pulled the young woman named Cindy down on his lap.

Steve glanced at Gina, indicated his lap, and smiled teasingly. "Shall we?"

Doubling up probably went against every rule on her list, but with the teenagers doing it and the cabby not complaining, Gina complied, climbing up on Steve's lap without looking at him. He wrapped his arms around her waist, giving her a playful squeeze.

Frowning she peered back at him.

"This is a bumpy road," Steve said. "I'm only holding you to keep you from falling off my lap, okay?"

"Relax, lady," Cindy's young man said, "and enjoy it." He grinned. "We are."

Gina finally relaxed but refused to look at Steve. She kept her eyes on the road ahead. Steve sent the young man a "thumbs up" sign, which didn't go unnoticed by Gina.

On their way out of town, they stopped at an antique shop because Gina loved antiques. She bought a very old and rusty flatiron, the kind women once used to remove wrinkles from clothes, back when ironing was a part of daily life. Then Steve bought her an old-fashioned blue bonnet that tied under the chin.

"This is for you," he said when he handed it to her. "A Texas girl needs a blue bonnet to keep her head warm during these scorching hot winters we've been having."

Gina giggled. "Thank you, sir."

They were both laughing by the time they reached the car.

GINA APPEARED to enjoy their day together, but Steve doubted she'd admit it. It wasn't a proper meeting between two business associates nor was it conducted in a professional manner. The laughing and joking around proved it. She appeared to try to turn things around, a sort of return to formal. It hadn't worked. Steve wasn't sure she wanted it to work.

At first she'd called him Mr. Bryson. Then it was Steve. He couldn't recall exactly when the change took place. All he knew was he hadn't had so much fun in ages and didn't want to give up his newfound joy any sooner than necessary.

An undeniable attraction had developed between them, and nobody comprehended it better than Steve. He also knew the probable outcome in all of this. Steve Bryson probably wasn't good news as far as Gina Hollister was concerned.

6

On the drive back to Austin, Gina's interest in Steve grew stronger. She wondered if he sensed it, too.

It was dark when they reached the outskirts of San Antonio, then on to Austin. To break the tension building between them, Gina pulled the blue bonnet from the shopping bag, the sack also holding the flatiron. "I'm putting this on." She tied the blue sashes in a bow under her chin. "On hot summer nights like this, the weather can change, grow cold. I want to be ready in case it snows."

He laughed. Nevertheless she wasn't sure the romantic spell was broken. Gina had to think of something fast or find herself in his arms. The list of rules she gave Steve popped into her head. So far he hadn't put his arm around her. As her grandmother would say, she needed to put on her thinking cap— discover why he hadn't.

Were her rules working? Was she keeping Steve at arm's length? Or was this merely a delaying tactic in hopes of a kiss goodnight at her door?

Steve was warm and friendly at Bluebonnet Hill and when they floated down the river. Yet at times he'd also seemed distant. Gina couldn't help contemplating what he might be thinking. Photographs of Steve with one beautiful woman after another had appeared in newspapers and on magazine covers all over Texas in the last couple of years. Were his thoughts focused on one of those women? If so, what business was it of Gina's?

Steve was nothing to her. Or was he?

In the hallway outside her Austin apartment, Gina unlocked the door. When she turned back to thank Steve for a pleasant day, his face was only inches from hers.

Her breath caught; she felt her eyes widen. It was obvious he intended to kiss her goodnight. No lingering doubts now.

"I think it's time we discussed another aspect of our future working relationship, Mr. Bryson."

"Mr. Bryson? I was Steve in the inner tube."

"We're not at the river now. I should never have called you by your first name."

"Why not?"

"We can't allow our business relationship to decay to that point. It's ... unprofessional."

Steve placed his hands on her shoulders. Her heart hammered against her chest. She felt herself moving closer to the curve of his mouth.

He reached down, lifted her chin with his forefinger, and untied the bow under her chin. Blue sashes fell to her shoulders.

"Is it so terrible I want to kiss you goodnight?" he asked.

"Yes," she whispered. But her heart wasn't in it.

He gazed down at her, with those dimples and a lopsided grin on his face. She hesitated to move for fear he'd discover more about her feelings than he needed to know.

"I'm not in the habit of kissing the fathers of my students," she finally said.

"I wasn't suggesting you kiss fathers with an *s*. I was talking about only one father." His voice softened still more. "Me."

SHE'D BECOME MUCH TOO fond of her boss and couldn't allow it to continue. Now all Gina had to do was figure out how to stop falling in love with Steve Bryson.

They still stood in the hallway outside her apartment. He lowered his head, aiming for her lips.

Gina reached up, covering his mouth with her hand. "The terms of the agreement I'll want you to sign include my list of ground rules. You aren't supposed to touch me while I'm living in your home in Colorado."

"We aren't living in Colorado yet."

Still holding the bag containing the items purchased at the antique shop, she tried to push him away. The heavy flatiron inside the bag bumped his shoulder. He jerked when the iron hit him. Gina tensed; regret pulsed through her. What was she thinking? He could be badly hurt.

"Bless your heart, sir," she said at last. "The flatiron must weigh a ton. I never meant to hurt you. I really am sorry."

"You're sorry?" Steve released her, lifting both his hands as if he thought he was under arrest. "Early American women must have been strong. That iron you said they used to press out wrinkles sure packs a hard punch. Nearly dislocated my shoulder."

Was he only pretending to be hurt while holding in a smile that begged to come out? She patted his shoulder. "I forgot about the iron," she said. "Is your shoulder still hurting?"

"A little. You don't happen to own a baseball bat or other dangerous weapons, do you?"

"No."

"That's good."

Gina was still concerned about his shoulder, though Steve didn't appear to be worried about much of anything. "You'll be all right, won't you?" she asked.

"Only if you'll put your lips ..." He pointed to his mouth. "... right here."

Here we go again. Doesn't this guy ever give up? She took in another of her now famous deep breaths of air, then slowly let it go. "Are you seriously suggesting I kiss my future boss?"

He nodded. "Seriously."

"No way."

"How can an innocent goodnight kiss hurt anyone?"

"This train we're on is running out of gas," she said. "I had a nice day, and I'm sorry about your shoulder, but this is where I get off." She spun around and faced the door.

"You mean you're going inside, just like that?"

She grinned back at him over her shoulder. "Just like that."

Gina wasn't fooled by Steve's feigned attempt at vulnerability, and she was fighting to keep from laughing. She glanced back over her shoulder. "Good-bye." After pausing to think for a moment, she waved. "And good night."

"But it's early yet. Couldn't you wait a while?"

She shook her head. "No. But I had a wonderful time."

Gina hurried inside, releasing a laugh she'd held in for several minutes. She pressed her back against the door, as warmth bubbled through her laughter, becoming an animated smile. Maybe she should throw away her misgivings and invite Steve in for coffee. He was, after all, possibly the most exciting man she'd ever met. Slowly her smile faded. He was also the most dangerous man she'd ever met, and he was wrong for her. *And I'm wrong for him.*

Setting her jaw determinedly, she locked the door. Yet she couldn't seem to stop herself from peering back at him through the door's tiny window. She expected to see him walking back down the hall toward the elevator, and he was. The problem was he'd managed to take a part of her heart with him, and she wanted it back. She'd always kept her heart under lock and key and wasn't in the habit of giving away samples. Yet the urge to call him back overwhelmed her. She managed to dispel it. They were too different; a lot more than a sheet of window glass divided them.

Gina hadn't forgiven herself for hitting him with the iron the way she did. *Iron*. The flatiron she bought at the antique store was the perfect item for her collection of survival gear—the perfect symbol of their day together. He bumped her heart. She bumped his shoulder a little with an antique iron.

Another thought came to her. She'd teach Amanda survival techniques as part of their regular tutoring lessons. What better way to teach history than to introduce simple tasks as they were done in the past? First she'd explain how to use the flatiron she bought at the antique shop. Maybe she should also visit a store where survival gear was sold and pick up a few more items to use during the lesson before they left for Colorado.

A mental list of steps to be followed when washing and ironing clothes the *old-fashioned* way filled her mind. *Let me see*, she thought ....

To iron clothes in Grandmother's day you brought the water and starch solids to a boil on the stove. Next you soaked the clothes, one-by-one, in the hot starch, dried them on a clothesline, and then dampened the clothes before ironing them. Antique irons like the one Gina now owned were heated until hot on a wood-burning stove and carefully pressed to a dampened garment until the wrinkles were gone.

She sighed. *If only the wrinkles in humans were as easy to iron out.*

IT RAINED all day on Wednesday, with lightning and thunder all around. On Thursday Gina dragged Nicole, nearly kicking and screaming, to Steve's lawyer's office to sign the Rent-to-Own document. Gina signed; Nicole also signed but grudgingly. Then Gina and Steve signed their personal agreement regarding proper behavior in boss-vs.-employee relationships.

On the drive home in Gina's Buick, Nicole started in again. "We should never have signed those papers, Gina, and you shouldn't go to Colorado under any circumstances. Steve Bryson will have you eating out of his hand before you leave the state of Texas."

Gina knew Nicole. She must calm her down before things got out of hand. It meant changing the subject.

"Is your cell phone working okay?" Gina asked.

"My cell phone?" Nicole sounded surprised and slightly confused by Gina's change of subject. "My cell's all right, I guess. Why?"

"Mine only works about half the time. Sometime my internet messes up, too."

"Really?" Nicole seemed concerned. "Maybe you should get another service."

"I'm considering that. Steve claims his phone and internet service work perfectly now; he talks to people all over the world. But when he tries to get me on the phone, it never works. Remember the big storm we just had?"

"Who doesn't?"

"The problem could be the weather, or maybe my timing is off. But there's more." Gina shook her head. "If all the rain, lightning, and thunder last night wasn't enough, I had to drive home from the mall in it. I think a small tornado might have been involved."

"You're kidding," Nicole said. "I hadn't heard."

"The convenience store two streets over was totaled."

"The one on the corner?"

"Yes."

"Oh, no," Nicole said. "How sad. I stop in there almost every time I'm in your neighborhood."

Gina paused before going on. "I have a lot more to say, and I'll say it as fast as I can." She hesitated again. "We had a blackout during the storm on Wednesday, and I was driving home in pouring down rain. When I got out of the car, I dropped my cell in a puddle of water. You know what water does to things like phones. Thankfully it's still under warranty.

They're ordering me a new one, but it's back-ordered. Now you know the rest of the story."

"My goodness, Gina, you *do* have problems! If there's anything I can do to help, let me know."

"Thanks." Gina smiled. "I needed to hear that."

Not only did she manage to pull Nicole out of her down mood, Gina had been able to share what was on her heart with a friend. She considered it a victory.

GINA SPENT the next few days moving from her apartment to her family home. Her mother had moved into an apartment in San Antonio shortly before Gina moved in, and she was slightly hurt by that. Was Mom trying to avoid being around her, or was there another reason she abandoned a house she owned outright in favor of an apartment she didn't own in San Antonio? At least Gina and her mother phoned back and forth, but only if all connections were working.

On the plus side the Hollister family home was closer to the mansion where Amanda and her grandmother lived than her apartment had been, making it easier for Gina to schedule Amanda's tutoring sessions. Also Gina had completed all the loose ends connected with her doctorate, making scheduling easier.

Gina arrived at Mrs. Lola Ford's Austin mansion right on time and ready for Amanda's tutoring session. Later she and Amanda went out the front door and onto the long front porch. The porch stretched across the front of the house and was supported by huge pillars, two stories high. Amanda's grandmother had all but insisted Gina see and smell the roses in her garden before they made their way to the summer house where the lesson would be held.

"Your grandmother's home is absolutely perfect." Gina

sniffed the roses. "The flowers and the trees are lovely. Be sure to tell Mrs. Ford how much I like everything here."

"Okay. I will."

Gina didn't add she'd noted the trees and flowers earlier when she first arrived.

They stepped off the porch and around to the back of the house. The summer house looked like the main house in miniature. Both had the same white-brick siding and the same southern-plantation design, but to Gina the summer house seemed warmer, less formal.

"So Amanda, what have you been up to since our last session, and how's your horse doing? Have you gone riding lately?"

"Cricket is fine, and I ride at the stable as often as I can."

"And how's your friend, the stable boy?"

The girl's cheeks turned pink, and her words took on a snippy tone. "Danny's fine. We like each other. You might say we're in a relationship just like you and Mr. Phil Arnold were."

"Mr. Arnold and I were engaged, Amanda. It's not the same, and I don't like your smart talk. What kind of a relationship are you and Danny in anyway?" Gina asked.

Amanda sent her a hard look.

Gina sent Amanda a harder one. "I'm waiting for an answer." The tension surrounding them built. It was a moment Gina hoped Amanda would never forget.

At last Amanda said, "I'm sorry, ma'am. I shouldn't have said what I did. Danny and I are just friends."

"That's better."

Gina had liked Amanda from the first day they met, and they grew closer after the death of her mother. Yet the teen had seemed a little stiff when Gina first arrived. Now she was downright disrespectful. Gina hoped Amanda and Danny really were just friends. But she planned to keep an eye on the boy at the stable—just in case.

Gina hoped the morning lessons and the charm of the summer house would put Amanda at ease and perhaps at peace.

With the death of her mother and the other changes in her life, she was an emotional time-bomb waiting to explode.

White wicker chairs and couches, pale green walls, and china vases greeted them as soon as they stepped inside the summer house. Marigolds added still more color.

Gina removed her shoes and stretched out on one of the couches. Amanda reclined on the couch opposite her.

"Amanda," Gina said before the tutoring began, "I know you don't want to move in with your dad, but—"

"I hate Daddy!"

Gina raised her eyebrows at the intensity of the girl's words. "Would you like to expand on that?"

Amanda grimaced, making it clear she found Gina's request distasteful. "I guess."

"Good. Now tell me why you don't like your father."

"When I was seven, Daddy divorced my mom and me. What's to tell?"

"How did you feel when he left?"

"I was sad at first. I missed him a lot."

Sympathy and compassion for Amanda surfaced because Gina knew exactly how Amanda felt. She wanted to grab Amanda around the middle and give her a big hug, but there would be a time for that. Not now. Gina stiffened, putting the motherly emotions now building into the smallest room in her heart.

"And then what?" Gina said at last. "You missed your father later on, didn't you?"

"No."

"Why not?"

"He hardly ever came to see us. Mama said Daddy was bad."

"Bad?" Gina froze, afraid to hear what might be coming next. "Did your father hurt you in any way?"

"He never hit me, if that's what you mean."

"But did he hurt you in any other way?"

"He said he was going to spank me once."

"Did he?"

"No." Amanda's forehead wrinkled, and the muscles around her mouth tightened. "But once he made me sit in the corner for five whole minutes. It seemed longer."

"What had you done to cause this punishment?"

"He said I lied."

"Did you?"

Amanda looked away without answering.

"Did you lie, Amanda?"

"A little, I guess." She'd turned her head and was looking toward one of the windows overlooking the garden. Amanda got up then, walked to the window, and stood there silently, looking outside for a long time.

Funny, Gina thought. *Sometimes people can know things about others, especially when circumstances are similar.* Gina had lied to her father more than once, and she never wanted to spend time with him after her parents' divorce.

*I*t was time for Amanda to end her two-minute sabbatical at the window. Gina believed she'd daydreamed long enough.

"Amanda," she said a little louder than necessary.

The teenager turned and faced her. "Yes?"

"You admitted lying to your father. Now tell me more about what happened."

"Daddy said not to eat candy before meals. I love candy as much as he likes ginger cookies. I can never get enough chocolate candy, and there was a whole box of chocolates in the refrigerator. So I ate a few pieces."

"How many?" Gina asked.

Amanda glanced away again. If it were possible to take a picture of the word *guilty*, a snapshot of the girl's face would win a prize in photography.

"How many pieces of candy did you eat, Amanda?"

"About three, maybe more. I don't know."

"Amanda, tell me how many pieces of candy you ate."

"There was only one layer." Amanda dropped her eyes for a moment. "Okay, I ate all the candy left in the box. But it was a small box."

Gina shook her head slowly. "You should be ashamed of yourself. Your grandmother said you ran away several times on days when you were supposed to spend time with your father. Was it because you were embarrassed after telling lies?"

"Maybe."

"Where did you go when you knew your father was coming to visit? Where do you hide?"

"A lot of places. The best place to hide is in a church."

"A church?"

"Yeah. Nobody ever looks there."

"You know, Amanda, at fourteen you don't have to do what the court suggested. You can probably live with Mrs. Ford if that's what you and your grandmother want."

"I know. But Granny said it wouldn't look good in a court of law if I keep living with her and something went wrong." Amanda smiled. "Besides, you're going to Colorado with us now."

"So you're going to Colorado for sure?" Gina asked.

"Yes." Amanda grinned. "If you're going, then I am, too."

Gina waited a long while before speaking again. She wanted to say fathers naturally loved their daughters, and therefore Steve Bryson must love Amanda, too. From personal experience she didn't believe it anymore and wouldn't pretend she did. Gina closed her eyes, turning a long blink into a short reprieve. She wasn't as relaxed as she'd like to be.

She took a deep breath. "Amanda, have you considered your father might love you very much?"

"If he loves me, he has a funny way of showing it."

"Did it occur to you he might not know how to show his feelings?"

Amanda looked away, and Gina realized it was time to change the subject. "Did you finish the math homework I gave you?" she asked.

"I couldn't."

"Why not?"

"I don't know how to do math problems when they tell a story—stated problems, as Grandma calls them. Okay?"

"You're a tad snippy today," Gina said. "I'm here to help you, you know."

"I don't want to do homework today. Granny will help me after you leave. I don't want to do school work either. But you're still going to do what you said, aren't you?" Amanda paused before going on. "I mean, you're not backing out or anything."

"Backing out on what?" Gina asked.

"Going to Colorado."

"I said I was going, didn't I?"

"Yes, but if you decide to back out, then I will, too."

"I'm going to Colorado. You have my word on it. In fact I've already rented a storage building to keep my furniture and other stuff in."

She studied Amanda for a moment. The teenager was more than pretty, standing there with her dark hair pulled back from her face. She was beautiful, very mature-looking, and physically well-developed for her age. No wonder boys found her so attractive.

"You don't need to worry, Amanda. I'll always be your friend, but you're too dependent on me. Your father is bound to remarry sooner or later. When he does, you'll need to be free to love and accept your new stepmother. The last thing you'll need then is me, hanging around somewhere in the background."

"I don't care who Daddy marries, or *if* he marries. Nobody else will be my mother ever again." Amanda picked up a magazine from a small table and leafed through the pages. After a moment she threw down the magazine and made a dash for the door.

"Amanda! Where do you think you're going?'

"Out!"

"Out? Why?"

"I'm stupid." She stopped at the doorway, her back to Gina,

as she peered out at her grandmother's rose garden. "That's why."

"You're not stupid," Gina insisted.

"I wish I could believe you."

"But it's true, Amanda. You've been tested. You're very smart. You need—"

"Need what?" Amanda whirled around and faced her. "If I'm so smart why can't I read that magazine?"

"Well ..."

"Mostly all I can do is look at the pictures."

"I've explained all that, remember?"

"I remember all right, but I don't believe I'm smart. I know better. You're just saying I'm okay to make me feel good."

"That's not true."

"It's the way I see it." Amanda went over to a display case next to one of the windows and picked up a carved race horse with a female rider on it. "The only things I'm good at are drawing pictures and riding horses. Now I have to move miles away from my mare." She'd put her hands on her hips. "Cricket probably won't remember me by the time we get back."

"There'll be horses in Colorado, you know."

"It won't be the same." Amanda hurried to the door again and glanced back. "I think I'll go outside for a while, walk around."

Gina thought Amanda should finish their tutoring session before she went out, hoping her disapproving facial expression affirmed her opposition. On second thought maybe Amanda did need to get away for a few minutes.

She forced a smile. "Don't be gone long. We have some things to go over before I leave. And remember you're intelligent and successful."

"Give me a break."

The door slammed, leaving Gina in the summer house alone.

Oh, how she empathized with Amanda! They shared many common bonds. Amanda would be considered extremely creative in some educational areas and very gifted, yet the teen honestly thought she was stupid.

Gina understood. Who better knew what it felt like to be in the lowest reading group in the entire school? Or what it meant to be shunned merely for being different? She didn't want others to know about all the problems she'd had in school as a child. It was too personal. To know her parents and former schoolmates knew the truth was bad enough.

She'd read somewhere that Steve was a straight-A student and graduated near the top of his class. She'd hate for him to know that in elementary school she was at the bottom of hers. It hadn't gotten much better in middle or high school either.

Memories of Trudy and Stella, two especially hurtful high-school bullies, invaded Gina's mind. The two were cheerleaders and the most popular girls in school. Like Gina they were also members of the high school choir. Gina was especially successful as a choir member and often sang the solo parts during performances. She could hardly wait to read what Stella and Trudy wrote in her year book.

And then she read them—and her heart shattered.

"Gina," Stella wrote, "why do you have to be so incredibly stupid?"

She hadn't wanted to read more but couldn't seem to stop.

"I leave you with a few suggestions for your last two years of high school," Trudy's comment had said. "First, learn to walk across the floor without falling on your face. Second, learn to read and spell. We all know you were the dumbest kid in your class. And please learn to sing. Can you?"

Gina swallowed, hoping those memories, along with the invisible something hard now lodged in her throat, would go down. Her experiences molded her into the person she'd become, including her sincere desire to help others. Still she could be hurt; hiding her past was like a shield of protection against stones and fiery darts, but for how long? Would a day come when all her secrets would pour down on her like a flood?

Amanda raced back inside and shut the door. "Daddy's coming!" she exclaimed. "I don't want to see him. I'm hiding in the hall closet. Please don't tell him I'm here."

"I won't lie for you," Gina said, "but I'll do what I can."

Amanda nodded her approval, disappearing down the hall.

STEVE SMILED when he first came in. Was he glad to see her? Gina smiled back. But what was he doing here?

Lola Ford must have told him her granddaughter was having her regular tutoring session in the summer house. For Gina the parent-teacher meeting with Steve was anything but regular.

He glanced around the room. "Where's Amanda?"

Gina didn't want to lie. At the same time she couldn't break her promise to Amanda. Gina shrugged. Her smile slowly faded.

"She couldn't be hiding because she didn't know I was coming," Steve said. "Did she take a walk somewhere?"

Gina nodded.

"That sounds familiar." He shook his head. "She always takes one of her walks or goes horseback riding to get out of doing what she doesn't want to do." He sat down on the nearest couch, looking like a little boy who'd lost his only friend.

Gina understood. She'd felt like he must be feeling more times than she could count. She sat down beside him without saying a single word. Maybe he thought she was being Shy Ann again, but at this particular moment there wasn't a shy bone in her body. She couldn't—wouldn't—betray Amanda. At the same time she saw a deep need in Steve's dark eyes, a cry for help. Being Gina she couldn't ignore it. Neither could she ignore the obvious strain between them.

They sat side by side on the couch, the silence between them growing.

"Nice weather we've been having," Steve finally said. "There was a cool breeze this morning. Maybe we'll get some rain."

"The weatherman said we might."

"That's good."

So he appeared to want idle talk instead of a parent-teacher conference. She decided she could sit there and listen, see where it led.

At last they discussed Amanda's progress in reading, math, and spelling. Still Gina refused to tell him Amanda was hiding in the closet. In fact she forgot the teenager was still there. She and Steve were getting along so well by that time that all thoughts of promises and closets were lost in her desire to help a man who needed encouragement.

He seemed to be reaching out to her like a drowning man, begging for someone to come and rescue him. The next thing she knew, she was in his arms. She didn't know how it happened, yet it seemed so right.

His sweet kiss was deep and life-shattering, and then—

A sudden banging sound startled Gina. She jerked around. The closet door must have opened, whamming back against the wall. Amanda stood in the doorway.

"What's going on in here?" Amanda demanded. "And don't think I didn't see what you two did."

Too stunned to speak Gina stiffened. Steve looked as uncomfortable and embarrassed by the turn of events as she was.

"Amanda." He motioned for his daughter to join them. "Come over here."

"No!" Amanda took a step back. The wrath in her eyes shouted her disapproval of the kiss she'd witnessed. "I thought you were *my* friend, Dr. Hollister. Not his."

"But I am your friend," Gina insisted.

"*Were*," Amanda exclaimed. "Not anymore. Now I know the real reason you said you'd go to Colorado. And it has nothing to do with me."

"It has everything to do with you, Amanda." Gina didn't move, though she wanted to reach out and draw Amanda into a motherly hug. "Please believe me. You're the reason I accepted the job."

"I wish I could believe it. I ...I can't anymore." Sobbing, Amanda ran outside and raced toward the main house. Gina started after her.

"No," Steve said. "Let her go."

With a feeling of helplessness, Gina turned, moving as far from Steve as possible.

I should have told him exactly where he could find Amanda and the location of the closet as soon as he came inside, Gina agonized. *If I hadn't gotten sidetracked, none of this would have happened. Now it's too late.*

She sat down at one end of the couch. Steve sat at the other. Neither spoke. In hindsight Gina wished she'd gone after Amanda instead of standing back as Steve instructed. Amanda needed comforting, needed a friend. And Gina had a strong desire to fill those needs.

After a few moments Lola Ford stuck her head in the doorway. "What have you two done to my poor little granddaughter? I think you might have broken her heart. And after all she's been through, too."

*M*rs. Ford claimed her granddaughter was out of control and said she wanted to die. It was enough to get Gina, Steve, Amanda, and Mrs. Ford racing to a local medical clinic to see a Dr. Walter Bennett.

The waiting room grew cold after Amanda went in to see the doctor, and not merely because the air conditioning unit appeared to be turned on high. Mrs. Lola Ford sat across the waiting room from Gina and Steve, glaring at them. It got colder when the nurse came in to say the doctor wanted to talk to Amanda's grandmother instead of Steve.

"But I'm her father," Steve said.

The nurse didn't seem to be listening. "Step right this way, Mrs. Ford."

If Gina could have erased the last two hours from the portals of time, she would have. She felt sorry for Amanda *and* Steve. He had to be hurting terribly now. It was time to pray.

"Steve, will you pray with me?"

"Pray!" His eyes filled with what Gina interpreted as anger. "You sound like Caleb Cantu."

"Who?"

"A friend of mine—or *was*. He's a Bible thumper, too."

"A what?"

"A Bible thumper," he said. "You know those people who talk about God in just about every sentence. Prayer is a private thing, Gina."

She speculated about whether or not he prayed at all, concluding he probably didn't. She wanted to hear more about Caleb but decided not to bring up his name again. The conversation might have heated up even more, but Dr. Bennett finally came in.

"As you know, Mr. Bryson," the doctor began, "your daughter is very upset. I've given her something to take when she gets home to relax her. Mrs. Ford is driving her home. They left through the back door."

Steve's eyes opened wide. "Left?"

Gina could see the hurt on his face.

"I thought it best they go on home," the doctor said. "Mrs. Ford said you plan to move Amanda to Colorado this summer. I strongly advise you to reconsider. Amanda has been disturbed since her mother died and doesn't want to go to Colorado. Have you considered leasing a house right here in Austin?"

"I have business interests in Colorado and elsewhere," Steve said. "Business I must take care of this summer. My assistant takes my place when needed, but I can't avoid all my obligations."

"I see." Dr. Bennett gazed at Steve, and his smile looked forced. "I know of a child psychiatrist who practices in Durango. Dr. Larker is also a medical doctor. Why don't you give him a call once you've settled in?"

"Psychiatrist? Do you think Amanda needs a shrink? I had no idea her problem was so serious."

"Shrinks, as you call them, can do wonders for people suffering from depression, Mr. Bryson. I think depression might be a factor here." Then Dr. Bennett got Steve to promise to call Dr. Larker once they arrived in Colorado.

The question was, would Steve keep his promise?

STEVE SAT at his desk at the office in Houston, studying his appointment schedule for the coming days. Bricot Oil and Natural Gas was his most important asset, and he'd need to acquaint himself with any new developments before leaving for Colorado to make sure there were no conflicts.

He should schedule a staff meeting with his entire crew as soon as possible, yet his thoughts were far from business meetings or trips to other locations. Steve kept thinking about the stronghold Gina had on his emotions and how the two of them had hurt his daughter.

He should have known Amanda would be somewhere nearby and wouldn't react favorably to a romance between her tutor and her father. Steve wanted to talk to Gina again and had tried phoning her, but she didn't answer. Then he texted her but without success.

Briefly he gazed out his office window at the construction site directly across the street, then reached for the stack of papers on his desk. Work on his new office building was coming along well. The Bryson Building would be almost finished by the time he and Amanda returned from Colorado.

His secretary, Josie, popped her head in the door. "Drake Rather is here to see you, sir."

Steve had fallen behind on his work and was counting on having some free time to catch up. Still he needed to talk to Rather. "Send him in." Steve winked at Josie. Then he sent her an insider grin meant to make her laugh. "Is Mr. Rather smiling yet?"

"No, sir." She giggled. "Not yet."

"Don't hold your breath."

Josie continued to laugh at their private joke and Steve joined in. Nobody appreciated Steve's brand of humor as much as gray-haired Josie.

Drake Rather, a somewhat rigid but trusted Brit, entered

Steve's office carrying a briefcase. Steve had always thought his no-nonsense assistant would have made a good Secret Service officer or FBI agent. Rather stood stiffly beside the empty chair in front of Steve's desk.

"Please," Steve said, "sit down."

"Thank you, sir." Rather sat down and put his briefcase in his lap.

"So." Steve crossed his arms and placed them over the edge of the papers on his desk. "What brings you to my office right at closing time?"

"It's about Dr. Hollister, sir."

Steve's antennae went up. "Gina Hollister?"

Drake Rather nodded. "My brother is married to an American, and Randy, my nephew, left a magazine at my apartment last night. I came across an article about Dr. Hollister in it." He handed Steve the magazine. "I thought you should take a look at it."

Steve glanced at the cover. Seeing nothing unusual, he looked back at Rather.

"Turn to page twenty-six."

Steve started flipping pages.

Rather cleared his throat. "I assume this student-published magazine of Randy's is illegal."

"Illegal?"

Rather nodded. "I was told student-published magazines like this are quite popular on some college campuses these days. Every issue contains stories and candid photos of faculty members in compromising situations—so I'm told." The wrinkle in Drake Rather's forehead disappeared, and the muscles in his face had turned to stone. "According to the article Dr. Hollister is especially popular among college-age men."

Steve tilted his head at an angle. "Considering her religious views this is amazing. Did she give her permission for this story to be written?"

"I would think not, sir."

Steve finally found page twenty-six: "Teacher-Babe of the Month, Gina Hollister." Steve swallowed. *Teacher-Babe of the Month?*

In the enlarged snapshot Gina was walking down a sidewalk in a business suit, carrying a briefcase. The story began by giving her dress size and other personal information. Steve wondered how the author of the article managed to get such detailed information.

"Turn to the next page," Rather urged. "It gets better."

Colored photos of Gina at the beach in a black bikini glared back at him. Steve sucked in his breath. "These pictures must have been taken before she got religion."

"That's possible, sir," Rather said. "But even Christians wear swimsuits from time to time, like everyone else. My nephew purchased the magazine at a campus rummage sale. This issue is over two years old." Drake cleared his throat. "I do know she wasn't *Dr.* Hollister when these pictures were taken. All this is explained in the article."

Merely to say Gina looked lovely didn't tell the whole story. She was nothing short of perfection. Steve wanted to build dream castles in those blue eyes of hers. And how could he forget her sharp wit and spark of intelligence? A man would never be bored with a woman like Gina around.

Rather peered at Steve. "If you don't mind my saying so, Dr. Hollister is not exactly the academic-looking type, is she?"

Steve tensed. "And why not?"

"I meant that, well ..." Rather shrugged. "She doesn't look like any of the teachers I had at university, if you see what I mean." Straight-faced Rather grinned for perhaps the first time since signing on at Bricot. "I wouldn't have minded having a professor who looked like her when I was a student, sir."

"Oh." Steve knew what he meant. What surprised him was Rather's reaction to the photos of Gina. He'd always avoided making personal comments, and Steve didn't like anyone putting

Gina in a bad light. Steve's reprimanding gaze zeroed in on Rather.

Rather's facial expression turned serious. "I didn't mean to offend you, sir."

"No problem." Steve examined the other picture, the shot of Gina standing by a man. "Who's the guy?"

"A stockbroker by the name of Phil Arnold. The article said they were engaged. My nephew thinks Arnold is married to someone else now."

"Did your nephew say why they broke up?" Steve asked.

"No. But if you like I can do some checking."

"That won't be necessary." Steve looked down at the photos again. "Anything else you wanted to discuss with me?"

"No, sir. Plans for the trip to France were cancelled as you requested."

"Good." Steve managed to manufacture one more unimpassioned glance at the photo of Gina. "We'll be having a short staff meeting at nine in the morning. Spread the word. We'll discuss the oil deal I'll be working on. The board's already approved my plans, but I wanted my staff here to know where the company is headed before I leave for Colorado."

"I'll see to it. But there is one more matter I would like to discuss with you, sir." Rather hesitated before saying more. "It concerns Dr. Ward Dremont."

"Who?"

"That scientist who was in the news recently, the astrobiologist. His secretary wants to get in touch with you."

"Why?"

"Maybe Dr. Dremont hopes to get you to finance one of his projects. I read that some in the press think you might be his secret backer."

"Secret backer? What do I know about astrobiology? If the secretary calls again, say I'm not available. And Rather, since I won't be able to attend the other meetings in Europe like I first planned, I want you to take over for me."

"Very good, sir."

"In fact the entire plan is already set up in my mind," Steve went on. "I'll have all the details mapped out for you and written down before I leave for Colorado."

"Yes, sir." Rather gathered his things and hurried out.

Steve needed to relax after the meeting with his assistant. He trusted Drake Rather, but the man was a Brit, a proper English gentleman. Rather's serious attitude sometimes put Steve's nerves on edge. Now was one of those times. Stretching briefly, Steve leaned back in his swivel chair and placed his hands behind his head. The tension inside him continued.

In spite of his concern for Amanda, the magazine article and photos of Gina had stirred up emotions of a different kind. Until now Drake Rather had never showed any kind of an interest in women. Did the normally serious Englishman blush when he talked about Gina? Or had Steve only imagined his assistant's interest in Gina because of his own growing awareness of her?

Josie once again peered at him from the doorway, interrupting his thoughts. "I'm leaving now, sir. Is there anything else I need to do before I go?"

"I can handle everything," he said. "And thanks for staying late." He paused. "Have a good one."

"Oh, I will."

Steve froze. The phrase, *Oh, I will,* brought back way too many unpleasant memories, and these memories played in his mind long after Josie left the building. *Oh, I will* was part of the last phone conversations Steve had with his ex-wife before she died.

He had said something like, "When are you going to send me a copy of Amanda's report card?"

Myra had said, "Oh, I will." But she never did.

Steve knew he shouldn't be bitter. Myra never did any of the things she promised she'd do, while always finding the time to do what she wanted to do.

Probably a lot of wives were unfaithful to their husbands, he reminded himself. Some had affairs with businessmen in competition with their husbands and told lies. However, he doubted many women had boyfriends who attempted to take over their husband's companies.

Before reaching for the stack of papers, Steve sneaked another quick look at the magazine story.

Rather was the one who first interviewed Gina for the job. Why wasn't he told she was beautiful? Yes, he wanted a relationship with Gina. But marriage? Never. He was married once and still in recovery as a result of the relationship. He'd sworn he'd never leave himself open to heartache again and saw no reason to break that vow. Furthermore Gina was super religious, while he hadn't attended a worship service in years.

Steve had the sudden urge to call Gina, and now he had an excuse to do it. He wanted to let her know he'd managed to convince Amanda to go to Colorado after all, but he hadn't had much luck getting in touch with Gina lately. He was about to grab the phone and press in her number again when he remembered she had said she could also be reached on her mother's landline. He had Josie track down the number, and then he touched in that number instead.

"Hello," an unfamiliar female voice said from the other end of the line.

Steve blinked. He must have called the wrong number. "I'm sorry, ma'am. I was calling the Hollister residence."

"This is Lucille Hollister."

"Oh, Mrs. Hollister, this is Steve Bryson. Is Gina there?"

"Not right now," the woman said. "I'm her mother and recently moved to San Antonio. I stopped by to pick up a few more of my things. I expect Gina later this evening."

"I left a message on her cell earlier, but she hasn't answered."

"Call her at this number anytime. Her cell phone doesn't always work."

"I tried texting her," Steve said. "No luck there either. I knew she planned to move into your house, but I didn't know she already had. I took a chance calling your number just in case."

"Would you like me to tell Gina you called?"

"That won't be necessary. I'll keep trying to reach her. Sorry I bothered you."

"You haven't. Thanks for calling."

Gina had said her mother would be visiting her grandmother in Oklahoma soon. Maybe the trip was delayed since Mrs. Hollister mentioned San Antonio. He couldn't help wondering if her mother would tell Gina he called.

Why was it so hard to get in touch with Gina Hollister?

ON A WARM AFTERNOON in late June, Gina, in navy pants and a matching jacket, waited for her ride to the airport. If not for Drake Rather, she wouldn't have known about today. She wouldn't have known for certain that she still had a job or about the flight to Colorado in less than an hour.

Gina hadn't heard from Steve in days. Apparently, his business trip to Europe was delayed, and he spent two weeks in Houston. At least her phone and internet problems were solved. But Amanda hadn't returned any of her calls. For a while Gina wasn't allowed to see Amanda at all or talk to her on the phone.

"My granddaughter isn't ready for you yet," Mrs. Ford had said.

Obviously Gina wasn't Amanda's favorite person anymore. They weren't even casual friends. Oh, she still cared for Amanda as much as always. But according to Mrs. Ford, Steve and Gina were at the top of Amanda's enemy list.

Gina had no idea how to make things right. Not only that but Gina questioned whether or not she was still Amanda's tutor. She'd only received one short note from Steve and nothing positive from Amanda since the terrible day at the summer house.

Three days ago, Gina had spent an uncomfortable five minutes trying to have a conversation with Amanda in her grandmother's living room while Lola Ford glared at her from across the room. The meeting was a total disaster.

At home on the same night, Gina had heard two radio sermons on forgiveness. As she listened she kept hoping Mrs. Ford wasn't one of the people she was expected to forgive.

The limo arrived at last. Steve and his driver carried Gina's suitcases to the car. Amanda remained inside the limo. Gina had no idea what to expect from Amanda or Steve.

"Ready to go, Dr. Hollister?" Steve asked.

Gina's heart did somersaults. "Yes." She forced an element of calmness into her voice. "I'm ready." At the least she could hold on to the hope Steve hadn't forgotten her completely.

The driver loaded her bags into the trunk, while Gina opened the car door. "Good afternoon, Amanda."

Amanda didn't utter a sound.

Steve came up behind Gina, motioned toward his daughter, and rolled his eyes. Gina interpreted his prolonged eye roll as a plea for help and perhaps a request she say nothing to upset the girl. Without another word Gina slid into a seat toward the back.

Steve sat by his daughter. The driver started the motor, and they wheeled in silence toward the airport.

"How have you been, Amanda?" Gina finally asked. "I've missed you."

"Yeah?" Amanda said barely above a whisper.

"Amanda," Steve said, "Dr. Hollister said she missed you. Aren't you going to answer?"

"Oh, sure." Amanda cocked her head to one side. "Now let me see. I'm fine, but lately I've been too busy riding my horse to miss anybody, okay?" The teenager turned away and peered out a window.

Gina had heard more than a trace of sarcasm in Amanda's

voice. What had become of the sweet young girl she'd known for three years?

Steve turned to Gina and shrugged as if he had no idea how to handle his daughter. Gina managed a smile she hoped would encourage him.

She'd assumed the teenager aired her frustrations because she was deeply hurt. In order for Amanda to be whole again, counseling as well as understanding was vital. Amanda also required a measure of correction. Would Steve give his daughter the kind of discipline the teenager needed?

Amanda's tense facial expression softened as if she'd had a pleasant thought. "Daddy, I want to buy a bathing suit before we get on the plane."

"Do you need one, honey?"

"I most certainly do. The ones I had last summer are faded and worn out. Besides they're babyish and out of style."

Steve pulled out his wallet and handed her several bills. "Will this cover it?"

Amanda smiled, examining the bills. "Thanks, Daddy." She rewarded Steve with a peck on the cheek. "You're great."

Gina suspected Steve had given his daughter some rather large bills. Amanda's attitude toward her father had improved accordingly, and Steve appeared unaware he was being manipulated.

Gina leaned over in order to speak to Steve in the seat in front of her. "I could take Amanda shopping, if you like," she said. "There are several nice shops near the airport."

The teenager shook her head. "No, thanks. I want Daddy to take me shopping."

He sat a little straighter, his inner glow seeming to shine brighter on hearing his daughter's flattering comment. "If that's what you want, Amanda, then that's what we'll do."

Gina pressed her back against the leather seat cover and tried to pretend to enjoy the drive. They would travel to Colorado on a private jet owned by Bricot International and spend one night at a hotel Steve owned in Colorado Springs. Drake Rather claimed Steve had ordered a new car to be delivered to the hotel.

Gina took a moment to think. Not exactly a direct route since the starting point was Texas, but Drake Rather had said Steve had matters to discuss with his hotel staff in Colorado Springs. The side trip there would give him the perfect opportunity.

Near the private airport Amanda found the most expensive-looking boutique in the entire city. "Let's go in here, Daddy."

"I'd feel foolish in a woman's clothing store with a teenager," he whispered to Gina. "Will you go with us? Please."

Gina nodded. "Sure."

Amanda went straight to the rack of swimsuits marked "small sizes" and grabbed a bright red bikini. Gina didn't think this particular swimsuit would be appropriate for a fourteen-year-old girl, but she hated to hurt Amanda's feelings by saying anything negative about it in front of Steve.

"I'm sure the swimsuit would look nice on you, Amanda, but it's more for someone older, don't you think?" Gina pulled out a more conservative bathing suit in the same shade of red. "I think this one is cute."

"I don't," Amanda said. "I want the other one."

"I think I like the bathing suit Dr. Hollister suggested better, too," Steve said. "Why don't you try it on?"

"I'm not five anymore, Daddy. Why do you always treat me like I am?"

"I just thought—"

"If my mother was still alive, she'd buy it for me."

Steve looked vulnerable, perhaps because he was. Amanda knew how to make him feel guilty. Didn't Steve realize he was about to make some of the same mistakes Myra made?

"Well," he said, "if this is the swimsuit you want, then ..."

"Oh, it is, Daddy. It's *just* what I want."

A warm fatherly gleam flashed in his eyes. "Then let's get it." He patted his daughter on the shoulder.

On tiptoe Amanda reached up and kissed her father on the cheek again. "Thanks."

Gina had attempted to convince Steve clothes would make a better gift for a girl Amanda's age than dolls and ginger cookies. But a string bikini swimsuit was not what she had in mind, and she certainly didn't consider it appropriate attire.

First he goes overboard trying to keep Amanda a child. Now he appears to be leaning the other way. She sighed. *Steve needs to develop some sort of balance, and he could sure use a lesson or two on how to compromise.*

STEVE'S PILOT finally announced their flight. Gina entered the plane along with Steve and Amanda. Never having been inside a private jet, she was amazed by the plush leather interior. She looked around, taking it all in, then put her handbag in a storage area above one of the seats.

"Sit here by me, Gina," Steve said.

He sat by a window with an empty seat beside him. But when Gina attempted to sit down, Amanda moved ahead of her, flopping down in the seat next to her father.

"You don't mind if I sit by my daddy, do you, Dr. Hollister?" she said, looking up at her with wide, innocent eyes.

Gina smiled. "Of course not."

When Amanda leaned over to whisper something to Steve, Gina moved to the seat across the aisle from them and picked up a book about Colorado, which she'd brought to read on the plane. After paging through it for a while, she glanced up to find Steve studying her as if he'd been doing it for a long time. Gina dragged her gaze from his and continued reading. When she looked up again, he was staring out a window.

AT LAST THEY arrived in Colorado Springs. Steve thought both Gina and Amanda looked tired. He knew he was, but it wasn't merely fatigue troubling him. Amanda's behavior on the plane baffled him. He'd thought his daughter hated him. Now he thought they had a real chance. While in Houston Steve had two weeks to think about his daughter's recent behavior. He'd thought he'd put it all in perspective. But now ...

Amanda required love and lots of attention; he understood that and intended to fill those needs.

They arrived at Steve's hotel after a long lunch at a nearby cafe. From across the lobby he waved to the manager of his hotel, hoping Kurt wouldn't come over and start a conversation, but he did. At last Steve followed Gina and Amanda to the line of elevators, hoping to get everybody settled in their rooms as soon as possible.

Three hotel attendants in green uniforms nearly stumbled over each other to help Steve with the suitcases. Steve, followed by the three attendants, trudged on toward the elevators.

He'd been watching Gina off and on throughout the trip, and he was certain she was worried about something. He smiled, but she barely returned it. Did Gina resent the attention he showed his daughter?

No, she's too professional to let real or imagined slights get in the way of her job. Maybe she's preoccupied. She looks as if she's deep in thought, but about what?

The elevator doors opened, and everybody crowded inside.

"Amanda," Gina said, "we can go exploring if you'd like. I hear the shops around here are great."

"You go if you want to," Amanda said. "I'm going swimming."

"Swimming?" Gina glanced over at Steve and directed her question to him. "Why is Amanda suddenly interested in swimming?"

He shrugged, offering the explanation Amanda had just recently given him. "Some of her friends here in town are meeting her at the hotel pool. Amanda said they've been texting back and forth for days."

Gina frowned. "I didn't know Amanda knew anybody in Colorado Springs."

"I met them when Mom and I were here," Amanda put in, "when we visited during spring break last year."

"I see." Gina was still gazing at Steve. "I don't suppose you've had the chance to meet any of her friends, have you?"

He shook his head, feeling a bit guilty but determined to cultivate his daughter's seemingly new interest in their relationship. "No. This is the first time she's been here with me. I'm sure the kids are all right though. I know some of their parents."

"Don't you think ...?"

Gina didn't finish, but Steve sensed she had plenty she wanted to say. He'd make sure she had the opportunity. A quiet dinner for two by candlelight might be the setting she needed to air her opinions. Such an environment would also allow him to air a few ideas of his own.

THE ELEVATOR STOPPED at their floor. "I'd like to have a meeting with you over dinner tonight, Dr. Hollister," Steve said. "My private dining room is up on the top floor."

"All right. I have some things I want to discuss with you, too. What time should we meet?"

"I'll be in business meetings until late. Is ten o'clock all right?"

"Ten will be fine."

The metal door slid to one side. Steve looked on as Gina followed Amanda out into the hall. Would he ever tire of watching Gina move? He reached down for his suitcase before following Gina, Amanda, and the hotel attendants into the hall.

Gina reminded him of someone. He'd thought so from the moment they met. But who? Did he think he was some kind of would-be prophet or something? Nevertheless there was a mystery here. Gina belonged in another place, another time in his life.

She followed one of the attendants to Steve's right, while Amanda drifted in the opposite direction.

"This way, Amanda," Gina called after her. "We need to unpack."

"Can't I do it later?"

"I thought you were going swimming. Won't you need to change?"

"Yes, but—"

Gina sent Amanda what Steve perceived to be an impatient gaze.

"Okay, okay," Amanda said. "I'm coming."

Steve's inner smile faded. Why couldn't Amanda have waited awhile before going in to unpack? After all she was just a kid.

Plainly Steve and his daughter's tutor differed on the subject of childrearing as well as religion. He still wasn't convinced Amanda needed the kind of help Gina provided.

Lola Ford had said Amanda read on a third-grade level. Why wouldn't a regular classroom teacher looking for a summer job work out as well as a high-priced specialist like Gina Hollister?

Of course he wanted the best for his only child and liked knowing Gina would be living in his house. But nothing was wrong with Amanda. Maybe she was never taught to read properly. And after witnessing that kiss, Amanda would naturally think Gina and Steve were attracted to each other. No wonder she felt left out. He should include her more.

Steve loved Amanda deeply and wanted her to know it. Could it be he didn't know how to share his feelings any more than his father had known how to share his?

Something he read—couldn't remember where—caused Steve to conclude that Gina and her father weren't on the best of terms. As soon as he got to his hotel room, he'd open his suitcase and take another look at the report Rather worked up on her. He might have missed something.

Gina was a delightful companion at the river, and he was convince she could be again. Steve resolved to do all he could to make that happen.

Forty-five minutes before her scheduled dinner date with Steve, Gina lazed in a scented bubble bath. As she sat there breathing in the sweet odor of spring flowers, she kept going over in her mind how she would present her opinions to Steve. Of course he wanted Amanda's love, but spoiling his daughter was no way to get it. She fully intended to tell him as much but prudently of course.

In order to get her point over, she hoped to project the image of an informed professional. For Gina that meant high heels, a tailored jacket, and matching pants. However she'd spilled a drop of coffee on the outfit she wore on the plane. Except for a pair of jeans, a knit shirt, and a yellow party dress, her clothes had been sent ahead to that oversized house of his. She'd planned to wear jeans and a shirt the next morning on the drive to his estate.

Gina didn't know why she packed the yellow dress. Maybe, subconsciously, she hoped to impress Steve by wearing it.

A maid at the hotel had said the private dining room overlooked a swimming pool. Since Amanda found it so interesting, Gina wanted to see it.

Revitalized after a nap and a warm bath, she slipped on the party dress and stepped into white heels. Sheer pale yellow fabric hugged her body from under her arms to her slender waist, then swirled out in a wide gathered skirt. The scent of her favorite perfume surrounded her. Her hair fell in loose curls, framing her face, while pearl earrings dangled from her ears. The yellow dress swished in time with her determined gait as she strode to the private elevator. Her confidence increased during the ride up.

The elevator stopped on the top floor, and the doors opened. Steve waited beyond the doorway. Something stirred deep within her at the sight of him. Her good intentions evaporated, along with her confidence.

Gina stepped into the secluded dining room, shivering like the heroine always did in all those romance novels she'd been reading. The possibility they might be completely alone disturbed her a little. Her true motivation for accepting his invitation had nothing to do with romance. Or did it?

She must concentrate or risk losing her entire focus. Oh, Steve looked dashing in his white dinner jacket, but it was not a problem she couldn't handle.

He smiled, and all her apprehensions washed away. She returned his infectious smile without looking where she was going. She took another step and plowed right into the serving table. Gina grabbed hold of the back of a chair to keep from falling.

He reached out. "You all right?"

"I guess," she whispered as softly as a small child.

A pitcher of water on the table had overturned. Icy water tumbled like a waterfall onto the skirt of her yellow dress and down to the blue carpet. The white tablecloth was soaked.

"You must be freezing," he said. "Would you like to go back to your room and change?"

"No, I'm fine." She refused to mention she had nothing else to wear except a pair of blue jeans. "The wet spot's not so big, really."

Accidents like this didn't occur when the hero and heroine met for a romantic dinner, nor did they transpire during business meetings between two equals. As a result of this turn of events, she had two alternatives. She could slip into her supercilious PhD mode, or she could pray and laugh it off. She chose the latter.

Gina leaned down to look for something she could use to mop up the mess. "Do you happen to have an old rag on you?" she asked without looking at Steve.

He laughed. "Sure." He reached for a white tablecloth on one of the vacant tables. "Will this do?"

Gina studied the cloth carefully. "It looks expensive."

"I got it at a garage sale."

"Are you kidding?" She cocked her head. "You don't expect me to believe you shop at garage sales, do you?

"Why not?" Still chuckling softly, he seized the tablecloth in both hands. "Garage sales save businessmen like me a lot of money." He got down on his knees and rubbed the carpet vigorously. "I'm always looking for ways to economize."

Gina knelt beside him, clutched the other end of the tablecloth, and started rubbing. "Were you saving money when you gave Amanda all those bills to buy a bathing suit?"

"That's different. Amanda's my daughter." Deep dimples punctuated his mirthful grin. "You know," he said, "I hire a cleaning staff to do jobs like this."

"Yeah?" Gina teased. "Well, my mother taught me a long time ago to clean up my own messes. She also told me never to trust a man who cleaned the floor with a linen tablecloth."

"I'm still concerned about your pretty yellow dress," Steve said.

Gina shrugged and tossed back her hair.

"What if a water stain's left when the dress dries?" he asked. "My grandmother always worried about such things."

"It won't happen with modern fabrics. But if it does I'll send my dress to the cleaners. They do have cleaning shops near your country home, don't they?"

"I'm sure they do. If not I'll have your dress flown back to Texas on the next flight."

Gina lifted her perfectly shaped eyebrows. "I'm impressed."

"You should be. It would probably cost me a bundle." He glanced down at the carpet again. "That's about as dry as we can get this rug right now. Would you like to keep scrubbing or have something to eat?"

"I think I'd like to eat." Gina got to her feet. As an afterthought she rubbed the front of her dress with a dry corner of the tablecloth.

"You look lovely, you know," he said. "Wet spot on the front of your dress and all."

"Thank you, kind sir," she said in her best southern accent.

He laughed and glanced at an intimate corner table by a window. "Should we order now?"

His deep voice sounded so southern Gina wondered if she'd been transported back in time to Civil War days.

"Or would you rather wait awhile, ma'am?" he asked.

"Let's order now," she said. "I'm famished."

His face looked tender, and his polished manners fueled her interest. He escorted her to the carved oak chairs. Now all she had to do was call up a desire to discuss his relationship with his daughter.

Steve pulled a velvet cord hanging from the ceiling, and a waiter quickly appeared. They ordered trout flown in from the coast, a light salad, and an especially tasty baked potato topped with melted cheese and a spicy sauce.

She'd once read a book about situations like this, and she'd learned she didn't have to let what happened with the water pitcher destroy her evening. She could and would let it go.

Almost as soon as she thought those words, her entire evening took on even more romantic overtones. Perhaps a discussion of Amanda and her problems could wait a while.

Since the breakup with Phil, Gina had concentrated on getting an education. She'd never attended a candlelight dinner quite like this one in her entire life. She felt almost shy as she watched Steve study her from his side of the table. She should look away, think about something besides him.

Above the door a carved shield and crossed swords in polished wood caught her interest. Instantly she pictured Steve, sword in hand, facing an unknown enemy from behind a metal shield.

Several men had flirted with Gina at the airport while they waited for their flight to Colorado Springs. Steve had turned them all away with a look of quiet authority. In spite of his rather indulgent outlook regarding his daughter, Gina had felt Steve's understated protection from the moment he arrived in the limo.

The waiter returned with their meal. Steve grinned as soon as the waiter left the room, then lifted his glass of wine in a silent toast. Ignoring her wine Gina lifted her tumbler of ice water.

"You don't drink?"

"No," she said. "I don't."

"Then I won't either." He connected his water glass with hers in a silent toast.

Gina blinked. *I'm blushing.* Somehow the clicking sound the glasses made when they touched had caused her cheeks to warm. She searched for something to center on, anything but Steve.

A beautifully carved maple hutch stood on the north wall, capturing her full attention. She'd visited every antique shop in Austin, looking for a hutch like that one but without success.

"I thought you'd like the sideboard," he said, following her gaze. "Want a better look?"

"It's called a hutch. And what about our meal?"

"The fish will still be here when we get back."

"Then I'd like to see it," she said. "Very much."

Steve helped her out of her chair. Careful not to stumble or hook the hem of her skirt on something, she went over to examine the antique hutch.

Gina ran the palms of both hands across the smooth finish with its interesting distresses and timeworn flaws. Steve stood directly behind her with his hands on her shoulders.

"What do you think?" He rubbed his chin against the top of her head.

"If you're asking about the hutch, it's wonderful." She glanced back at Steve, and his affirming smile dissolved all her feelings of self-consciousness. "Where did you find such a beautiful piece of furniture?"

"Here," he said, "in the hotel."

"You mean you didn't pick it up at a garage sale?"

He squeezed her shoulders. "I don't claim to know as much about old furniture as you appear to, but as they say, I know what I like."

"That's a good enough reason. Where in the hotel did you find it?"

"Up in the attic. As Chairman of the Board of Bricot Corp., I was looking around up there among the junk on the day I signed the papers to buy this place, and there was the sideboard."

"Hutch."

"Okay, *hutch*, and it had dust on it an inch thick."

"Amazing. Find anything else?"

"Not like this."

"I hope to own an antique as lovely as this one someday." Pulling her gaze from his, she moved around to the other side of the hutch and safer ground.

"I don't know if it's true." Steve's tone warmed. "But they say sometimes priceless treasures are found without looking for them."

Her cheeks felt warm again. *He's talking about me.*

"I found a very special treasure recently," he went on, "in a place I would never have thought to look." His eyes were on her, yet his voice sounded as calm and steady as ever.

She'd done it again, let this romantic fantasy exploding between them get out of hand. She was supposed to be a sophisticated professional. At that moment, she felt like anything but.

They had a whole summer ahead of them, and she'd be seeing Steve almost daily. If he could tear down her resistance so easily now, what defense would she have later?

Gina should go to her room immediately. But how would she explain why she left?

"I think I'd like to get back to my fish," she announced. She whirled around and returned to her place at the table.

To avoid another of his heart-stopping looks, she glanced out the window. Her gaze moved downward, focusing on the swimming pool below. A young man chased a beautiful young woman in a skimpy red bikini around the pool. Both had dark complexions and were possibly Italian. If she didn't know better, she'd swear the young woman was—

Amanda? Amanda!

What was Amanda doing at the pool with a boy, and at this time of night?

"What are you looking at down there?" Steve asked.

"That girl. I think she's Amanda."

"Impossible. My daughter's downstairs in her room and probably asleep by now," he said. "I tucked her in myself."

"I looked in on her earlier, too. But it's Amanda all right. The swimsuit she's wearing is the one she bought today."

"How can you be sure?" he asked doubtfully.

"I was there. Remember?"

"So was I, but ..." He followed her gaze downward. Then he laughed. His tone had a mocking ring to it. "That's not my daughter. Even from here I can see she's wearing too much makeup to be Amanda. And shoes with super high heels? Really, Gina."

"The shoes could be mine," Gina said. "Besides most young girls nowadays own pumps with high heels. Maybe several pair."

"If she's wearing your shoes without your permission, then of course I'll have a talk with her. But I strongly doubt—"

"Are you saying you'd scold your daughter for wearing my shoes but not for sneaking out with a boy?"

"What's so terrible about sneaking out to go swimming?" he asked. "I did it a few times myself when I was her age."

"Then you're not going to do anything about it?"

"Well, it isn't as if her parent isn't watching her," he said. "And in my opinion she isn't doing anything so terrible. Besides it's probably not Amanda anyway."

"I can't believe your permissive attitude," Gina shot back. "I've seen a big change in Amanda since her mother died. I think she needs strong discipline, especially now."

"After all she's been through this year?"

Steve sounded like Amanda's grandmother. "Children have a way of using misfortune to their own advantage." She'd tried to keep her tone as calm as possible. "To get their parents to do exactly what they want," she added.

"But surely you don't think ..."

"You should be aware of the possibility Amanda might try to take advantage of you, sir. She tried it with her mother."

"I'm nothing like Myra," he said, "and I care deeply what happens to my daughter. So what do you suggest I do? Lock her up?"

"No, go out to the pool and tell Amanda to go to her room immediately. And ground her for a stated length of time."

"Ground her?" He shook his head. "I'm not sure I agree with that idea. Come to think of it, I'm not so hot on some of your teaching methods either."

"Are you saying you don't plan to do anything?"

"I plan to finish my fish."

"Then I'm afraid you'll be forced to eat your meal alone because I'm leaving." Gina got up from the table.

"Don't go," he said as she headed for the door. "I'm sure we can work this out."

"I doubt it."

"At least give me the chance to apologize."

She sensed he was following her, and she raced to the elevator without looking back.

"You're really going?" he asked, closer now.

Nodding quickly she darted inside. It was unlikely a man like Steve Bryson was accustomed to being turned down flat by a woman.

As the doors closed she glanced back, forcing a weak smile. "Goodnight, Mr. Bryson."

His eyes widened, but he didn't reply. The elevator jerked downward at a rapid speed, throwing Gina against the back wall. She had to grip the railing with both hands to stay in an upright position.

The lift stopped suddenly, leaving her stomach far behind. She must look ridiculous, standing there in a damp dress, holding on to the railing for dear life. At least nobody stood in front of the doors watching her as she got off the elevator. However Steve would surely recall every embarrassing detail of their disastrous dinner.

Gina slammed her bedroom door. The yellow dress soon fell in a heap around her ankles. When she finally cooled down, she changed into her nightgown and repacked her suitcase.

They were leaving for Steve's lodge early the next morning. However she considered flying back to Texas immediately. Of what use was she as Amanda's tutor if Steve refused to act on Gina's suggestions?

Ten minutes later the connecting door opened between Gina's bedroom and a private sitting room. Amanda charged inside, glaring at Gina.

"Thanks to you, Daddy sent me to my room tonight."

"Good for your father. That's exactly what he should have done."

"Not!" the teenager shouted.

Amanda wore heavy makeup, causing her to look older and perhaps more worldly than Gina's idea of a proper fourteen-year-old.

"Why are you so mean to me now?" Amanda demanded. "You used to be nice."

"I'm still nice."

"You sure don't act like it!"

"You aren't acting very nice either, Amanda. You told your father and me you were going to sleep, not going to the swimming pool to meet a boy."

"I woke up. Okay?"

"We trusted you, Amanda. You knew you didn't have permission to sneak out to meet a young man, especially one we don't know." Gina glanced down at Amanda's shoes. "You're wearing my shoes, not to mention entirely too much makeup."

"Well, par-don me." Amanda's sarcastic tone of voice was hard to miss. She removed first one black pump and then the other, letting them drop to the floor. *Thump. Thump.*

Frowning Gina picked up her shoes, wiped them off with a hand towel, and put them in her suitcase. "Your father will hear about this."

Amanda put her hands on her hips. "What's so terrible about wearing makeup? All the girls my age wear as much as I do. Maybe more."

"The way you applied your makeup tonight wasn't flattering," Gina replied. "I'll be glad to show you how to do it correctly if you like."

"Who made you an expert?" Amanda asked. "Paulo thought I looked great."

"Paulo being the boy you were with, I suppose? Where and when did you meet him?"

"We met at the pool this afternoon."

"He looks too old for you," Gina said.

"Well, he doesn't think he's too old for me."

"Did he kiss you, Amanda?"

"Maybe." She shrugged. "We're friends. I was having a great time until you ruined everything."

"Does he know you're only fourteen?"

"He knows," Amanda said. "And I'm not saying one more word about him. Daddy already asked me enough questions for one night. If you want any information, ask him."

"Go to your bathroom, Amanda," Gina demanded. "And wash your face. I have a lot more to say about all this."

Amanda turned and stomped from the room.

Gina's phone rang. She glanced at her caller I.D. *Daddy!* Why was her father calling at this hour of the night? Would he ever give up? She counted to ten. Then she touched the disconnect icon. Her phone went dead, along with part of her heart. Guilt flooded her.

Should she call him back? Maybe, but not now. Amanda topped her list, and what Gina had to say to her couldn't wait until morning.

*G*ina entered Amanda's bedroom and shut the door behind her. "Let's talk about what's-his-name. *Now!*"

"Paulo." Amanda was stretched out on the bed. She sat up. "His name is Paulo."

"And what is Paulo's last name?'

She shrugged. "I don't know. He's a foreign student from Italy and only in Colorado Springs for the summer. He attends the university at Boulder."

"University?" Gina's mouth opened of its own accord. "How old is this guy?"

Amanda didn't reply.

Gina stood there without saying a word, waiting for Amanda to answer her question. When no answer came she decided to put off the confrontation until later.

"It's late," Gina said at last. "We'll discuss this in the morning."

She turned, crossed the sitting room, and went back to her own bedroom. But during the night Gina heard Amanda crying. She raced back to the teenager's room without bothering to knock.

"Amanda." Gina sat on the edge of the bed and touched her shoulder. "Can I help?"

"No!" Amanda buried her head in her pillow, sobbing. "Go away!"

Gina didn't go away. She moved over to a chair and sat beside Amanda's bed until the teenager went to sleep.

Early the next morning Gina found a note under her door.

"Sorry about the misunderstanding last night. You could be right about Amanda. I should have listened. Steve"

Could be right? Gina shook her head. *I am right. But Steve would rather walk on hot ashes than admit it.* She tucked the note in her luggage, along with the one Steve sent with the flowers, and closed the suitcase.

Amanda slept late the next morning. Gina didn't want to wake her, forcing a delay in the move to Steve's estate. Gina also postponed the talk she planned to have with Amanda. Instead she engaged in a little private investigating of her own in hopes of finding out all she could about the young man at the swimming pool.

A few minutes later she stood in front of the hotel's main desk, waiting to speak to the desk clerk. A little old lady with white hair and a long story to tell was in line ahead of her.

With those thick glasses and her dark hair pulled back in an old-fashioned looking bun, the desk clerk looked like Gina's childhood memory of the Wicked Witch of the West. Gina read the name on a nameplate in front of the desk clerk: Mrs. Mable Rosen. It was probably against hotel rules to answer the kind of questions Gina planned to ask, but she'd give it a try anyway.

Gina stepped forward, forcing a smile. "Good morning."

The desk clerk frowned. "And what can I do for you?"

"Well, I have a question."

"Let's hear it."

"It's about ...about Paulo, a young man working here in the hotel."

Now she really frowned. "Do you have a complaint?"

Yes didn't sound like a good answer. "No," she said, forcing a smile. "Not at all. He seems very helpful. I wanted the hotel staff to know."

The wicked witch grinned—at least the edges of her lips turned up a little. "We like Paulo here, very much. We're glad you like him, too."

"He seems so nice."

"He *is* nice," the desk clerk replied.

"I would love to hear more about him."

Miss Mable Rosen glanced away briefly, as if checking who might be watching. "I'm not allowed to share private information about our employees with our guests. But in *my* opinion, Paulo Ponte is the kind of young man we dream of having our daughters marry. If I'd ever married and had a daughter, I'd want her husband to be just like Paulo."

This was good news, but why was Paulo interested in Amanda Bryson? She was a beauty for sure, and maybe he thought she was older. Or could his real interest be Steve Bryson's money?

They checked out of the hotel after a late breakfast. Gina never got the chance to have another talk with Amanda or to tell Steve what she'd learned about Paulo. Later she got two more phone calls and a text from her father but refused to answer any of them.

The note Steve sent before they left the hotel had softened her feelings toward him but changed nothing. She'd keep him at arm's length and tell him her opinions every chance she got.

Yes, Gina had to admit she might be falling in love with Steve, but she'd keep her love well hidden from him and everyone else.

They'd be leaving Steve's plane in Colorado Springs and driving to his estate in the van he ordered. His pilot would fly his plane to Durango later.

Steve had said, "The drive through those mountains is something to see." She was certain that was true, and she could hardly wait to view the mountains for the first time. Steve couldn't have been more considerate during the long journey, but Amanda complained about everything from the food to highway conditions. Nevertheless Gina fell in love with the hills and Colorado's white-capped mountains long before they reached Steve's estate.

The quaint shops and gingerbread houses she saw along the way fulfilled her deepest expectations. She also liked the state's cooler mountain air. The charm of the immediate area made her feel like a child who'd entered a fairyland. She tried to forget everything else.

At last they reached the city limits of Durango. "My place is some miles out of town," Steve said. "We'll drive through town and on down the highway a ways. Then we'll turn off the main road. We'll have to rough it for a few more miles down a narrow country road."

Some minutes later Gina leaned over to speak to Steve in the seat in front of her.

"Mr. Bryson, your assistant, Mr. Rather, said your home here was large and in the middle of a big estate you inherited from your grandfather. Is the lodge strictly for vacationing and winter skiing, or does it also have another purpose?"

"It's not a ski lodge. In the winter we ski over in Purgatory. In the summer and fall, the house is used for hiking, fishing, and swimming in the waterfall pond I mentioned earlier."

"I can hardly wait to see everything, especially the waterfall." She looked out a window. "Are we almost there?"

"We're turning off the highway right now."

As they turned onto a country road, Gina was happily surprised when green pastures, flowers, and tall pines greeted her. Beauty surrounded them, and nothing looked as Steve had described it.

"If this is roughing it," Gina said, taking in a deep breath of country air, "then I'm all for it. This place is wonderful."

He flashed her a grin in the rearview mirror. "Wonderful, huh? Well, you haven't seen anything yet."

The road curved upward and around a hill. A few minutes later a huge mansion appeared in the distance, sitting on a flat surface near the top of another hill. Surrounded by a heavy mist, the outline of the structure was all Gina could see, but it was enough to identify its shape. Was one of her dreams about to come true?

"Who lives there?" she asked.

"We do," Steve said. "At least we will as soon as I can get us inside."

"It's fantastic." Gina was amazed. "Is *this* what you call a large house?"

"Yep."

"I was expecting something large but quaint."

"I call this quaint," he said. "Don't you?"

"I'd call it a castle."

"In a way it is. It's similar to the Neuschwanstein Castle in Germany but on a smaller scale, of course."

Steve wheeled down an impressive drive, while Gina recalled what Nicole had said about Steve locking her in the tower of a castle. At that precise moment she spotted a tower bursting through the mist.

"My German ancestors would have loved to know my grandfather had the place built here in the mountains of Colorado," he said.

"Are you German, too?"

His quick smile broadened. "Afraid so."

"Is there any group of people you're *not* related to?" Gina asked.

"I'm still checking."

Gina couldn't believe Steve had an interest in castles. He seemed to be more of the modern flashy type.

"I would never have built such an expensive structure," he

said again, as if he'd read her thoughts. "But my grandfather was into genealogy and something of a romantic."

"I can believe that."

"Like you, Gina, my grandfather liked antiques."

"Well, that speaks highly of him, doesn't it? And please, stop calling me by my first name."

The edges of his eyes crinkled charmingly. "Grandfather had this big old house built after he visited a small village in Germany."

"And your German ancestors came from the village?"

"They were peasants, but yes."

Steve's van climbed through the mist and on toward the top of the mountain. Gina thought the house fit its inspiring surroundings perfectly. Not only did it look as if it were a part of the hill, it reminded Gina of a Grimm's fairy tale, complete with knights in shining armor and maidens in distress.

"What do you think?" he asked.

"It's wonderful. What else would I think?"

"The panoramic view from the tower room is spectacular," he said, "and I want you both to see it."

Gina smiled. "I can hardly wait."

"What about you, Amanda?" he asked.

"I'll see it ...sooner or later."

Besides the house the estate contained a ten-car garage. Gina counted them. She also noticed three or four small houses, two storage buildings, and a large barn. Before Steve parked, Amanda started to get out of the car.

"Whoa." Steve killed the engine. "Where do you think you're going, young lady?"

"Swimming in the waterfall."

"Swimming?" Gina tensed. "Well, I don't think ..." Gina stopped herself lest she interfere. Memories of Amanda and Paulo at the swimming pool in Colorado Springs flooded her mind.

"You don't think she should go off alone again," Steve said, "do you?"

"No, I don't."

"She'll be safe," he said, "I assure you."

"She's your daughter. What else can I say?"

"When anyone is here," he said, "I keep the compound heavily guarded. One of my employees is at the pool right now, serving as a lifeguard."

Gina looked around. "I don't see any guards."

"Trust me. They live right over there." He pointed to the largest of the quaint little houses.

"I'm going now," Amanda put in.

"Have you got your swimsuit?" Steve asked.

"I'm wearing it under my clothes." Amanda got out of the car and started running.

"Be careful, honey," Steve shouted after her.

"I will."

"Will she know how to find the pool?" Gina asked.

"How can she miss? I've been talking, off and on, about the pond and the waterfall since we left the hotel."

"That's true."

STEVE SPENT ALMOST an hour showing Gina around his enormous home. She enjoyed every second of it and hoped a tour of the castle would give her the opportunity to discuss Amanda and her problems. She simply had to select the right time.

They climbed winding stairs to what Steve called the tower room. *Tower room.* Gina had to smile when she heard those words, recalling what Nicole had said about towers. They finally reached the top floor and a small landing.

The door straight ahead was open, but another door to the right was closed. She wondered what was behind the door but thought maybe she shouldn't ask.

Steve motioned for her to enter the door straight ahead, and she did.

"The tower room is a combination office and studio," he said.

Gina noticed a telescope pointing out one of the windows.

"Want to take a look?" he asked.

"Yes." Gina took the telescope in both hands and peered at her surroundings. "Wow!" She glanced back at Steve. "The mountains are absolutely picture-perfect, aren't they?"

"I think so."

Gina studied her environment a little longer. As she turned back around, she noticed the tower room was divided into two unequal parts with a wall at the north end. She wondered what was on the other side of the wall but again kept the thought to herself. Then a toy-sized castle grabbed her attention, pulling her to the opposite side of the room. Gina went over and stood in front of Steve's castle in miniature, set up on a long table. "What's this?"

"I've been working on a design for remodeling the castle, as you call it, and love doing it." He sent her a warm side glance. "It's part of what I meant when I said I have business in Colorado this summer. It all started when I was in college and had the opportunity to help a kid who attended an elementary school near my dorm." He glanced through one of the windows. "Just look at that view."

"Yes, it's beautiful." And the landscape *was* beautiful. But she wanted to hear more about the kid. Who was he, and how had Steve helped him?

"As I was saying, after I met the kid, remodeling this estate and helping children became one of my goals in life. I never regretted it."

"Never regretted what? Remodeling, or helping kids?"

"Both." He laughed. "So I plan to convert this big old house into a shelter for homeless children. With an entire summer ahead of us, I should have plenty of time to arrange for the remodeling job ahead of me."

"What a beautiful idea." She hoped to learn more about his plans for the shelter and could hardly wait to hear what he'd say next. When he didn't say anything, she dropped the subject and studied the model again. "You didn't do this excellent work, did you?"

"I did, though I'd hardly call it excellent." He grew silent for a moment. "I have a lot of hobbies. At one time I intended to become a football coach, and as I said, I like working with kids. My BS and MS are in business management with minors in architecture, science, art, and physical education, among other things."

She must have given him a strange look because he certainly seemed to pick up on it.

"I know." He nodded. "My minors don't exactly go with my major, do they? But when you have as much money as my family has, you're allowed to do strange things like that." He shrugged. "I never got around to working on my doctorate."

"So you trashed your dreams in favor of your father's company."

"Bricot was started by my grandfather."

"The grandfather who built this castle?"

"The same." Steve didn't say anything for a moment. "I always knew I'd have to take over and head Bricot sooner or later. Now it's Bricot International. I thought I'd hate bossing the company but was pleasantly surprised to find I actually enjoy running the family businesses."

"I've heard your genius is what pulled the company out of the red and caused it to start showing a profit again."

"No," he insisted. "The company was already in recovery by the time I took over the reins at Bricot."

Steve's artistic ability overwhelmed her, and he was also modest. His gentleness, kindness, understanding, and interest in helping others touched her heart. Maybe he was more of a humanitarian than she first thought.

The guard who carried their suitcases in from the car came

into the tower room with a large package wrapped in brown paper. If its shape was any indication, it could be a large picture frame.

Steve smiled. "Oh, the package I ordered came."

"Yes, sir," the man said. "Where should I put it?"

"Put it under one of the windows there."

The guard leaned the package against the wall as he was told. Was there a photograph inside the mysterious package? Gina was too polite to ask.

The man left the room, and Steve turned to Gina. "The package is in honor of you, Doctor."

She blinked in surprise. "Me?" If this was a gift from her boss, Steve was out of line. Maybe she misunderstood. She would wait and see.

"I'd been looking for an excuse to buy a new picture to decorate the walls up here in the tower," he said. "You inspired me with your love of bluebonnets. So I found an oil painting I like. It reminds me of Texas. I think you'll like it, too." He paused. "Open it."

Gina didn't move an inch.

"Please." His deep voice had compassion tucked inside and a dash of tenderness.

"I'll need a pair of scissors." Gina knelt down in front of the package. Why did she always feel obligated to respond every time he said *jump?*

"Try this." Steve handed her a pocket knife.

Carefully Gina cut a small slash in the brown paper, big enough to get three fingers in, and began ripping the paper. The wooden frame had an old–fashioned look to it, and she did like antiques. To Gina the painting was a masterpiece in shades of blue, lavender, and green. She grabbed the frame with both hands, holding it up to the light.

"What do you think?" he asked.

"What would I think? It's wonderful."

"I knew you'd like it."

Suddenly some of the degrading stories Myra told about Steve's private life and his ability to draw women to him flashed before her. The smile, forming in her mind, died before coming to the surface. Was the painting another of Steve's tricks to get her to fall in love with him? He must never know she was already falling. After all, she was in Colorado to help Amanda and for no other reason. She should focus on that. Myra had warned her about all this before she died.

"You're uneasy about something, aren't you?" Steve said. "Please tell me what it is."

"We need to talk about Amanda and about the way she's been acting lately. By now you must know how worried I've been. And then last night—"

"She went swimming with a boy," he finished. "I've already talked to her about that."

"That boy, as you call him, is a student at a university."

He sent her a thoughtful look. "I was eighteen my freshman year. Some of my friends were seventeen."

"Yes. He could be a freshman. On the other hand he could be a senior."

"A senior? Really, Doctor, my daughter isn't stupid."

"I agree with you. But it's her attitude. Amanda was rude to me last night after you sent her to her room. And it's so unlike her."

"Amanda was upset with me," he said. "She took it out on you. I'm not saying she was right, but her actions were certainly understandable, considering all she'd been through in the last few months. And I promise to speak to her regarding this matter. Now why don't we walk down to the pool and check on Amanda? I know you'll feel better if we do, and so will I."

He'd made light of Amanda's problems. Ignoring them altogether was more like it. So why was she allowing him to escort her to the waterfall as if there were no problems?

In the distance Amanda stood in the pond, showering under the waterfall.

"See?" Steve said. "Amanda's fine."

"She seems all right, and I see a lifeguard standing by." The situation suggested Gina change the subject before arguments surfaced, but she had a couple of things she wanted to discuss. "Never having visited a castle before, I don't know the rules. Do we dress for dinner as they do in the movies, or would something less formal suffice?"

"Anything you want to wear will be fine. We'll be dining early tonight and in the kitchen. I'm wearing exactly what I have on now."

"Then I will, too."

If she was going to bring up religion, it was now or never. "I'm what you might call a Bible believer. I try to attend worship services as often as I can. Do you have a local newspaper? I'd like to find out when and where services are held." She hesitated. "I try not to miss."

"Gretel puts a newspaper on the table in front of my plate every morning," he said. "There's probably one on the table now. Feel free to borrow it any time." A sort of half-smile formed on his lips. "Come to think of it, I know of some folks like you, but they don't have a church. They meet in a private home."

"A church isn't a building," she explained. "A church is a group of people who gather together to worship God. Some call the building where services are held a church."

He cocked his head to one side as if trying to remember something. "I can't recall the address where these people meet. I'm sure it'll come to me sooner or later. I'll do some checking and get back to you."

I'll get back to you said the conversation had ended. Besides it was time to go inside and find the newspaper.

"I have to unpack," she said. "And I have other things to do. I better get back to the ...to the ..."

"Castle?" He laughed.

"Yes, the castle." She chuckled. "But I'll need directions to find the kitchen and my room."

"Glad to do it. I can also give you a detailed map if you need it."

'That won't be necessary."

When he'd finished giving directions, she thanked him again and walked away.

"Oh, that reminds me," he called after her. "This is Gretel's night to serve homemade apple dumplings. They're the best in the world. Of course there are always ginger cookies in the cookie jar if you're so inclined."

So inclined? There's that term again. Does Steve think I'm a sugar junkie or something? Gina took another step and looked back. "Thanks for telling me what's for dessert. I'll try to save some tummy space."

SHE'D LEARNED a lot about Steve Bryson, maybe more than she wanted to know. Gina hoped he never learned more than he needed to know about her, including secrets she was unwilling to share, and she could hardly wait to find the newspaper.

A rose bush to the right of the castle's side entrance caught her attention; it was dotted with yellow flowers with an especially large rose near the top. Gina's mother once raised flowers like those. She paused to take in the sweet scent. A rush of unpleasant girlhood memories sent her tumbling back in time.

She'd pulled a big yellow rose from her mother's bush before getting on the school bus one morning. The bus was yellow, too, with the words "High School" written on the side. She'd found a seat by a window. As she looked down at her flower, she heard two of the older boys laughing from the back of the bus.

"Hey, Gina," one of them shouted, "you may not be very smart, but you sure are looking good, especially in your yellow sweater."

Totally humiliated she'd pretended not to hear. Then more male laughter exploded from somewhere behind her.

"I wish I had that swing of yours in my backyard," the other boy said.

The boys laughed again, louder this time.

"And Gina," the first boy yelled, "in case you don't know, he's not talking about the kind of swing you find on playgrounds."

She'd wanted to fall through the cracks in the bus floor.

Gina stepped through the side door of Steve's castle and into the present, trying to ignore the recent flashback. She headed for the kitchen. The question was, would she be able to find it using Steve's instructions, and later her room?

It took a while but she found the kitchen and the newspaper. She flipped to the ads. "Welcome to Open Doors Fellowship," she read in an ad on the religion page. "We open at seven o'clock every evening, seven nights a week, for prayer, Bible study, and fellowship. We are also open on Saturday, Sunday, and Wednesday mornings at ten. Call for individual counseling any time." A telephone number and web address were listed, and the ad was signed "Caleb Cantu—Group Leader."

Cantu? The name sounded Spanish. And wasn't Caleb the Bible thumper Steve mentioned? Gina copied down the contact information listed in the ad, and an inner peace filled her heart. Now she knew *exactly* what group of Christians she wanted to be a part of, and there was no reason to discuss it with Steve.

Gina kept her private thoughts and decisions in an inner jar with the lid closed securely. Her special jar not only contained all her secrets, including her own reading problem, it also contained information on how dyslexia had affected her as a child and also later in life.

School had been difficult for her. Gina tensed, remembering. She'd kept trying, harder and harder, to keep up with other students. Studying and trying became a way of life for her. Other girls her age were getting married, having babies. And what was Gina doing? Working on her PhD. She was never smart enough, good enough.

Defects of any kind should be treated and then forgotten, and that was just what she taught her students. When was she going to start practicing what she preached? Could telling others about the cross she'd had to bear since childhood help them carry theirs? She wasn't ready to reveal all her secrets. But she could tell her story as if it had happened to someone else. It might be therapeutic.

A few minutes later she climbed the stairs in hopes of reaching her room, reminding herself she wasn't a failure. Her life was filled with successes, recently at least. She might never get her views across to Steve Bryson, but it was no reflection on her.

She looked down. The mansion was huge. Like the web of halls below, stretching in all directions, there were many untried paths in life from which to choose. Merely because the first one didn't improve her position with her new boss, it didn't mean all of them would lead to a dead-end.

But she had an immediate problem. She was climbing to the top of the stairs when the problem became clear. Yes, she found the stairs, but which of these hallways should she take to get to her bedroom?

GINA MET Gretel and her daughter, Netty, when the two women served the family an early supper.

"Netty and Gretel are the only servants on staff at the Colorado house fulltime," Steve explained after they started eating. "They're completely in charge of the area of the house where the family lives, but with a home as big as what you call a castle, a team of cleaners and home-repair experts come in at least once a week to clean the rest of the house. Gretel and Netty also have other household duties, especially for large parties and events."

"About how many team members should I expect?" Gina asked. "And will I be told in advance when they're coming? Or will they simply show up?"

He chuckled. "You'll be told in advance. We can expect between fifteen and twenty team members at any one time. All depends on need. If a big party's in the works, we need more. If not, less, and you'll hardly know they're here. The team is very professional."

Gina was amazed by all she heard, but the only reply she could come up with was, "Oh, I see."

After supper Gina went up to her room, took a shower, and finished unpacking. Later she went out on the balcony for a breath of air. As beautiful as the hills had looked during the daylight hours, she wanted to have a look at them at sunset.

The mountain air felt cool against her skin. Her surroundings thrilled her. She'd moved closer to the metal railing for a better view when she heard someone talking. Amanda's clear voice rang out from the bedroom next to Gina's.

"Oh, I miss you too, Paulo," she heard Amanda say.

Paulo! Gina didn't wait to hear more. She charged through the French doors and barged right into Amanda's room.

The teenager was stretched across her princess-like bed, holding the phone near her ear. Strands of long dark hair fell across her face, and she didn't look up when Gina came in.

"Who are you talking to?" Gina demanded.

Amanda glanced up and frowned. She jerked the cell phone from her ear and held it out, gesturing for Gina to leave with her free hand.

Gina didn't budge.

"Go away!" Amanda said in a loud voice. "Can't you see I'm on the phone?"

"You're talking to Paulo, aren't you?"

"Hold on a minute," Amanda said to her caller, glaring at Gina.

Gina didn't move an inch.

Slowly Amanda's expression softened. "Don't tell Daddy on me," she whispered.

"I won't if you'll promise never to call Paulo Ponte again. Is it a deal?"

"Okay."

"Did he call you, or did you call him?" Gina asked.

"I called."

"All right. You have one minute to say goodbye and tell him you'll never talk to him again." She glared at Amanda. "And don't think we won't know if you call him. There are ways of finding out such things. Do I make myself clear?"

"Yes."

"Okay then." She left the room so Amanda could finish her conversation.

Once she'd trusted Amanda and Gina desperately wanted to believe the teenager would never phone Paulo again. She wouldn't tell Steve about the phone call, but if the calls continued, she'd share that and her other concerns with Steve whether he wanted to hear them or not.

Initially Amanda must have felt betrayed when she saw Steve kissing her, but it was no reason to let Amanda hold the reins now. And why did Gina keep thinking about Steve? He was even showing up in her dreams.

Instead of returning to her room, she headed for the main hall. She wanted to have another look around or risk forgetting how to find her way to the breakfast table in the morning. A few minutes later Gina was about to climb the stairs to her room when she heard footsteps coming up behind her.

"Vait," Gretel called from somewhere behind her.

Gina turned. The woman's heavy German accent was hard to miss. The elderly servant hobbled toward her as if gasping for breath.

"Are you all right?" Gina asked.

"Yah." Gretel frowned. "Now, vhat vas I going to do?"

Gina shrugged.

"Oh, yah, now I remember." She handed Gina a letter.

"Thanks. And Gretel, are you sure you're all right?"

"Yah, yah. Mr. Bryson's secretary delivers all da mail here," Gretel said. "But Josie von't get here from Houston for several days, so I am da mail person today."

Gina peered down at the letter. Her mother's large handwriting made it easy to identify the writer. *How sweet. But why a letter?* Her mother was a phone-caller and never texted. She seldom wrote letters unless it was very important.

In the small office upstairs next to her bedroom, Gina opened the letter. Yet for a moment questions about Steve's recent behavior overshadowed her desire to read it. She shoved the thoughts aside and concentrated on the letter.

"Dear Gina,

"Hope you're enjoying your new job. Your Oklahoma kinfolks send their love. I received the letter you mailed in Austin before you left, and I know you're eager to know who I'm dating now. I only wish I could tell you. But we had a lot of fun when we went out on that Friday night.

"I promised *him* I wouldn't reveal his name at this time. Please try to understand. As soon as I can, I will tell you anything you want to know.

Love,

Mom"

Gina had hoped to learn the identity of her mother's new love interest before she left Austin. Why was Mom being so secretive about this man? Was she ashamed of the guy? Was he a criminal or a mafia type? Maybe he was the billionaire financing the mad scientist. The thought made her smile.

Gina read the letter again, learning nothing new. She put her letter back in the envelope and turned on the radio. A news program was in progress. It didn't sound interesting until she heard the name Dr. Ward Dremont at the tail end of the broadcast. A commercial followed, and then the topic was sports. Gina hurried to the computer and typed in the name "Dremont," but nothing new surfaced.

Why did she find this so called "mad scientist" so intriguing? She'd known science professors while in college, even dated one or two of them. *But none of them caught my interest as much as Dr. Ward Dremont, and I don't even know the man.*

BREAKFAST in the kitchen with Steve and Amanda the next morning was not what Gina would have expected. Not only did Gretel and her daughter prepare all the food, but they also sat at the table with them and shared the meal. Gina loved every minute of it.

Later she searched for the scientist via her computer again. This time a long list of topics appeared on the computer screen. She was about to click on the first one when she heard a noise, as if someone was creeping up behind her. Gina jumped, then jerked around.

"Hi."

She hadn't expected to see Netty—or anyone—appear from out of nowhere, but now Netty stood directly behind her with a mop in her hand.

"Sorry, Miss," Netty said. "I didn't mean to scare you. I came to tell you the cleaners will be here on Monday."

"The what?"

"The cleaners. The cleaning staff Mr. Bryson hires. I was told to remind you about it, boss's orders. They come here and clean once a week, sometimes twice in one week, but you'll probably never see them. We clean here where the family lives. We also clean the family entry hall and the tower rooms.

"They clean the ballroom," Netty continued, "the party kitchen, the big dining room, the main entry to the mansion, and all the other rooms on all other floors. You'll see their trucks and vans parked out back, but you probably won't see them. They're practically invisible."

"Sounds mysterious. I hope I get a look at them at least once, and I'm looking forward to seeing the grand ballroom again," Gina said. "I only saw it briefly."

"I could take you there if you want."

She smiled. "I want."

Netty giggled. "So what are you up to, Doctor?" Netty asked. "Catching up with your emails? Or do you text mostly? I did a search of Dr. Ward Dremont last night. Ever heard of him?"

Gina couldn't believe her ears. "You know who Dr. Dremont is?"

"Of course. Why are you surprised?" Netty asked. "I listen to television talk shows like everyone else."

"I didn't even know Dr. Dremont was on talk shows," she confessed. "And I was a little surprised to hear the news. I've heard some call Dr. Dremont a mad scientist."

"I wouldn't be surprised," Netty said. "Mama thinks he looks like Mr. Bryson, and with the laboratory up in the tower room, I —" Netty stopped herself mid-sentence, and her mouth opened in a sort of gasp. "I wasn't supposed to mention that. Oh, please,

Dr. Hollister, don't tell Mr. Bryson what I said. It was all in fun, you know."

"I won't tell," Gina promised. "And you could be right about Mr. Bryson and Dr. Dremont. They do look something alike— about the same size and everything. But with Dr. Dremont's long black beard, it's hard to tell for sure." A thought came to her then. Could the beard be fake?

"Oh," Netty said, "that reminds me." She pulled a letter from the pocket of her white apron. "Here's another letter for you, Doctor. Mother forgot to give it to you, and the return address says California."

*C*alifornia? Gina tensed. The letter had to be related to her beloved great-aunt, the one who raised her father. At ninety-five Aunt Rose probably wasn't in the best of health. Gina wanted to read the letter but would rather not do so in front of Netty or anyone.

"Are you okay?" Netty asked, cutting into her thoughts. "You look a little pale."

"I'm fine." Gina produced a weak smile. "And I was enjoying our conversation about Dr. Dremont. I'd like our discussion to continue, but I think I should go to my room now and read my letter. I hope you understand."

"Of course. I could take you to the ballroom later."

"Thanks." Gina hurried up the stairs.

Her aunt's home address was written in the upper left-hand corner of the envelope, but the letter came from her father. *What's Daddy doing in California? Is Aunt Rose ill? Or worse?* Her fingers trembled when she finally opened the letter.

"Dear Gina,

I know how much you and Aunt Rose love each other, and I hate giving news like this in a letter. But since I was unable to reach you by text or phone, I have no choice. Aunt Rose passed away in her sleep on Wednesday night.

I'm in California now, making arrangements. The funeral is pending until we hear from you, and I think you're mentioned in the will. Come to California if you can. If you can't we understand. But please contact me. And remember I love you.

Dad"

Tears gathered in her eyes. Gina wiped them away with the back of her hand, then put the letter back in the envelope. Her daddy tried to tell her, but she wouldn't even answer his calls. She would have to go to California now. She'd simply have to tell Steve about the funeral and go. But she would return as soon as possible.

HER FLIGHT to California arrived on time. The funeral service was sweet but sad. Gina sat next to her father during the reading of the will, trying to appear kind but aloof while counting the bricks on the back wall of the lawyer's office.

The lawyer turned his full attention on Gina. "And to my dear niece, Gina Hollister," he read, "I leave all my furniture and eight hundred and forty thousand dollars."

What had he just said? Gina braced herself to keep from falling out of her chair. She'd expected to inherit the furniture, since she and her aunt had shared a love of antiques. But eight hundred and forty thousand dollars? *I'd have enough for a generous down payment on the center, and maybe pay off all my other debts besides.*

This also meant she didn't have to return to Colorado. With money for a down payment, she and Nicole would be able to get a bank loan. She could choose never to see Steve Bryson again, but it would also mean abandoning his daughter at a critical time in her life. Amanda needed her, whether the teenager knew it or not. Forgetting Steve wouldn't be easy, but she was confident she could do it. Yet she felt drawn to Colorado, as if the "Man upstairs" wanted her there.

Nobody but her father and the California branch of the Hollister family knew about her inheritance. Gina had no intention of telling anyone else, except her mother, of course.

She would return to Colorado as if nothing changed and see what happened. *But saying good-bye to Daddy in California won't be easy. The other relatives will wonder why we took separate flights.*

As it turned out Gina's worries were groundless. Her father played along with her plan as if traveling separately was his idea, too.

On the flight back to Colorado, Gina found herself thinking about Dr. Dremont and Steve. She had to know whether the gossip about a connection between Steve and Dr. Dremont was true. It seemed unlikely, but she had to know for sure.

THE NEXT MORNING Gina got out of bed before sunrise and raced downstairs. She couldn't remember when she'd needed to hear a good sermon more, and she hoped Amanda and Steve would change their minds and attend the services with her. When she got to the kitchen, she was pleasantly surprised to find Steve was awake too, reading the morning newspaper.

He looked up. "Oh, I found the church I was telling you about. They worship in a private home. And I sure am glad you're back." He paused. "I ...I mean Amanda missed you while you were away."

Gina offered a smile. "Thanks. Nice to hear I was missed. Actually I found the group of believers I want to visit today, so that's where I'm going. Hope you'll attend the service with me."

Steve shook his head. "I can't. Sorry." He motioned toward the breakfast bar as if he hadn't heard a word she said. "There's coffee on the stove if you'd like some, and donuts."

She'd wanted both Steve and Amanda to attend the services

with her, but Amanda too had declined the invitation. She still hoped Steve would change his mind and agree to go. But time was running out. It would soon be time to leave.

As she changed into an expensive pair of designer jeans and a rust-colored blouse, practically every doubt, every worry, and every unfortunate incident in her life flashed before her. She did her best to shake them off, but the random thoughts continued.

Shortly after nine Gina went down the stairs for the second time. Steve stood at the bottom of the stairs in a dark gray suit and a dark tie. He looked overdressed, but she hoped this meant he planned to attend the service after all. The word *handsome* echoed inside her head.

"My, don't you look sparkling his morning," he said, covering his eyes with both hands as if a sudden light had blinded him.

His flair for wit was obvious, but she didn't think he'd changed his mind about the service. He was funny all right, but she didn't feel like laughing.

"Don't let my clothes fool you." He went over, opened the front door, and looked back at Gina. "I'll be attending a meeting with one of my associates in town during the service. Then I thought I'd take you to lunch."

"What about Amanda?" she asked.

"She watched TV movies until late last night, probably won't wake up until noon. So are you okay with me driving you?"

"Whatever you want to do is fine with me."

He took her arm. As they headed for his car, she noticed dark clouds in the distance.

A blanket of rainclouds rolled toward them. Gina and Steve stepped up onto the front porch of a rather large two-story house in a rural area just as lightning cracked the sky. Thunder rumbled in the distance beyond the hills. Could this also be the private home Steve was talking about? She still hoped he'd change his mind and go inside with her.

"Well," he said, "I'll see you around twelve, I guess."

A loud blast of thunder boomed overhead. Gina and Steve jumped simultaneously, then exchanged brief smiles.

"That was a big one," he said. "You all right?"

"I'm fine so far."

"So far?" He laughed. "You'll be okay. Wait for me outside the church—I mean, the house. I wouldn't want you to spend time looking for me." He glanced up at the dark clouds again. "If it's raining I'll look for you on the other side of the front door."

A sudden loneliness swept over her, but she dismissed it. "All right."

Gina turned to go inside. Out of the corner of her eye, she saw Steve wave to someone. She turned back as a couple moved toward him.

Steve motioned for her to come close. "These are the people I was telling you about." He turned to the two strangers. "Dr. Gina Hollister, meet Caleb and Bonny Cantu."

So they were Steve's Bible-thumping friends. "I'm so glad to know both of you." Gina shook Bonny's hand, and then Caleb's; she liked them immediately.

"They're both friends of Dr. Larker," Steve put in. "The one Dr. Bennett wanted Amanda to see."

"Oh, yes, I remember." Gina was especially pleased Steve hadn't forgotten the doctor in Austin wanted Amanda to see Dr. Larker.

Caleb glanced down at his watch. "Guess it's time to go in. I hope you two will visit Bible study this morning. I'm the teacher. And come again tonight for fellowship."

"Gina might," Steve said. "I have a meeting to attend this morning. My nights are pretty full, too."

She thought Caleb and Bonny looked disappointed. Gina knew she was.

"Maybe next time then." Caleb looked up at the sky. "Did a raindrop just land on the tip of my nose?"

"Yes," his wife said in a teasing tone of voice. "So we need to go inside. It's starting to sprinkle."

Bonny and Caleb hurried toward the front door. Gina stood on the wide porch in front of the door a while longer. The sprinkle had become a light rain. She still felt a little lonely, but somehow the patter of raindrops on the tin roof above her head had a comforting effect.

She watched Steve get in the van. When he'd pulled out of the parking lot, Gina went inside.

Gina followed Caleb and Bonny down a long hallway behind what they called the main auditorium to one of the bedrooms.

Caleb glanced around the small room, filled mostly with empty chairs. "Most folks get here early. Some are late this morning; probably the rain." He sent out a welcoming grin to those present. "Glad *you're* here." He turned to Gina. "Sit anywhere."

Bonny touched a chair on the first row. "I want Gina to sit by me. Right here."

Gina returned Bonny's smile with one of her own. "Thanks."

By a quarter to ten, most of the chairs were filled. Caleb opened with a prayer. When the prayer ended he turned around and wrote "Peculiar People" on the chalkboard in big letters. "Ever met a peculiar person?" he asked.

Many in the group chuckled, including Caleb himself. Gina stiffened. She'd been called hurtful names for most of her life and hated name-calling.

"I'm going to read what the Bible has to say about peculiar people," Caleb added. "You might be surprised." He lifted his glass and took a sip of water. "First Peter, chapter two and verse nine." He waited, giving everyone time to find the scripture in the Bible. "It says, 'But ye are a chosen generation, a royal priesthood, an holy nation, a peculiar people.' From reading the scripture, I think God loves peculiar people."

He hesitated. "I don't know about you guys, but I'm about as peculiar as you can get."

Laughter exploded inside the room. Gina exploded mentally, but not in a joyful way.

"When I was a kid," he went on, "other kids called me names worse than peculiar, especially in elementary school. It hurt a lot. Maybe some of you had problems like mine."

Caleb knows what I'm feeling. A smile birthed in her heart. *He's been there.*

"I thought everybody hated me," Caleb went on. "Instead of turning the other cheek, I hated them back. Then one day I got to thinking about forgiveness. The Bible says we have to forgive others if we expect God to forgive us for our sins. It's here in the Good Book." Caleb held up his Bible, tapping a certain page again and again with his forefinger.

He really was a Bible thumper, Gina decided.

"While Jesus was still on the cross," he continued, "He forgave those who were crucifying him. Stephen did the same thing as he was being stoned to death. It's in the Book of Acts, chapter seven, verse sixty. Here's what Stephen said: 'Lord, lay not this sin to their charge.' We must do what Jesus did, guys. We must hate the sin but love the sinner, and we must forgive. Everybody!"

Then Caleb said, "When Jesus was on the cross, He said, 'Forgive them, Father, for they know not what they do.'" He paused again as if he wanted his teaching to sink in. "The Bible says the sword of the Spirit is the Word of God. So when we quote verses from the Bible, we're using our swords against the devil, our enemy." He reached out as if he was holding an invisible sword in his hand. "On guard!"

Everybody laughed. Caleb closed his eyes. Gina thought he might be praying.

"Peculiar people do strange and unusual things," he said. "As Christians we must turn the other cheek and truly forgive those who harm us. Now *that's* peculiar."

When everybody laughed again, Gina joined in. Something wonderful had happened, like someone turned on a light she didn't know she had until this very moment. Gina had no idea what caused this new and exciting knowledge but wanted to learn more about it.

"If you're depressed," Caleb went on, "worried, or can't get unpleasant thoughts to leave your mind, try memorizing a Bible verse or two—or a hundred. Recite those scriptures aloud or mentally when you're discouraged and need cheering up."

He grinned. "It works, believe me. If you can use your remote to change the channel on your television, you can replace negative or unpleasant thoughts and memories with positive ones. I recite uplifting Bible verses either aloud or mentally in the name of Jesus as often as I think to do it. And remember what Proverbs 15:1 says: 'A gentle answer turns away wrath.'"

Gina leaned forward hoping to hear more. Not only had she found someone who understood what she'd gone through, but his answers made sense. However, for now she preferred not to think about forgiveness and reciting Bible verses. *I'm not ready. I'll leave it for another day.*

BY THE TIME Bible study ended, the rain was more of a sprinkle. They headed for a large living room, the room Caleb referred to as the main auditorium. Seated with Bonny and Caleb on the front row and waiting for the sermon to begin, Gina studied a nearby window. Raindrops made a slow downward journey from the top of the window glass to the window sill below.

The pastor sat in a big chair to the right of the podium. He got up, walked to the pulpit, stood there a moment, and said, "Today's sermon is on forgiveness."

Gina suppressed a giggle. He'd said exactly what she expected.

THE SUN WAS out by the end of the service, the rain but a fading memory. Steve waited for Gina on the sidewalk in front of the two-story house.

"We'll have lunch at a fancy restaurant I know," he said. "But first we'll go back to the house for Amanda. I want out of this suit and tie. After lunch I thought we'd go bowling and see a movie." He lifted his eyebrows with a touch of mischief and then lowered them. "Who knows what else we'll get into?"

She liked the lighthearted expression on his face and the agenda he planned. But did Steve ever relax? Was he "chairman of the board" 24/7? Yet his jovial mood was catching. For a moment or two, she laughed internally.

But when at last they arrived at the castle, Amanda had rarely looked more disagreeable.

"I don't want to go with you and Dr. Hollister, Daddy. I want to stay right here."

"Why, sweetheart?" Steve asked.

"I just don't want to go." Amanda glared at Gina. "You two go on."

Two. Gina frowned. *So that's it. Amanda feels left out again.*

"You know," Gina put in, "it might be fun if the two of you had a father-daughter get-together without me. What do you think?"

Steve moaned his veto to her suggestion.

"Now wait a minute." Gina raised both hands to silence him. "I think this is a good idea. Frankly I have things I want to do. Tonight I'd like to attend services at the same place I visited this morning. This will give me the perfect opportunity."

"How would you get there?" Steve asked. "Walk?"

"I can drive if you'll kindly let me borrow one of your vehicles."

"I don't think that's such a good idea."

"Why not?" Gina asked.

"It's a long drive into town. If something went wrong who would help you out there on the road at night?"

She held up her cell. "I also know how to change a tire, Mr. Bryson."

"That's not what I meant."

His apprehensions were about as transparent as his views on religion.

"I'm not the helpless type," she said.

"Never said you were. So how about this? We'll all have a meal together. Then I'll drop you off at Caleb's house, and you can go to the service with them."

His recommendation rated a weak okay as a possible solution to her transportation problem. Gina liked doing things on her own and hated feeling pampered. Still her wishes weren't worth fighting about, so she decided to do it his way.

GINA WAS RELIEVED when she saw Steve and Amanda pull up in front of the Cantus' home fifteen minutes after the service ended. From the expression on their faces, she made a prediction: The father-daughter outing was a huge success.

On the way home when she told them a little about the services, she half expected Steve to make some crack about Bible thumpers. He didn't say a word. So much for her account of her evening with the Cantu family. At least Amanda seemed more approachable.

"Amanda," Gina said. "would you like to play a board game or something before you turn in for the night?"

"I think I'll go up to my room and watch a little television."

"Mind if I join you?" Gina asked.

"You want to watch TV with me?"

"Sure. Why not?"

"Okay, but I get to control the remote."

"Deal."

Gina and Amanda watched television in the teenager's room for almost an hour. Then without a word Amanda started channel-surfing.

"You know," Gina said, "it's impolite to change the channel while someone else is watching."

"Sorry." She clicked back to the program they'd been watching.

"We could talk if you like," Gina said.

"Is this a sneaky way to slip in a lesson?"

"No, it's real for-sure talk. I'd like to tell you about our lesson for tomorrow morning. I think you'll like it."

"Okay." She shrugged.

"Have you ever wanted to step back in time? Learn what life a hundred or two hundred years ago was like?" Gina paused, hoping to take and hold the girl's interest. "Don't you think it would be fun to do something like that?"

Amanda hesitated, shrugging again as if she didn't have an opinion. "I guess so. Why?"

"Well, we can't actually step back in time, but what we can do is learn how people lived back then and how they did things. I bought a flatiron at an antique store a while back. They were used to press out the wrinkles in clothes the old-fashioned way. It's called ironing. I thought we could do some ironing as one of our lessons this summer, see where it goes."

"You mean iron a bunch of clothes?" Amanda shook her head. "I don't think that sounds like fun."

"Why don't we try it? If you don't like it, we'll stop."

Amanda turned her head to one side. "I don't know."

"Okay," Gina said. "I'll do the ironing. All you have to do is watch. If it looks like fun, you can take over. If not we'll stop and do something else. Now let me think. What else could we do besides the lesson I mentioned?" Gina feigned a facial expression she hoped made her appear in deep thought. "Oh, I know." She smiled as if a special kind of light had turned on inside her head. "You'll write a nine-hundred-word essay on ... on forgiveness. And I'll sit in a chair with my feet up and watch."

Amanda laughed, maybe for the first time since the summer house disaster. "You wouldn't really do that, would you?"

"Well, I don't know." Gina shook her head. "But if I were you, I wouldn't risk it." She paused, hoping her point would soak in. "It's pretty hard to get me to change my mind once I'm sitting in a chair with my feet up."

Amanda's laughter had downgraded to a smile. Then it disappeared completely.

"We've spent enough time talking about the lesson," Gina said. "Let's have the little talk I mentioned earlier. Okay?"

Amanda's sigh sounded louder than usual. "Okay." She sighed again. "We used to talk a lot ...back when we were friends."

"I hope we can be friends again." Gina nodded as if to confirm her deepest hope. "The kiss you witnessed in the summer house was not what you think."

"I saw you and Daddy kissing. Are you saying what I saw wasn't real?"

"I'm saying what happened just happened. It wasn't planned. I'm sure it will never happen again. Your father and I are friends, nothing more." Gina sent her a stern look. "I know you've been through a lot, but it's time you tried showing a little respect."

The sea dividing Gina and Amanda was still there, but maybe it wasn't quite as wide now.

STEVE PINCHED the bridge of his nose, hoping to dissolve a tension headache starting to bother him. Was it caused from thinking about Baylee? *Again?* She was always beneath the surface of his mind. How many times did he need to remind himself she was gone and never coming back?

Memories of Baylee, which he'd tried unsuccessfully to forget, had returned, and it was getting harder and harder to push them away. Was he still running from God? And why had he wished he and Amanda were inside the two-story house with Gina instead of waiting in the van?

Gina deserves to know why I'm so opposed to Christianity. But how do I explain a loss of faith to someone like Gina Hollister?

He'd intended to tell her about the backsliding, the doubts, everything, as soon as they returned to the castle. He would have if Gina had stayed downstairs instead of going up to watch TV with Amanda. Now he'd lost his nerve and had no idea when he'd be able to retrieve it. Gina was not the type of woman he usually hung around with. The term "guilty as charged" summed up this thoughts when they were together. He kept wanting to impress her, like a seventeen-year-old kid, but he doubted he was being very successful

GINA SLEPT LATE ON MONDAY. Upon awakening she discovered she was alone in the castle with only her thoughts and the housekeepers to keep her company.

"Where are Mr. Bryson and Amanda?" Gina asked the women.

"They went to town right after breakfast," Netty explained. "I saw them leave."

"Well, Netty," Gina said, "guess my lesson for this morning went down the drain. Is it too late for breakfast?"

"No, ma'am."

After breakfast Gina hung around the kitchen with Gretel and Netty, hoping Netty might mention the laboratory again.

"I'm bored this morning with nothing much to do," Gina said. "Do you mind if I stay and help y'all clean up in the kitchen?"

"Mind?" Netty's bubbly laugh rang out. "Why would we mind? Mama will be doing the wash this morning, but we'd love to have your help."

"Yah, yah," Gretel said. "Ve vould."

"Then it's settled."

Gina grabbed a dishtowel and dried a china plate. Gretel went into the wash room, leaving Gina and Netty alone in the kitchen. Gina was eager to tell Netty what was on her mind but decided to step carefully into all possible conversations.

She placed the dish she'd dried on top of the cabinet and reached for another one. "Netty, why aren't you using the dishwasher?"

"Mama thinks dishwashers are bad, especially for expensive china like this."

"Oh, I see."

But Gina was still thinking about the laboratory. She couldn't get it out of her mind. She pictured a typical laboratory, like a mad scientist would have in a horror movie, with glass globes filled with bubbly liquids soaked in evil. She'd tried to block such thoughts from her mind, but it hadn't worked. Now what was it Caleb said about problems like that?

"Would it be possible for me to visit the laboratory?" Gina asked.

Netty shook her head vigorously. "No, no. We can't do that." Her whole body kind of pulled inward, arms pressed close to her sides. Then she took a step back. It didn't take a genius to know Netty was serious about not wanting to take her to the tower.

"Never mind," Gina finally said. "I didn't want to see the laboratory anyway." But it was a lie because she did. "So," Gina continued, "how about showing me the ballroom? You never did, you know."

"Now *that* I can do," Netty said. "Come this way."

Gina followed Netty to the ballroom. Her thoughts, however,

weren't focused on the large and beautiful ballroom or the size of the huge dance floor. She kept thinking about Steve, contemplating what his next move might be.

They returned to the kitchen ten minutes later. Gina climbed up onto a barstool. "I'd like to ask a question."

Netty nodded. "Sure. Go ahead."

"How long have you and your mother known Steve Bryson?"

"Mama has known him since his mother brought him home from the hospital." Netty pointed to the location on the shelf where the plates were kept. "Put them there."

Gina set the stack of plates on the shelf with care, almost as if the china were her own.

Netty hunched over. Her hands slipped back into the pan of hot soapy water. "I'd like to explain about Mama. You see, she gets a little confused sometimes. It's getting worse. I thought you needed to know. Nobody but Steve Bryson would keep us on in a job like this."

"Your mother seemed all right at supper last night."

"She still has her good days," Netty said. "And her cooking has never tasted better. I have to keep a watch on her though. She's constantly getting lost in this big old house."

"So do I," Gina explained. "I have trouble finding my way around here all the time."

Netty laughed. "Me, too." She paused, gazing out the window above the kitchen sink. "Did you know Mr. Bryson plans to convert the castle into a shelter for homeless children?"

"Yes, I do know that. And I think it's a very admirable thing, don't you?"

"Of course," Netty said. "Mr. Bryson is a very admirable man."

Gina examined Netty for a long moment. There were so many questions swirling around inside her head, and Netty might be able to answer them. But maybe this wasn't the right time. "You like working for Mr. Bryson, don't you?" Gina said.

"Oh, yes. As I said, he's good to us." Netty frowned, rolling her eyes. "Not like Mrs. ..."

"Bryson? Steve's mother?"

"My, no," Netty said. "She's an angel."

"Then you must mean Myra?"

"Yes."

etty ducked her head. "I'm sorry. I've said too much, haven't I?"

"Please," Gina said, "I want to hear more."

"Very well then." Netty paused. "Promise never to reveal what I'm about to tell you."

"Of course."

"Mrs. Bryson—Myra—was a bad woman."

"Bad?"

Netty nodded.

"In what way?"

"She sneaked out with other men while she was married to Mr. Bryson and did a lot of other terrible things."

Gina had liked Myra and didn't want to believe what she'd heard.

"We were all living in Houston when Mrs. Bryson started seeing Mr. Greg Carson," Netty went on. "He was Mr. Bryson's lawyer then. Mama and I would see her sneak out to meet him when Mr. Bryson was out of town."

Gina wrestled with her emotions. How could this be true? And yet why would Netty lie about such a thing? "What happened when Steve found out?"

"He fired his lawyer." Netty rinsed the soap off a china cup and handed it to Gina.

"And then?"

"Mr. Carson broke up with Mrs. Bryson and moved away. Then Mrs. Bryson started telling all those lies about Mr. Bryson."

"What lies?"

"I've known Mr. Bryson all his life," Netty said. "I know the kind of man he is, and he was always faithful to his wife while they were married. Myra Bryson was the unfaithful partner in the marriage."

Gina was stunned at the revelation. "I had no idea."

"He tried to save the marriage," Netty said. "It was Mrs. Bryson who wanted the divorce."

"Why would Myra do such terrible things?"

"I don't know. Maybe she wanted to get even with Steve for destroying her relationship with Mr. Carson."

Netty's words astounded Gina. They were the exact opposite of what Myra had told her.

"I'm not ashamed to say I think Mr. Bryson is a saint," Netty continued. "Please, Dr. Hollister, don't ever believe otherwise."

"I'm sure he appreciates your loyalty."

"I'm not doing this to sound loyal," Netty said. "I'm speaking the truth."

"Still I want to thank you for telling me. And don't worry. I won't betray your confidence."

"I knew you wouldn't, Dr. Hollister, without being told."

Gina had a lot to contemplate. After she completed her chores in the kitchen, she moved into the library, hoping to come up with an idea for a lesson Amanda would like. But Netty's revelations kept getting in the way.

Netty and Gretel obviously liked and respected Steve. *So why do I still have doubts about a man I'm half in love with?* Gina blinked. *No. More than half.*

Gina was confused. She'd always thought Myra was

trustworthy and honest, and she sensed Netty certainly was. Did one of them lie about Steve's character? *Maybe my doubts are like a giant myth created in the gossip centers of my brain. I want to believe Netty told the truth. But how can I know for sure?*

She gave up trying to get any work done. Steve had invited her to go swimming, so now she would go. Alone. She hurried upstairs and changed into her swimsuit. On the way to the pool, she noticed a lot of cars, trucks, and vans on the big parking area beyond the waterfall.

The cleaners must have arrived, but I haven't seen a single one of them.

BY THE TIME she returned to the castle, Steve, Amanda, and a young girl by the name of Polly Newton were seated in the green sitting room. Gina had suggested Steve find a friend for his daughter, someone her age to hang out with. Apparently he had. The sparkle in Amanda's dark eyes confirmed it.

"Polly and I are going outside." Amanda's tone of voice spelled excitement. "I'm gonna show her the waterfall."

"Now be careful, okay?" Steve said.

"We will," Amanda called back over her shoulder.

Gina saw Steve shift his full attention to her. The cover-up she wore over her swimsuit was made of material so thin you could see through it, and his gaze made her want to hide under the couch. Gina grabbed the two sides of the cover-up, pulling them together in front.

"I want to thank you for finding a friend for Amanda," she said.

He shrugged as if he didn't know how to reply.

"I know Amanda appreciated it too," Gina went on. "This could make a difference."

"I hope you're right." He looked away briefly as if uncomfortable with her compliment. "Look, I got a phone call while you were down at the pond from somebody named Phil Arnold."

Her mouth fell open as if it had a mind of its own. "Phil called? Here?"

Steve nodded. "He said he'd been trying to reach you for weeks and finally talked your mother into giving him the main phone number here. She wouldn't give him your personal number."

"Mom wouldn't give him any number. He must have tricked her somehow."

Steve motioned for Gina to follow, then headed down the hall in the direction of his downstairs office. "We need to talk."

"Do you mind if I go up to my room and change first?" she asked. "I'm still wearing my swimsuit under—"

"I noticed." His grin beamed amusement, erasing the frown he'd been wearing.

Steve needed to back off. Gina hoped her body language served as a warning. She couldn't handle it if he closed in on her again. More kisses were out of the question.

"Go ahead and change," he said. "You're probably cold and wet."

"I am."

"Did I mention you're also very beautiful?" he asked.

"Did I mention sexual harassment is now a crime?"

He chuckled under his breath. "I'll be in my office."

Gina climbed the stairs to the second floor and hurried down the hall to her bedroom. Being alone with Steve in his office again could spell trouble, but it was a gamble she'd have to take.

She shut the door just as the land line rang. "Hello?"

"Hi. This is Phil."

"Phil! I thought we said our goodbyes back in Austin."

"I can't get you out of my mind, Gina."

"Try taking a cold shower."

He laughed. She didn't.

"I'm serious, Phil. We're history. Let's make our history the good kind. I read a lot of romance novels. We already shared the time in every romance where the hero and heroine shake hands and walk away in different directions."

"I don't want us to walk in different directions."

"Sorry, but I do." She tried to come up with a tactful way to say what had to be said, then gave up trying. "I don't know an easy way to say this, but I'm not in love with you. That will never change. If you call me again, Phil, I'll hang up on you."

He didn't reply.

"I'm hanging up now," she said. "This is my final goodbye." She clicked off.

To a sensitive person like Gina, conflict of any kind was difficult. Name-calling was out of the question. She hadn't wanted to hurt Phil, but in his case, saying what she did seemed like the right thing to do.

Ten minutes later she joined Steve in his office. She was wearing a blue-checkered dress with white buttons all the way up to her chin. Steve sat at his desk. He got up when Gina entered the room.

"I expected you to change," he said, "but not so drastically." His slow grin reached out, causing her to almost forget what she wanted to say. "You look fresh," he went on. "Well-groomed and ... conservative."

"Exactly the way I intend to look from now on."

An amused glint still lingered in his eyes. "Won't you sit down?"

"Maybe later." Gina continued to stand in front of a chair. "I've said all I care to say about Phil. What else did you want to talk about?"

"Phone calls. I forgot to mention the second one."

"I got a second phone call? From whom?"

"Nicole Danton." His eyes still held a trace of merriment. "You know I got the impression your friend, Dr. Danton, doesn't like me very much."

"Frankly she doesn't. Nicole thinks you plan to lock me in the tower at some point and throw away the key."

"What a great idea." He feigned a monster-like facial expression, ending in an animal sounding growl. "Just kidding."

Gina rolled her eyes to keep from laughing. After a moment she couldn't hold in her true feelings any longer; cocking her head to one side, she laughed. Then she sat down in the chair across from his desk, leaning back in hope of looking relaxed. Steve sat down, too, and leaned back in his chair.

"You make me crazy," she said. "Did you know that?"

"How so?"

"Neither one of us has said anything serious or consequential since I came in here."

"Oh, that." He waved her off. "Well, let's get serious then, by all means. You can start by telling me all there is to tell about your friend Phil Arnold."

STEVE HADN'T EXPECTED Gina to talk about her ex-boyfriend, but he'd decided to give it a shot anyway. "Come on, Gina. Is old Phil still important to you?"

"I didn't come in here to discuss Phil Arnold. And I'm not prepared to discuss my private life, any more than you're prepared to discuss business matters with me."

"We can discuss business matters if you like," he said. "What do you think of the stock market?"

"I read the report, Mr. Bryson," she said. "Oil and natural gas stocks are down."

"Only temporary."

"Is that why you're always flying off here and there on such short notice?"

"It could have a slight bearing on it, yes."

"I thought so." In the chair opposite his, she leaned toward the desk between them.

Steve stiffened. Gina intended to lower the boom again; he could feel it. She would either engage in a long discourse on how he should or shouldn't handle his daughter's problems or hit him from another direction. He had a corporation to run, for goodness sake. If all Amanda's difficulties had to do with business matters, he'd know what to do. To hear Gina tell it, he was in the dark—totally unprepared for childrearing.

"I know more about oil and natural gas than you might think," Gina said, interrupting his thoughts. "But it's not the reason I came in here."

He shook his head. Gina's no-nonsense persona reminded him of his ex-wife. Sometimes Myra lifted her chin in exactly that way before she delivered one of her outrageous demands. The granddaddy of them all happened the day he found out Myra was scheming behind his back in hopes of taking over his company, the day she made her plans for Bricot all too clear.

He shook his head again as if he thought it might clear his mind. Gina wasn't a bit like his ex-wife, but for an instant, her facial expression reminded him of Myra. With a little luck he could steer Gina in another direction.

"How do you know so much about the oil and gas industry?" he asked.

"Daddy was an executive for an oil company until he retired. He used to let me sit in on some of his business meetings."

"That's right. You're Tip Hollister's daughter, aren't you?"

"Unfortunately."

"I've never met him." Steve forced normalcy into his tone. "I know him by reputation. And I hear he was a fine oil man." Steve shrugged offhandedly. Since reading the article on Gina, he'd suspected she and her father had problems. Her answer confirmed it.

"Why do you keep putting me off like this, changing the subject all the time?" she demanded. "We should be discussing Amanda's reading disability, not my father."

The muscles in his jaw tightened. "Disability?"

"Don't let the word scare you. I should have said reading and spelling problems."

Gina was punching all his buttons, the wrong buttons. He needed to shut his mouth before he said something he'd regret. "It's after one, and I'm hungry. It's time to take a break, have some lunch. We can continue this conversation later."

"Later?" Gina lifted her chin again. "Mr. Bryson, I came to Colorado to help your daughter overcome some serious problems. These problems could affect her for the rest of her life."

"I realize that, but—"

"Let me finish," she said with a halting gesture. "I'm trained and more than willing to do my job. But you've avoided the issues I've wanted to discuss at every turn. I think we should stop playing games, join forces, and solve this problem."

It was not the response he wanted to hear. After the long-distance phone call he'd had with Drake Rather earlier, he'd heard enough bad news and negative feedback to last for days. How could he think about Amanda's problems when the entire meeting in Naples was about to blow up in his face?

He'd hoped a dash of light banter with Gina would reduce the pressure a little. Instead their conversation went downhill from word number one. Steve glanced down at his watch. "I converse better on a full stomach. Suppose we put off this discussion at least until we finish eating."

"As you wish," Gina said with a frosty edge to her tone. "But can we schedule a time for this future meeting you mentioned—right now?"

"I'm sure we'll be able to settle all the details to your satisfaction, Dr. Hollister—over lunch."

Steve had promised to meet Gina in the garden at three o'clock. Shortly before that Netty presented her with a note from Steve: "Sorry I have to break our appointment for this afternoon. Something came up. I'll be in meetings at my office in town for the rest of the day. I'll try to reschedule our meeting as soon as I can. Steve"

Steve Bryson was a smart man. Nobody knew it better than Gina. She also knew time was money in his eyes. His business dealings were extremely important. Why then couldn't he see his only child was important too—in fact, more important even than work?

He still hadn't made Amanda an appointment with Dr. Larker, the child psychologist the doctor in Austin recommended. He hadn't scheduled a time when Amanda could visit her grandmother in Austin either.

Gina's phone rang, and her mother's number appeared.

"Hi, Mom."

"Hi. I'm so glad you answered because I keep forgetting to ask whether or not you plan to attend the Hollister family reunion. I don't have an actual date yet, but I know it's coming up toward the end of the summer or early fall. You're going, aren't you?"

"I don't know. I haven't given it much thought."

"You should go, Gina. You know you should. Your cousins from California will be there, and all the ones from Texas you love. Your father will probably be there, too. Is that a problem?"

"Maybe."

"You've got to break down the wall you've built between you and your daddy. It's not healthy. In fact I just heard a sermon on forgiveness ..."

"Not now, Mom."

"Yes, now." Her mother paused before continuing. "It just came to me. The reunion is scheduled for early September, the third, fourth, maybe the fifth. I can't remember which. So keep all those dates open, and ... and I hope you come."

"Maybe I will, but only if Daddy doesn't."

"Gina."

"After the uncomfortable situation in California during the reading of the will, dealing with Daddy at the reunion could be difficult, Mom, if not impossible."

IN THE LIBRARY the next morning with Amanda, Gina checked her materials to make sure everything was in order for her tutoring session. They hadn't done the lesson with the flatiron yet, but today was the day.

Then Steve arrived. How could she explain a lesson like this to someone like him? She needed to hide today's lesson immediately. And what was he doing here anyway?

He still stood in the doorway.

Go away, she thought. But she said, "Won't you come in?"

He nodded. "Thank you."

Quickly Gina switched gears, turning to the next page in her lesson-plan book. It would be hard to explain why she chose a lesson on early-American ironing practices as a topic, but a lesson on reading and phonics should work.

"If you don't mind," he said, stepping inside, "I think I'll sit here a while and watch."

"Please do." Gina tensed because she *did* mind. Yes she was glad Steve was interested enough in his daughter to show up, but she had other reasons for wishing he weren't there. Students tended to behave differently when their parents were in the room. "We're glad to have you," she added.

He glanced around, studying the room carefully. "I'm glad to be here, Doctor. I see you've brought in the flatiron you bought and an ironing board."

"Yes." *He noticed. If only I'd had time to hide those things.* "I've found items from other times in history help my students create an appreciation for the past as well as the future."

"Interesting."

Myra Bryson had given Gina permission to begin each lesson with silent prayer. She saw no reason to change her daily routine merely because Steve Bryson was watching.

Gina bowed her head. "Let us pray."

"Wait a minute. Is this an example of one of your lessons from the past?" Steve didn't say more, but the heat in his eyes communicated his disapproval.

Amanda glanced at Gina smugly and looked back at her father. "Do I have to pray, too, Daddy?"

"Prayer is optional here," Gina put in. "Nobody's forcing Amanda to do anything she doesn't want to do."

"Why are you suggesting she do it then?" Steve asked.

"For several reasons. For one thing I've found it helps my students calm down before the lesson starts."

"Frankly," he said, "I found the opposite to be true."

"I once knew a girl with problems much like Amanda's," Gina said, trying to sound as calm and cheerful as possible. "Prayer seemed to help her focus on what she was doing. It also gave her the confidence she needed to keep trying. You might be interested to know she graduated near the top of her class.”

“Bravo.” Steve checked his watch. “Since those facts are out of the way, can we get on with the class, Dr. Hollister?”

Gina moved over to a long library table and picked up a stack of papers, trying not to look at Steve. After what happened in Dr. Bennett’s office back in Austin, she should have known what he’d say about prayer. She handed the papers to Amanda.

“This is a diagnostic test to determine your current reading level,” Gina explained. “Read the stories, then answer the questions at the end of each story. Take all the time you need.”

Amanda rolled her eyes upward. “All right.”

As soon as Amanda began reading, Gina felt Steve’s eyes on her again. She refused to give him the satisfaction of returning his gaze. She sat down at the library table she called her desk, pretending to read an article in a magazine she’d brought along. She’d actually looked forward to reading the article, but now it was a shield to hide behind as he continued to watch her.

What can he possibly be thinking? Am I about to lose my job?

Steve got up out of his chair and started toward her.

She swallowed, touching her throat.

“Dr. Hollister,” he whispered, “may I speak to you out in the hall for a minute, please?”

She was sure her heart rate must have increased radically. “Of course.” Without another word she stood and preceded Steve into the hallway.

“I appreciate your religious convictions, Dr. Hollister,” he said as soon as they were out of Amanda’s earshot. “My mother is a churchgoer, but please keep your religious views out of the classroom.”

Here it comes.

“I didn’t hire you to lead my daughter in prayer,” he said. “Bowing your head and saying ‘let us pray’ sure sounds like praying to me.”

“We pray silently here, Mr. Bryson. Bowing one’s head is

merely a physical act. 'Let us pray' is an invitation, not a demand." She raised her chin. "In the future I'll try to keep my chin up whenever possible."

His eyes laughed briefly. "I didn't mean to upset you."

"Who's upset?"

"As my employee," he went on, "I thought you needed to know how I felt."

"Yes I do need to know." Her jaw firmed. "If you'll recall I have a few things to say to you, too. So, Mr. Bryson, if you have nothing else to say right now, I'll go back to the classroom."

"Go right ahead."

She opened the door to the library.

"Wait," he said. "I forgot to mention something."

She looked back.

"I've had one of the small cottages set up for you and Amanda to use as a classroom. I came here to tell you about it."

"Does this mean I'm to continue working here?"

"Of course." He chuckled. "The cottage should be ready right after lunch today. Netty has the key. I told her to walk you over there."

"I appreciate it." With her hand on the doorknob, she continued to study him. "I'm still waiting for you to reschedule the private parent-teacher appointment you cancelled. I'd also like to know when Amanda will be spending the weekend in Austin." She swallowed. "I could also use a weekend off as promised in my contract, but since I spent a short time in California recently, we can wait a while before my next weekend off."

"Fine."

"However," she added, "Amanda needs to visit her grandmother now and then, and I hope you haven't forgotten your promise to make an appointment for Amanda with Dr. Larker."

"I'll have to check," he said, "and get back to you on that."

She nodded. "Now if you'll excuse me, I need to get back to

my student." Not waiting for a reply, Gina whirled around and hurried to the door. She opened it, walked in, and let it close on its own.

Bang! Amanda looked up from her reading. Gina hadn't slammed the door, but the sound it made when it closed was louder than she'd intended.

She sat down at the library table, drained. She'd never felt more humiliated or more like crying. The urge to put her head down on her desk the way she did as a child had never been stronger. Instead she lifted her chin defiantly and straightened her back.

Who did Steve Bryson think he was, dictating her head movements the way he did? She should have listened to Nicole and never taken this job in the first place. Gina could always resign, but she wouldn't think about that now.

Gina glanced down and folded her hands on her desk. She'd never considered how symbolic such a simple gesture might appear to others. Was it an implied call to prayer?

She could pray with her head up as easily as she could with it down. It was the act of praying that was important, not the method of doing it. In the future she would pray silently for her students in the classroom, but she'd keep her head lifted up toward heaven.

Gina was still upset with Steve. Why wouldn't he listen? Regardless, when the school day ended she visited the new classroom, loving what she found.

Steve had converted the smallest of the little cottages into a schoolhouse. She didn't get the opportunity to finish their discussion on Amanda, but he left another note. This time it was by her plate at suppertime: "Dr. Hollister, I'll be having supper at my office in town tonight. I leave on an unscheduled business trip to New York City afterwards. Sorry I didn't know about the trip sooner, so you and Amanda could head back to Austin for a few days. Maybe next time. Steve"

GINA GOT UP EARLY on Thursday morning, her first full day of actual classes in the cottage. She didn't expect to accomplish much but intended to try. With Steve out of the picture for a while, she and Amanda could do the lesson with the flatiron, though not today.

"Amanda," Gina said, "before we begin our lesson this morning, I wanted you to know you did very well on the tests you took. I'm proud of you."

"You are?"

"Yes." Gina smiled. "And I brought in colored overlays again since you liked the results the last time."

The sound of a door opening caused Gina to glance up. Steve stood in the doorway. *Again!*

"What's a colored overlay?" he asked.

"I thought you were in New York."

"The trip was delayed."

"Thanks for letting me know." Gina forced a smile. "I would like to explain about colored overlays." She cleared her throat. "Colored overlays help students with reading problems keep their eyes on a sheet of print. The pale yellow ones seem to work the best for Amanda."

The expression on Steve's face said he didn't agree with her conclusions. "Will you step out in the hall, Miss Hollister? I have a few more things I'd like to discuss with you privately. It should only take a moment."

Not again! Gina manufactured another fake smile. "Of course." She turned to Amanda. "Read the first short story in your reader, using one of the yellow overlays. It's about horses; I think you'll like it."

Gina followed Steve to the door, expecting a scolding. "I'm sure you disagree with the instructions I just gave Amanda."

"On the contrary, I was impressed. Amanda loves horses. But it's not why I'm here," he said. "I'm leaving for New York in a few minutes, but I have a little time. Maybe we could have the meeting you've been wanting."

"Thanks for the thought. But what I have to say will take more than a few moments out here in the hall. Let's reschedule when you return.'

"Fine."

Rather than the reprimand she'd expected, a halfhearted apology came out of Steve's mouth. What could have been a command became a restrained pat on the back.

Could there be a light at the end of this dark tunnel after all?

Steve returned from New York City shortly after lunch on Monday. Gina canceled classes for the rest of the day so Amanda could visit with her father. Later Polly dropped by for a sleepover. Then Steve requested a meeting with Gina in his office at the castle at three that afternoon.

She wondered if their long awaited meeting was now in the headlights. Gina looked down at her watch. Five minutes until three. She headed for his office, trying to put her worries behind her. *Steve seems to be trying to get along now. Is he beginning to like me ...a little? Probably not.* She sighed. In the words of her late grandmother from California, their discussions were always "over-the-top."

He ushered her to the seat across from his desk, then settled in his chair facing her. He did not look pleased. "I did some checking. Dr. Larker is a medical doctor, all right, as well as a child psychiatrist. But he's also a Bible thumper."

Gina ignored his last statement. "I've had some basic training in the area of medicine," she said. "I think Dr. Larker might be exactly the person to help Amanda come to grips with all the changes in her life."

"First I want to know what kind of Bible-thumping child psychiatry we're talking about," he said.

"I would say he's a devout churchgoer who's also a doctor."

"Devout," he said. "Just as I thought. Now I know for sure, and I don't want Amanda to see Dr. Larker. Understand?"

Stunned, Gina nodded. Was this the parent–teacher meeting she'd been waiting for all this time?

"I'm a churchgoer myself—or *was*," he said. "But I'm not inclined to take it to the extreme."

"You're talking about me, aren't you?"

"Did I say that?"

"You didn't have to."

"Look," he said, "I apologize for every cross word I've ever spoken to you since the day we met. Why don't we forget the past and start over?"

Start over? As far as she knew, they never started anything in the first place. But he did sound a little more repentant now.

"I accept your apology."

"Thanks."

Gina was working for Steve. It was a fact. She must accept his ideas, hoping he'd consider hers. If she ever got to give him her ideas, of course. As a tutor, she must go about her duties in a professional way. And if Steve asked her out on a date, the answer was *no*.

LATER ON MONDAY afternoon Gina paced back and forth across the cottage floor. Steve had said he'd stop by the school room. *Again? Maybe I should provide him with his own desk so he'll have a special place to sit during his numerous visits.*

The question was why? Weren't the earlier meetings enough?

She'd gathered some magazines she wanted to read and some of her teaching materials in hopes of rest and maybe a little work in the cottage. Then she got the memo. Steve was on his way.

Should she change her plans, put on her Dr. Hollister persona? No.

She settled onto the far end of the couch, removed her shoes, and put her feet on a footstool she'd moved in. Sitting here like this, she probably looked ... The word *stupid* popped into her mind, followed by a series of unhappy memories she'd tried to forget.

Was she stupid? If she knew the answer, she'd write a book on the subject and make a million dollars.

Gina still wasn't sure how to stop unpleasant thoughts from entering her mind, but she knew how to stop annoying tunes playing in her mind over and over. She'd found the answer in elementary school as a child.

Her teacher had said, "It's easy to stop all those irritating tunes playing inside your head. All you have to do is think of another tune you like and sing it in your mind, pushing out the annoying tune you don't like. You could sing the song aloud, if you prefer. It's like changing the channel on your television."

A stack of magazines stared at her from the coffee table. She picked up the one on antiques and thumbed through it. Yet Steve dominated her mind.

Steve claimed to be a churchgoer, but if he practiced his religion at all, he was probably lukewarm. And the Bible said to be hot or cold, not lukewarm. So why was she attracted to Steve? His views on religion alone disqualified him; in Gina's book, he sure wasn't husband material.

Gina wasn't convinced Steve would ever consider her as a possible wife. Should he marry again, it would be to someone rich, like a movie star, a fashion model, or a socialite. She turned to the next page in the magazine just as Steve entered the room.

Gina straightened the skirt of the gold dress she'd changed into for the occasion. What could he possibly want this time?

He sat down on the couch beside her. According to the text he sent, he had something important to say. Well, so did she, starting with her views on Dr. Larker.

She'd met Dr. Larker at Caleb's church the second time she visited there and liked him instantly. She'd spent time thinking about exactly what she'd say to Steve if the right moment ever came, and she hoped she was ready.

"I like the dress you're wearing," he said.

"Well, thank you." Was she blushing? She hoped not. "I'm glad you like it."

"You look good in dresses. Gold's your color."

"Thanks again."

"You should wear dresses more often. That gold one reminds me of the yellow dress you wore at the hotel."

"Will you ever forget the water pitcher incident?" she asked with a hint of sarcasm.

"I meant it as a compliment, Gina. You look great in both those dresses."

She didn't know how to respond at that point. Apparently neither did he. Total silence surrounded her, and somehow she got the feeling he was hiding something. Was he laughing on the outside but not so much inside?

"I've been doing a lot of thinking," he said finally. "We need to talk about Myra."

Myra? The last thing she expected was for Steve to start a conversation about his late wife.

"It might help you understand Amanda better," he added, "if you knew more about her mother. It might also help you understand me."

This was not what she expected to discuss with him. It would take a moment to change channels.

"Amanda's mother was nothing like you, Gina," he said. "But like you Myra did make suggestions I couldn't agree with."

"Like prayer in school?"

"Not that, but we had many differing opinions. For example Myra insisted on sitting in on all my important business meetings."

"I would have thought you'd have welcomed her interest," Gina said.

"I did ... at first."

"And then?"

"She demanded I make her a full partner. In fact I was in the process of doing it when ... when things got out of hand." He didn't say another word for almost a full minute.

What was going on? And what did any of this have to do with her? As Gina sat there watching Steve, she viewed his facial transformations, ranging from sad to desperate. A lump formed in her throat. He'd been hurt. She could see it in his eyes. Gina recalled her own pain, and waves of sympathy rolled over her and out to Steve. Regardless of what might have happened in the past, she longed to reach out and comfort him in some way.

"What I'm about to say is known to a lot of people," he said softly, "but I don't like repeating it."

"Please don't feel you have to tell me anything."

"You need to know if we're going to work together." He cleared his throat. "Myra and I met during my senior year in college. I'd transferred to the University of Texas from a small college in Oklahoma. I thought Myra was the prettiest girl in the senior class. We married rather suddenly, before the end of the school year. Amanda arrived a few months later." He glanced out the window.

Steve was still in love with his late wife; she just knew it.

"Myra came from a middle-class family," he went on. "I think she was always more interested in Bricot International than in me."

Gina couldn't help gazing out the window to see what he found so interesting. The view of the mountains took her breath away. Yet she was sitting on the edge of her seat, waiting to hear what he might say next.

"It's not surprising I trusted her," he said at last, "but from a business standpoint, I should have kept a closer eye on my wife.

When I finally decided to do so, Myra and my lawyer were in the process of taking over my company."

And Myra was having an affair with the lawyer, Gina wanted to add. But of course she didn't.

"I was gone a lot, tending to business matters," he said. "I guess it's never good for a marriage. I tried to fix things between us; it didn't work." His weak smile looked forced. "And that's about it."

More questions bombarded her mind. Gina knew instinctively the importance of keeping them to herself.

He glanced down at the magazine she'd been reading. "'The Modern Day Antique Lover,'" he read aloud. He lifted his brows up and down several times. "Sounds heavy."

"It is. Did I ever mention I like antiques?" she asked with a dash of humor, hoping to lighten the mood.

"I believe you did." His easy grin softened. "You're a very kind, thoughtful person, Gina Hollister."

Her cheeks warmed. If only she could think of an appropriate reply.

"I'll be flying back to New York again on Saturday," he said.

"Business no doubt?"

"Of course. I'll be spending part of the next two weeks there. Maybe it would be a good time for you and Amanda to head back to Austin."

"I'll think about it."

"The meetings in New York are important, just not as important as the ones I'll be hosting in Brussels. The success or failure of my entire company depends on the outcome of those meetings." He reached in his pocket and handed her a sheet of paper. "I thought you'd need to know my schedule, where and how I can be contacted."

"I appreciate it." She slipped the paper inside her notebook.

After what he'd told her about Myra, joking around seemed almost criminal. Yet he appeared to crave the light touch.

"Brussels, huh?" she said, faking an air of humor. "Sounds to me like you're going to be awfully busy this summer."

"Not too busy for a candy bar. Do you like chocolates, Doctor?"

She blinked and frowned. "Who doesn't?"

"Well, I happen to have a candy bar in my hip pocket. I'd consider giving you half if you're interested."

She laughed. "Thanks for the offer, but I'm trying to cut back." She put the magazine on the coffee table along with her plans to discuss Dr. Larker. "You know you remind me of an article I read some time ago. The author claimed to love sweets and called himself the Gingerbread Man." She didn't mention she'd called Steve the Gingerbread Man, silently of course.

"I do like sweets."

"I figured," she said. "As I recall the article also said the Gingerbread Man liked antique toys and visited antique shops in his home state of Maine as often as possible."

"Antiques?" His grin was seasoned with amusement. "Sounds like we have something in common. I like sweets; you like antiques. Now we both like the author you mentioned."

She chuckled softly. "Guess we do have things in common. But we also differ on some important topics." Gina hesitated before going on. How could she explain the truth about a child to a loving father?

"Okay, Doctor, let's hear it. How do we differ?"

The time had come to say what must be said. Was she ready? She cleared her throat. "First you sent Amanda dolls and ginger cookies as if she were five years old. Then you let her go swimming with an older boy without permission. And you're always running—as fast as you can. In the child's story 'the Gingerbread Man,' the cookie claimed nobody could catch him." She sent him a long searching gaze. "Can anybody catch you, Mr. Bryson?"

He grinned, but she knew he was serious. "Not if I can help it."

hy had she asked such a personal question? Steve's answer floored her, but she managed to smother a grin. Maybe he *was* the Gingerbread Man.

"As I believe I said earlier, you and Amanda are welcome on any or all these short trips."

"Aren't you afraid we might cramp your style?"

He shook his head. "Nah. And it might be a learning experience for both of you. New York City is something to see, even this day and time, and you'd be perfectly safe. My guards are available at all times."

"I'm sure it's interesting," Gina said. "But what about Amanda's studies? I think we should stay right here, at least for the next few weeks, and continue with her schoolwork. Maybe later we could visit New York or fly back to Austin for the weekend."

"Amanda could study in my New York apartment."

"The question is, would she?"

"I would," Amanda said from the doorway, "if Polly can go with us."

Both girls giggled. When had Amanda and Polly come in? Did they hear her conversation with Steve?

"Amanda," Steve said, "I thought you and Polly were down at the pool. How long have you been standing there?"

"A while" They laughed again.

"Dr. Hollister thinks it would be best if you stayed here," Steve said, "at least for the next few weeks. But you and your friend are welcome to visit back and forth."

Amanda's disappointment showed on her face.

"Polly's mother invited you to spend this weekend at their house," Steve said. "Would you like that, Amanda?"

"I'd like it a lot, Daddy."

"Sounds like you and Polly are cooking up something. Am I right?"

Polly nodded. "Yes, sir."

"Then it's settled," he said.

Amanda and Polly left the cottage, laughing and talking among themselves. Amanda would spend Friday, Saturday, and Sunday nights at Polly's. However nothing was settled as far as Gina was concerned. With Amanda staying in town for the entire weekend, Steve was making it entirely too easy for the girls to get into all kinds of mischief.

"Maybe I'll spend Saturday and Sunday night at a hotel or motel in town," Gina said. "I have a little shopping and sightseeing I'd like to do on my own."

"Perfect," Steve said. "And by the way I have to attend a boring dinner party in town on Friday night and need a dinner partner. Would you do me the honor, Doctor?"

There he goes again. Didn't he realize she wasn't like the women he normally went out with? She wanted roots, a family, not glitter and fancy parties. But mostly she wanted a husband who shared her faith in God. Steve could never be that man.

It would be foolish to pretend she wouldn't like going out with him, but they wanted different things in life. Still a dinner party in a town sounded like fun.

One glance at those dimples and listening to his voice for an evening would be worth the effort. Contrary to her firm resolve, what could be wrong with going out with him once? It wasn't as if she expected him to fall in love with her.

"All right," she said. "I'll be your dinner partner for one night. But bear in mind we both signed an agreement before I promised to come here."

"How could I forget?"

Evidently Steve had no intention of leaving the cottage. He picked up one of Amanda's textbooks and turned to the table of contents.

"I thought we might discuss our differing opinions," Gina said.

"I thought I'd made my views quite clear."

"Then maybe my views need to be clarified." She took a deep breath before continuing. "When I first decided to begin my teaching lessons with prayer, I told Myra exactly where I stood. She agreed with my teaching methods as well as my opinions on prayer and Bible reading."

"Bible reading," he repeated. "I didn't know about that one. Does my daughter have Bible reading in class too?"

"When it seems appropriate."

"I'm dying to hear how often that might be."

"I assumed you knew all this when you hired me," she said. "I never tried to hide it."

"All I knew was you'd been Amanda's tutor for three years, were a PhD, and Amanda liked you."

"I'm sorry about this, sir, and I'll be glad to hand in my resignation immediately."

"No need for that," he said. "Why don't we wait a while and see how things go? Frankly I would miss you. I think Amanda would too, but she might not be willing to admit it right now."

Gina found herself in the embarrassing position of not having a logical comment.

"Anything else you want to say?" he asked.

"Nothing." She blinked, then as diplomatically as possible said, "And if you don't have anything else to say either, I have some work I need to do to prepare for my next session with Amanda."

"Go right ahead." He reached for another of Amanda's textbooks. "Don't let me stop you."

It was becoming harder and harder to work for a man who neither appreciated what she was trying to do nor respected her wishes and opinions. Steve's motto was probably "my way or the highway." She'd missed the perfect opportunity to resign. But he said he'd miss her; she knew she'd miss him, too, and there was his daughter to consider.

He put down the textbook, picked up a news magazine from the coffee table, and began to thumb through it. Gina reached for a stack of teaching materials on the floor by her feet.

"Before you get started," he said, "I need to tell you about Otto Geller. He's one of my employees. He'll be your bodyguard now to protect you."

"Protect me? I can understand your concern for Amanda," she said, "but I don't need protection. I'm neither your wife nor your child. I assume I'm not your slave."

"You're an employee as well as a guest living in my home," he said. "As long as that's the case, I'll do all I can to see you're safe."

She bit her lip to keep from saying something she'd regret. Talking to Steve Bryson was like having a conversation with a bull moose.

All at once he turned and pointed his finger at the stack of plastic sheets on her lap. "What are those for?" he asked. "Are they the famous colored overlays you've been talking about?"

"Yes. As I explained sometimes children with reading problems are able to achieve more if they put a colored plastic overlay on top of the printed page before starting to read."

"Hogwash. Modern education junk, a waste of time."

Gina sucked in her breath, hoping to avoid kicking him in the shin. "Research suggests plastic overlays sometimes work very well. And as I told you, I've been using them with Amanda."

"Been, past tense. I thought after our little talk in the hallway you'd have stopped using them, period. Why don't you try teaching her to read instead? Seems like, so far anyway, nobody has bothered to do that."

Gina counted to ten. Unlike most in her field, she knew as much from personal experience as she did from textbooks and research. The teaching methods she used were tailor-made for someone like Amanda Bryson. What would Steve say or do if she put her misgivings on hold, told him the truth outright? What if she told him she was a dyslexic?

Out of the question.

Like most parents Steve probably meant well but couldn't possibly understand a problem like Gina's. She knew if she ever did break down and tell Steve about her own problem, he'd never see her in the same light again.

"Amanda's been thoroughly tested," Gina explained. "She's quite intelligent, but ..."

"You don't have to tell me she's smart," he said. "I've known it all along. I want to know why she can't read."

"She *can* read. But because of her learning disability, she—"

"Learning disability? There you go again. I don't take kindly to hearing my child is retarded."

"I never said that," she insisted. "Amanda has a learning problem. It's not the same as being retarded."

"Sounds the same to me."

"Amanda processes information differently than most people."

"What's that supposed to mean?"

"Her brain works in a different way. But it doesn't mean she can't learn."

"And I'm paying all this money so my daughter can play with colored sheets of plastic, huh?"

"I've been trained to teach students how to bypass certain trouble spots so they can learn faster and retain what they've learned longer."

He shrugged as if he didn't believe a word she said.

"I know what I'm talking about,' she informed him. "Because of the way their brains work, children with learning problems have to try harder than other children their age to get the same results. But there's a bright side to all this."

He sent her a sour look. "I can hardly wait to hear it."

"Sometimes because of the extreme effort they put forth, children with learning disabilities become super-achievers and are quite successful in life. It's like the story of the rabbit and the turtle. Rabbits are fast runners," she explained. "Turtles are slower but determined. Rabbits stop running and eventually retire. Turtles never retire. They keep going and going, maybe because they don't know how to stop trying."

"Is that a fact?"

She nodded. "Albert Einstein comes to mind."

"He must have been a rabbit."

"No. He was more of a super-turtle. Several PhD students I knew in college also had learning problems."

She didn't add she was one of them or that learning problems never go away. People like Gina simply learn to cope.

"All this sounds interesting," he said, "but I want you to forget all the overlay baloney. Teach my daughter to read the way I was taught when I was a kid. And you can forget all the religious stuff, too."

"Perhaps you should have hired someone whose views were more like your own."

"Look," he said, "all I want you to do is teach my daughter to read so she can catch up with her classmates."

"Exactly what I plan to do." She put down the stack of overlays. Rejection was the last thing she needed. She'd had enough. "I know I promised to attend the dinner party you mentioned, but I changed my mind. I'm not going."

"What?"

"You must know plenty of classroom teachers who share your

views on doctors, education, bodyguards, and prayer. I'm sure one of them would be happy to take my place."

Without waiting to hear what he might say next, she got up off the couch and stalked to the door. "I'll be in my room if you need me. Just rattle my chains, and I'll come right out."

Steve threw down the magazine he was reading. *Women.* He gave Gina's desk a hard look as if she were still seated behind it. Then he went over and stood in front of the fireplace. *Gina Hollister is a hard-headed female.*

But when she was around, he couldn't keep his eyes off her. She reminded him of someone. Sometimes her actions made him think of Myra but certainly not her looks. Myra was a pretty young girl and a pretty woman. Gina was beautiful.

He had to stop looking at her, not to mention thinking about her all the time. Steve was supposed to be a professional. Besides he didn't think Gina liked him—not to mention loved him. He frowned. Where did the word *love* come from?

He never had the opportunity to tell her that prayers weren't always answered, and he never told her about Baylee either and probably never would.

Steve didn't care for some of Gina's teaching methods. He could do a better job teaching Amanda than Gina Hollister was doing—if he could spare the time. Nobody in his family had problems learning. He didn't think Amanda did either. If there was a problem, it must have come from Myra's side of the family.

Amanda merely needed to be taught in the right way. Gina wasn't doing that.

He went over to the bookcase he'd had Otto set up on the back wall behind the couch area. So far there were only a handful of books displayed there. He picked up one of them and gazed down at the title. *Good Morning, Virginia*, he read.

Virginia. He'd heard the name somewhere .... All at once it came to him. Virginia was the kid he helped that time. Steve was a student in junior college in Oklahoma back then, and his roommate was a guy named Caleb. Caleb Cantu was his best friend. They played basketball on the same team. They did almost everything together.

But Caleb wasn't with him on the day he substituted for a physical education teacher at a nearby elementary school and met Virginia. Steve could almost see the playground now. The kids were picking on a cute little girl named Virginia, and he put a stop to it.

Steve was a rich kid, and he had never really helped anyone. But he stood up for Virginia. As a result his life was changed. He'd long dreamed of becoming a high school football or basketball coach, and suddenly he wanted to teach little kids like Virginia, help them in some way. And he knew he wanted to do that for the rest of his life.

The minute he walked into his dorm room, Caleb gave him the news. His mother called, and he was to call her back as soon as possible. Steve called and heard the worse news of his life. Daddy was—was dead! *Dead*! He could barely say the word.

He was expected to quit college immediately, return home, and take over his father's businesses. Later when the time was right, he could finish his education at the University of Texas with a degree in business. Any dream he had of a career in physical education or teaching in elementary school also died.

Thoughts of Gina interrupted his memories of what happened back in college. He'd been thinking about her a lot lately, too often to suit him, and his recollections weren't all regarding her tutoring skills or the lack of them. He should keep an eye on Gina, see what developed.

On second thought he'd keep both eyes on her. She might not be his idea of the perfect educator, but she was the most beautiful woman he'd ever met.

Regardless he'd wasted enough time thinking about Gina Hollister. He had a dinner party to attend and then another quick trip to New York City. Was there no rest for the weary?

STEVE RETURNED from his business trip before lunch on Monday with repentance in his heart. He was much too harsh with Gina before he left, and he wanted to make things right. He intended to go in and make that happen as soon as possible.

He'd barely put down his briefcase when Amanda reminded him of the agenda for the day. They'd leave for Purgatory, Colorado, right after they finished eating lunch, and Polly Newton would be going with them. Then Polly joined them at the lunch table. Steve liked Polly and had a special reason for being glad she consented to go on the outing with them.

"Where's Dr. Hollister?" He glanced around and didn't see Gina anywhere.

"I guess she's still in Durango," Amanda explained. "Otto drove her into town early this morning to pick up a dress she left to be altered."

Steve was eager to see her, but they'd be driving right through Durango on their way to Purgatory. He wouldn't mention it, but Gina could have picked up her dress then.

They'd already started eating when Gina arrived. She stood in the doorway connecting the dining room to the kitchen. "I'm back, everybody."

Steve nodded. "Amanda tells me we'll be leaving for Purgatory right after lunch."

"That's the plan," Gina said.

"I'll want some of my guards to go with us then," Steve insisted. "Otto and Frank can take my truck. But they'll stay way behind us, out of sight. We'll hardly know they're there."

"I'll know," Gina said.

Steve had assumed Gina wouldn't approve of his decision regarding guards. From her tone of voice, he now knew for sure. He hoped she understood and accepted his thoughts on the matter, and if she attempted to persuade him to leave the guards behind, it wouldn't work.

It wasn't unusual for someone as wealthy as Steve to hire bodyguards to protect his family, especially after what he'd heard in town earlier. A local child had barely escaped being abducted. But it wouldn't happen to Amanda or Gina if Steve had anything to say about it.

He turned to Amanda. "I suppose Polly's parents know about the trip to Purgatory."

"Of course they know," Amanda replied.

"You girls are getting thick, aren't you?"

Amanda nodded and smiled at Polly. "Yes, we are."

"I'm glad you have nice friends here in Colorado, Amanda." He grinned at Polly. "And Polly, I think the world of your parents."

"Thank you, sir."

He slanted his head to the side, hoping to read the secretive expression on his daughter's face. He might not know a lot about children and teenagers, but he knew when someone was hiding something. His daughter wasn't being completely honest with him. He hated to admit Gina could be right about her.

"Amanda." He paused. "I heard you've been hanging around the horse barn lately. I know you're a good rider, but you wouldn't try to ride one of those wild horses, would you?"

"No, Daddy."

"Good. Now hurry up and finish eating so we can get started. We have a big day ahead of us."

THE SKY COULDN'T HAVE BEEN CLEARER or the setting more majestic. Gina could think of few things she'd rather do than take another drive through the mountains of Colorado. Polly would spend the next couple of days at the castle with Amanda. In return Amanda would visit Polly at her home as well.

Steve and Gina loaded everything into the van.

"Okay, guys," he said. "Pile in."

He sat behind the wheel, and they wove their way through the San Juan National Forest. Gina found it an adventure worth remembering. For now she put all her troubles behind her.

In the passenger seat beside Steve, she turned to him. "The word 'Purgatory' has religious overtones. Tell us more about our destination, Mr. Bryson. Tell us about Purgatory, Colorado."

"Well, it's July." Steve released a big breath of air. "The slopes of Purgatory should be green and lush instead of white with snow as they are in winter. But white powder tops some of the mountains surrounding the castle. It's probably true everywhere around here now." He sent Polly a quick glance. "But none of this is new to you, is it, Polly?"

"No, sir."

"I didn't think so, since you live here year around. So if you think of something interesting to add to the conversation as we roll along, please share it, will you?"

"Sure."

"Great. And that goes for you, too, Amanda. Do you have any questions?"

Amanda shook her head. "No. None I can think of."

"Well, if you do have questions, ask them. I'll try to answer. If I can't maybe Polly or Dr. Hollister can. After all the doctor is a very educated woman, and a nice one, too."

He sent a tender smile in Gina's direction. "Now back to my job as your personal tour guide. So Purgatory, Colorado, is halfway between the towns of Durango and tiny Silverton, and the entire area is known as a wonderland, whether in summer or winter. My mother said the first time she saw Silverton she felt like she'd stepped back in time. She said visiting Silverton was like being a character in a western movie set in the 1880's."

"How exciting," Gina put in. "I can hardly wait to see it."

"And you will," he said. "Now back to our outing." He cleared his throat. "In winter Purgatory is the skiing haven we've all read about, and the green beauty all around us will lift your spirits. We'll shop, visit all the usual tourist attractions, and on our way home, we'll have an early supper at a family-owned restaurant that specializes in home-cooking. How's that for a day trip through the hills of Colorado?'

"Well done, tour guide," Gina said, clapping her hands.

Polly clapped, too, but Amanda seemed lost in her own thoughts, barely responding at all. Something was going on in Amanda's life, something new and something all wrong, and neither Gina, and maybe Steve, seemed to have any idea what it might be.

AMANDA WAS SPENDING a lot of time in Steve's horse barn where his half-broken animals were kept, including Hitler, Steve's wild stallion. Yes, Amanda was a good rider, but in Gina's opinion, she wasn't prepared physically to handle a truly spirited animal. Gina had warned her not to ride one of her father's unbroken horses, but she wasn't sure the message penetrated Amanda's thick head—or Steve's, for that matter.

She tried to warn Steve of this problem, and he did finally tell Amanda not to ride wild horses. But was it enough to stop someone like his headstrong daughter?

Steve said not to worry. He also said his horse trainer wouldn't arrive until early September. Until then either Otto Geller or one of his other guards promised not to allow Amanda to ride unsafe animals.

Gina had also suggested Steve have Cricket trucked to Colorado so Amanda would have a safe horse to ride, but his head was thicker than Amanda's. So far he hadn't listened.

THEY'D LEFT the restaurant and had almost reached the castle. "A surprise is waiting for you when we get back to the house, Amanda," Steve said.

"A surprise?" Amanda sounded truly interested in what he said for the first time since they left the castle. "What kind of surprise?"

"You'll see."

But it wasn't until they rounded a hill and Gina could see the castle in the distance she got a hint of what the surprise might be. A big truck pulling a horse trailer with two horses inside was on the road ahead of them and seemingly headed for the castle.

"Is Cricket in the trailer?" Amanda nearly shouted from the backseat.

"We'll have to wait and see."

"Oh, Daddy, I hope she is!"

He chuckled. "I kind of figured you'd say that."

Nevertheless Gina was amazed when the truck pulled to a stop in front of Steve's horse barn. By the time they arrived, one of his guards had bridled Amanda's mare, Cricket. Another guard followed the first one, leading a second horse.

Amanda jumped out of the car and ran around to the driver's side to hug her father. "Oh, Daddy, thank you!"

"Don't thank me," he said. "Thank Dr. Hollister. She's the one who talked me into having Cricket brought here from Texas."

"Oh, thank you, Dr. Hollister," Amanda said in animated tones. She glanced back at Steve. "But who's the other horse for?"

"Polly," he said.

Polly grinned. "For me?"

"I bought the bay at a ranch outside of Durango so you'd have a horse to ride when you visit Amanda."

"Oh, Daddy, thanks," Amanda said. "You're so special."

The two girls raced off toward the horse barn.

"Don't ride too long," Steve called after them. "It'll be dark soon."

"We won't," Amanda called back.

"I'm so glad you brought the horses here," Gina said. "It was a nice thing to do, and I know Amanda appreciates it."

"Were you surprised?" Steve asked.

"That you had the mare brought here?"

"No, that I could be nice."

She grinned. He'd be surprised if he knew how she truly felt about him. But if Gina had her way, he never would.

They strode on toward the family entrance to the castle. "You got several telephone calls yesterday while you were away," Gina said. "Does the name Lydia Bracken mean anything to you?"

"She's a movie actress I date occasionally. Did she call?"

"Twice."

"You're kidding!" He opened the front door. Then he waited, motioning for Gina to go in first. "Lydia was in *Below the Level* with Bryan Ashley. If you'd known who she was, you could have requested she autograph photos for you and Amanda."

"Frankly I'd rather have Bryan's autograph."

He laughed, indicating the hallway to their left. "Think he's pretty hot?"

"The hottest."

They were still laughing as they headed for the green room, finally settling in front of the fireplace with a big TV on the wall above it. But unanswered questions hid under the laughter—and Gina wanted answers.

2 0

Otto Geller, Gina's bodyguard according to Steve, drove her into town on Friday. She was in the passenger seat of Steve's van beside the tall Texan because Gina and Otto were on a mission to stop by the pharmacy and pick up a prescription for Gretel. The girls stayed behind to ride their horses.

Gina glanced over at Otto. Her bodyguard wasn't merely a big man; he reminded her of a middle-aged prizefighter who worked out. He wore a brown suit, a dark green tie, and cowboy boots, making him look even taller. His thick neck bulged above the white collar of his dress shirt. Were it not for the gentle warmth so clear in his green eyes and his friendly smile, he'd look frightening.

"Hey, Otto," she said, "can you suggest a good place to have a late lunch?"

"You're asking *me*, ma'am?" He appeared uncomfortable. "I ain't no education person such as yourself. You choose."

"I'm no smarter than you, Otto, believe me. Besides you said you'd always lived around here. I'm a newcomer. So where should we eat?"

"I know a café where the food is real fine. Can't remember the name of the place though. I call it the Snack and Yak." He grinned, revealing crooked teeth in front. "It's one of them fast-food places. They sell ice cream, too. I done planned to get me a hamburger with cheese and the biggest chocolate milkshake they got. How about you, Doc?" He reached for his phone. "I could order something good for you, too."

"You've sold me, Otto; phone in the order. I want a hamburger, fries, and a chocolate milkshake. But I think I'll go with the small size today."

"That'll do her," he said. "Them chocolate milkshakes sure leave a sweet taste."

"And I'll bet you like the taste of gingerbread, too."

"Gingerbread? Yes, ma'am."

"Mr. Bryson likes gingerbread," she whispered. "Don't tell anyone, but sometimes I call him the Gingerbread Man, but not where other people can hear." She paused, studying Otto's face for a moment. "You won't tell on me, will you?"

Otto shook his head. "No, ma'am. I won't tell."

"Fantastic!"

They finished their cheeseburgers and chocolate shakes, picked up the meds, then Otto drove Gina around town, pointing out the sites of interest and giving her space to think. But as it turned out, she spent most of her time trying to dissect the real Steve Bryson. Was he the gentle, fun-loving charmer who escorted her to River Hill, the womanizer Myra Bryson talked about, the out-of-touch Gingerbread Man who loved sweets, or the mad scientist with secrets hidden in the tower room?

GINA NOTICED that during a supper of fish and fries that Friday night, Steve didn't eat a thing. He looked a little pale—perhaps preoccupied. He could be ill. He'd seemed eager to leave the table. Then she remembered. His business dinner in town was scheduled for that night, and she'd refused to go with him the last time they met. He could be remembering the day she turned him down.

She could hardly wait to leave the table, and there was a book in Steve's library she was dying to read. But first she'd check on the girls. They planned to go horseback riding again, and she wanted to remind them to be careful. Wild horses were stabled in the barn as well as gentle ones.

At last Gina grabbed the mystery novel from one of the shelves in Steve's library. Then she hurried to her bedroom, crawled to the middle of the bed, and started reading.

She'd already read chapter one when a knock sounded at her door. "Gina," Steve called and knocked again.

She got up and opened the door.

Steve wore a white dinner jacket and held a bouquet of flowers. The white roses smelled delicious. But what was he doing here? He should be on his way to the dinner party, not chatting with her.

Gina joined him in the hall, pressing her back against her bedroom door. She heard a click. Did she just lock herself out of her bedroom? No, it couldn't have happened.

She looked up at Steve. "Why aren't you at the dinner party?"

"I'm on my way, but I wanted to stop by and see how you're doing first." He tossed her an irresistible grin, and he didn't look pale at all.

She managed to resist.

"Am I forgiven for speaking against your teaching methods?" he asked.

"Yes. As I Christian I always try to forgive."

"Then may I come in?"

She shook her head so hard her hair went every which way. What was Steve doing here? And why? They'd spent an entire day together, driving through the mountains. He should already know he'd been forgiven—sort of anyway.

"We should be able to discuss whatever it is you want to say out here in the hall," she said after a long moment. "Besides I wouldn't want you to be late to your dinner party."

"I have time."

"I don't. I have a lot of reading to do."

"I'm glad I don't pay you by the hour," he said. "I'd never be able to afford you." He handed her the flowers. "These are for you. And you'll never know how much I regret saying what I did about ..."

"Overlays?"

He nodded sheepishly. "Yeah."

She took the flowers, gripping the stems with both hands and creating a sort of barrier between them. *I should put them in water, but it would mean going inside. Steve would be right behind me, and that wouldn't be good at all.* At the same time tender feelings streamed through her, the result of his kindness in bringing the flowers. A stronger resolve would be required if she hoped to keep her emotions in check.

The sweet fragrance of roses mingled with the scent of his aftershave. Gina feigned a lack of interest in both the flowers and the man who gave them to her, accepting the white roses without looking at them as closely as she'd like.

"Thank you for the flowers. They're lovely," she said. "Now what can I do for you?"

"I just heard from my mom, and I'll soon have a couple of those pipes we talked about."

"What pipes?"

"You know, the kind pipe-smokers use. Maybe they'll get the peace process going."

"What in the world are you talking about?"

"My late father and grandfather were pipe smokers. My mother will be sending me two pipes in the mail; one belonged to my father, and one to my grandfather." He grinned. "They're simply carved wooden pipes, but they're special to me because they belonged to Dad and Grandpa. I thought you might find them interesting since you like old stuff."

She nodded. "I do like old stuff. But what does that have to do with anything?"

"We kind of got off on the wrong foot," he said. "I thought the pipes might wipe the chalkboard clean, so to speak. We could use them as a kind of symbol of peace. So what do you think? Will pipe-smoking work for you?"

"No!" She threw her head back and giggled like a teenager. Yet she couldn't stop wondering. Was Steve playing the humor card in hopes of a romantic relationship with her? If so it wasn't going to work.

He'd laughed, too. Now he smiled. She didn't.

"From the way things are going," he went on, "we might need both of those pipes."

Gina still refused to smile, though she wanted to.

His grin slowly faded. "I have to be out of town on business a lot. When I'm home I want to spend as much quality time with my daughter and you as possible."

Me? Did he just say he wanted to be with me? She'd have to make sure those feelings swirling around inside her heart didn't show on her face.

"I'm so glad you brought Cricket here," Gina said, tweaking the subject a bit. "Remember when I warned you Amanda was hanging around the horse barn? Well, one of your guards caught her when she was about to saddle up one of those wild horses of yours."

His eyebrows lifted. "Hitler?"

"Yes. Otto kept her from riding the animal, and I don't think Amanda will try it again now that Cricket's here. But I thought you should know."

"Thanks. I'll talk to her. But like you said, Cricket's here now." He hesitated. "Oh, I forgot to thank you for answering the landline recently. I think I told you Josie, my private secretary from Houston, broke her leg in a bike accident. Anyway she'll be all right, but she won't be arriving for six weeks or more."

"Sorry to hear about Josie. How will you manage?"

"I already have several secretaries who work at my office in town, but I don't have anyone to answer the phones at the castle except Gretel and Netty. You did it in the past, and I wondered if you might consider doing it when they can't until I can hire someone else."

"Is that all you want me to do? Answer the telephones?"

"Yes."

"Then there's no need for you to hire anyone. I can man the phones *and* tutor Amanda when needed. But I do have a question. Why the landline here?"

Steve pressed the palms of his hands on her door frames, penning her in with one hand to her right and the other to her left.

"Landlines are all but dead and buried," she added.

He inched closer. "Gretel can't seem to catch on to modern things like cells, stuff like that." He lowered his head.

With her back pressed against the door, she'd have no means of escape if he decided to kiss her.

"I won't detain you any longer." She hoped he wouldn't guess how much she wanted him to stay. "It's late. I know you want to get to the party on time."

He reached out and traced her chin with his forefinger. A tremble filtered through the invisible wall she'd built between them. She almost gave in to the awesome desire to be held.

"Where's that pretty smile of yours?" he asked.

"My bodyguard's holding it for me for safekeeping until I fly back to Texas."

He laughed. "You do sound like my mother." Then he glanced toward the stairs. "I'll be flying out early in the morning and probably won't see you again until next weekend."

She ducked under his arm, resolving the kiss problem but still standing beside him. "Have a nice trip."

"I intend to."

"Good-bye," she said.

"Good-bye?" A muscle in his jaw tightened.

Gina sensed Steve wanted to say more. Instead he turned and strode toward the stairway.

She'd tried to disregard the truth for too long but couldn't anymore. She loved Steve Bryson even if it turned out he was the mad scientist and had some kind of hidden laboratory in the tower. No realization ever frightened her more. But why did everything have to be his way or the highway? Steve needed to learn to compromise.

He took part of my heart the first time I saw him. Now he's managed to make off with the rest of it. She turned around and gripped the doorknob. It wouldn't budge. She tried again. Nothing. It wouldn't turn at all. Gina turned back around and pressed her body against the bedroom door. Steve knew her pretty well now. At least he didn't know she'd locked herself out of her bedroom.

With a little help from Netty and Gretel, Gina managed to open her bedroom door, close it again, and lock it. As to the return of her heart, the outcome was doubtful. It was behind an iron door, and Steve had bolted it to the ground. How did she get herself in this predicament? Nicole was right. She should never have left Austin.

She'd heard another sermon on forgiveness, couldn't stop thinking about it. Caleb had said she was expected to forgive *all* her enemies. But surely it didn't include Stella and Trudy. And Phil? Really? Her father and Lola Ford were on the list, too—and then there was Steve. He was probably on everybody's need-to-forgive list.

Off and on she'd considered quitting her job and going back to Texas. The desire grew stronger by the day, but the timing had to be right. Such a time hadn't arrived yet. When and if it ever did, Gina would know.

STEVE HAD NEVER TRULY FORGIVEN his mother for forcing him to become a business tycoon when he'd wanted to work with kids. Sometimes Gina sounded exactly like her. His mother was also a sort of Bible thumper, but not the twenty-four-hours-a-day kind like Gina. And why did the word *forgive* keep playing in his mind?

He remembered the time when he accidently turned on the wrong channel. A television preacher pointed a finger at him and said, "Forgive your parents and honor them." If only he could wash those memories from his mind.

Steve still planned to go to the party, but first he'd take control of his feelings before they took control of him. He'd become too emotional. Things that shouldn't bothered him anymore still did, and Gina and Amanda dominated his every thought. Lately the kid he helped when he was in college was always somewhere in the back of his mind.

He had seen the child for less than an hour, but meeting her changed Steve's complete outlook on life, as he learned for the first time he had the ability to help someone in need. He had no memory of ever helping anyone until he met little Virginia. Yes, Virginia. That was her name.

Steve had kept his true goals in life a secret, hiding his interest in science, drawing, painting, and teaching kids from his mom, dad, and the world. Though his parents seemed proud of his athletic abilities, they expected Steve to become a businessman like his father and grandfather.

He thought he'd hate becoming the big business Steve Bryson he was today. How could he have guessed he'd like it? Steve had no desire to go to the party, but good businessmen were expected to attend functions like this. It was part of the job. But maybe he wouldn't go—this time.

He went to his room on the second floor, called in sick, and changed into jeans and a tee-shirt. For a change he'd do something *he* wanted to do. Steve glanced down at his bed. What he wouldn't give to stretch out and read the book he bought at the bookstore last week. But first he had telephone calls to make regarding his plan to convert the castle into a home for children.

He could text them instead, but a call was more personal. Steve hoped to get started on the castle renovation by late August and had a lot to do before that.

He could make those calls in the morning before he left on the plane, but he knew he should make them now while he was thinking about it. *Should.* That one word echoed inside his head. Would his "I should" ever become his "I want"? Not likely. Now where did he put those papers he needed?

He stopped to think. He knew they weren't in his briefcase. Then he remembered. They were in his office, top drawer of his desk. He glanced toward the door leading to the stairway. He'd work in his office, then he'd go back to his room, pack, and read the book.

Dusk approached, but it was still daylight outside. Maybe he'd go up to the tower first and then to his office. He always felt better after a visit to his laboratory.

Once Gina managed to open her bedroom door, she couldn't get the laboratory off her mind. It was time to search for truth.

As for the book she'd read chapter two later. The big question was Steve. Was he the mad scientist, or at the least, the scientist's financial backer? How was it possible to love a man she didn't know? There had to be ways of finding answers to questions like this. She just needed to find them. And was Steve involved in some kind of scientific experiments in his so-called laboratory?

She couldn't ask Netty or Gretel for help. They were too loyal to Steve. She'd do the investigating on her own. She'd heard of a hidden stairway in Steve's office and intended to find it. He'd be at the party by now. This was the perfect time.

She crept down the stairs, aiming for his office. Gina was about to open the office door when she heard sounds like steps coming toward her, a lot of them. She turned back and stood still, her body pressed against the door as a parade of men and women in blue uniforms marched down the hall straight for her. They carried mops, brooms, and vacuuming machines with electric cords. Was this the cleaning staff she'd been hearing about? *Finally?*

The apparent leader of the group stopped the march like he wanted to talk. "I'm Jason Potts," he said. "We're the cleaning staff here and about to borrow some of Gretel and Netty's equipment. You must be Dr. Gina Hollister."

"Yes I am. I'm glad to finally see you in person." Gina put out her hand; he shook it. "I was beginning to think you people didn't exist."

"Oh, we exist all right, and we've heard a lot about you."

"We sure have," the elderly woman behind him said. "Mr. Bryson talks about you all the time. I think he's sweet on you."

Impossible. Gina felt her face warm, knowing she was likely blushing.

"Hush, Matilda," Jason said. "You're embarrassing the doctor."

Gina did her best to produce a smile. "I was out for a late evening stroll, but now I think I'll head for the kitchen and get me a cold glass of water before turning in."

"We won't keep you then," Mr. Potts said, herding his group on down the hall. "And we do hope you have a great evening."

"You, too."

As soon as they were out of sight, Gina went into Steve's office, and the search began. She combed every square inch of the room for some kind of hidden door or secret stairway but without results. At last she gave up, concluding the so-called gateways didn't exist. She pointed her inner compass toward the kitchen. At least the stairway part of the puzzle was resolved.

Gina poured herself a glass of water and sat down on a kitchen chair to drink it. She was about to take her last swallow when Steve appeared in the doorway between the kitchen and the family dining room.

"Mr. Bryson, what are you doing here? I thought you'd be at the party by now."

"As you can see, I didn't go." Steve wore jeans and a blue tee-shirt, and he wasn't smiling. "I'd been looking all over for you when Mr. Potts said I could find you here." He looked a little ticked. "Caleb and Bonny Cantu are here, looking for you. That Dr. Larker is with them. I was headed for my office when they came in the family entrance. We met in the entry hall."

"Where are they now?"

"In the green room." He started to walk off, but he turned back and faced her. "By the way, Doctor, I saw the girls leave the house after supper. They were headed for the horse barn. With their horses here now, I guess they went for a late afternoon ride. But it'll be dark soon."

"I haven't seen them, but I'm sure they'll be in at any moment. Amanda doesn't like to go riding after dark. I'll go in and check on the girls again as soon as our guests are settled in."

"*Our* guests?"

"You're going to join me in the green room; aren't you?" she asked. "After all, this is your castle."

"They came to see you, not me—something about a Bible study group they want to start."

"You're not interested?"

"No, frankly, I'm not."

"It would so please me if you were," she said. "Sometimes we do things merely to be kind. It's called compromise."

He put his hands in the pockets of his jeans. "I have some work to do. Then I plan to go to my room and grab a book on dyslexia I've wanted to read for a long time. I need to find out why my daughter can't read."

A sarcastic comeback shouted from the center of her mind. Gina ignored it, instead hurrying to the green room to greet Caleb, Bonny, and Dr. Larker. But her heart wasn't in it. She needed time to let things settle, come to some kind of conclusion.

The four of them gathered around a small table, talking and drinking the coffee Steve had sent in.

"So where's Mr. Bryson?" Dr. Larker asked. "I'd like to get to know him better."

Gina tried to think of an answer, but nothing came to mind. At last she said, "He said he had some work to do tonight. Should we get started?"

"By all means." Dr. Larker reached for the stack of papers on the table in front of him and handed a sheet to each of them. "If you'll please read the objectives listed here, we can get started."

They were in the middle of a discussion on the objectives when the double doors opened and Steve burst into the green room.

"It's after dark," he exclaimed. "Amanda and Polly still haven't gotten back from their horseback ride." Deep worry lines wrinkled Steve's forehead. "Otto checked the horse barn. Amanda's mare is there. Hitler and the bay mare are missing!"

"Hitler?" Gina gasped, and rose from the table. "Oh, no!"

"I already called 911," Steve added.

"We'll form a search party immediately," Dr. Larker said.

"Yes," Caleb and Bonny said together. Then without a word, Caleb, Bonny, the doctor, and Gina joined hands.

"Why aren't you doing something?" Steve demanded. "My daughter could be hurt out there."

"We *are* doing something," Dr. Larker explained. "We're getting ready to pray."

"A waste of time," Steve said under his breath. "And we don't have time to waste. I'm leaving, with or without you Bible thumpers." Steve stormed from the room.

"Steve!" Gina dashed after him, out of the house and onto the front porch. She knew the others would stay behind and pray, then join them in the search.

Moonlight illuminated the outline of a man. "Steve!"

He ran on ahead as if he hadn't heard her call out. She knew he was frantic because she was getting that way too.

"Steve!" Gina shouted. "Wait!"

He didn't slow down.

She darted through the tall trees, her initial jogging becoming an all-out run. Her chest tightened; her breathing was labored.

At last she couldn't see Steve anymore. It was dark and getting darker. It would be pointless to continue. She turned around, backtracking to the castle to join the others. They *had* to be successful.

GINA TOLD the household staff what happened. Netty provided each of them with flashlights. Dr. Larker instructed everybody to spread out systematically. With the guards fully alerted, Gina teamed up with Dr. Larker for the actual search.

They started across the well-tended yard toward a dark cluster of towering trees.

"You're worried, aren't you, Gina?" Dr. Larker asked.

"Is it that obvious?" She wiped her eyes with the back of her hand.

"We must have faith our prayers are in the process of being answered."

"I know. But sometimes it's hard to do," she said. "In a way I feel partly responsible for all this."

"You shouldn't."

Gina had already told him about Myra's recent death, the kiss in the summer house, and every other important thing hidden in her brain. Somehow she had the desire to inform him of all these events again as if she thought he might have forgotten.

Dr. Larker flashed his light through a heavily wooded area thick with underbrush. "It doesn't look like we can get through here. You know faith is like that too. We could choose to turn around and go back to the house, go in a different direction, or plow on as if we expected a miracle. I'm going for the miracle."

"Me too, and thanks."

Gina heard shouts coming from somewhere up ahead. "Did you hear that?"

"Yes!" Dr. Larker said. "Hurry!"

"Help!" The shout sounded louder.

She charged through the underbrush, hardly feeling the thorns and spiny twigs tearing at her clothes. Dr. Larker was right behind her. Somehow his mere presence had a calming effect on Gina. The shout rang out again.

"Is that you, Amanda?" Steve called from the darkness.

"It's me and Dr. Larker," Gina called out. "Over here."

In an instant Steve stood beside her, breathing heavily. "Know anything yet?"

"We heard somebody yell," Gina said, pointing. "Just over there."

"I heard it, too." Steve moved ahead of her. "Follow me."

Twigs snapped under their feet. An owl fluttered out of their path. The shout she'd heard earlier had vanished.

"Who's there?" the voice called from the shadows.

Gina shivered. "That's Polly! She sounds terrified."

"It's me, Polly," Steve yelled back. "Amanda's father."

"Oh, Mr. Bryson! I've been praying you'd come." Polly stepped into a stream of moonlight. Her blonde hair looked darker in the dim light. "Amanda's hurt. Hurry!"

Steve bolted forward. "Is she all right?"

"I ...I don't know. She's under that tree."

Dr. Larker rushed ahead and knelt in front of Amanda's still body. "She's breathing, but at this point it's all I know for sure."

"Can she be moved?" Steve asked, clearly worried.

Gina held her breath as Dr. Larker opened his doctor's bag. "I'd advise against it," he cautioned.

Steve got down on his knees beside his daughter, then glanced over at Gina. Her lips were moving. *She must be praying.* Gently he touched Amanda's face. The doctor checked her pulse.

"What can I do to help?" Steve's voice sounded weak, even to himself. Was this what they called parental distress?

"Mr. Bryson," Dr. Larker said, "why don't you and Dr. Hollister take Polly and go back to the house? Call an ambulance, and I'll stay here with Amanda."

"I've already called an ambulance," Steve explained. "It should be here in minutes." Somehow he knew his daughter's condition was serious. "I want to stay, but I know I should go."

"Yes you should," Dr. Larker agreed. "You know the grounds and would be a much better guide for the ambulance than Dr. Hollister or me."

"Then I'll stay," Gina put in. "Amanda will need to be with someone she knows when she wakes up."

Dr. Larker nodded. "That's probably a good idea."

Steve grabbed Polly's hand. "Come on, Polly, let's go."

"No." She tried to pull her hand away. "It's dark out there!"

"I could make better time without her." Steve released her

hand and shifted his weight from one leg to the other. *Okay, so I'm nervous.* "Why don't I leave Polly here and go?"

"That might be wise," Dr. Larker said.

Steve took off, racing through the aspens and tall pine trees, on toward the castle. Visions of Amanda's unconscious body assaulted his thoughts. He didn't trust that right-wing medical doctor-slash-psychiatrist, doubting Amanda would survive unless she got some real help. He had to get her to a hospital before it was too late. Panting he pushed on.

STEVE STOOD in front of the castle. He pulled his cellular phone from the hip pocket of his jeans, called Polly's parents, and told them what happened. The ambulance still hadn't arrived, but Polly's parents had suggested their physician, a Dr. Springfellow.

He hung up and phoned Dr. Springfellow's answering service. They picked up. Steve requested they take Amanda's case, and the answering service promised a quick reply.

If only he could stop and catch his breath. But he pressed ahead and made another call. "Otto, Steve Bryson here."

"Yes, Mr. Bryson."

"Amanda fell off a horse. She needs to go to the hospital immediately. Park my van at the entry gate of my property. When the ambulance gets there, have them follow you to the house. Pick me up out front. Dr. Hollister and the others will ride back with you."

"Yes, sir," Otto said.

And then Steve waited. He wanted to pray. But how? Did people forget things like that? He couldn't even recite the Lord's Prayer from memory anymore, but he remembered praying to save Baylee. He'd prayed to save his marriage to Myra, too. After neither of those prayers were answered, Steve came to a conclusion: prayer didn't work.

A lump formed in his throat. Would God hear his prayers for

Amanda now?' He closed his eyes and bowed his head. *It's time to try.*

Steve finished praying and was about to call Dr. Springfellow again when his phone rang.

"I understand there's been an accident at your estate, Mr. Bryson," the doctor said. "Would you mind telling me a little more about what happened in the woods earlier? I'm here at the hospital. According to the answering service, you sounded understandably distraught on the telephone."

"I don't … I don't know much." He paused to catch his breath. "But she fell off a horse."

"Just hold on and try to relax."

After what seemed an eternity, the ambulance arrived. Steve sat in the front seat next to the driver, directing him to where his daughter lay. Red lights flashed through the trees with Steve's van right behind it. The ambulance parked near Amanda's tree. Healthcare workers jumped out, checked Amanda's vitals, and loaded her onto a stretcher.

"I appreciate all your help," Steve said to Dr. Larker. "But Dr. Springfellow will be taking Amanda's case now and admitting her to the hospital. He's also the Newtons' doctor."

"Very well," Dr. Larker said soberly. "Dr. Springfellow is an excellent doctor."

Polly sniffed. "Where are my mom and dad?"

"They're on their way," Steve said. "I bet they'll be waiting for us at the castle." Castle? When did he start calling his estate a castle? Gina was having more of an influence on him than he liked.

While Dr. Larker, Gina, and Polly crowded into the van, Steve stayed in the ambulance with Amanda, and they started off. Steve knew Gina and the others would get out of the van at the castle to wait for the Newtons. Accelerating rapidly the ambulance sped down the road toward the hospital emergency room.

GINA LOOKED up at Dr. Larker before going inside. "I'm sorry about Dr. Springfellow taking the case. I know you must be disappointed."

"Yes. But as I said, Dr. Springfellow is an excellent surgeon and physician. The girl couldn't be in better hands."

"You're excellent at what you do, too," Gina said. "And you pray for your patients as well as healing them physically and emotionally. I heard you're also an ordained minister."

"Yes, I am." The elderly doctor wouldn't meet her eyes, perhaps embarrassed by her generous praise. "But we can pray for Amanda whether she's my patient or not." He paused and smiled. "And Dr. Hollister, drive Mr. Bryson's car to the hospital right now. He'll appreciate your kindness, and I know it's where you want to be."

"Yes, it is." Dr. Larker's kind words and offer of help reduced Gina's apprehension a bit. Yet she couldn't stop worrying about Amanda.

LATER GINA SAT beside Steve in the hospital waiting room. She glanced down at her watch. "My watch stopped. Do you have the time?"

Steve studied his own watch for a moment. "It's after midnight. It's Saturday now in case you'd forgotten." He turned his attention to Gina. "I wish that fancy doctor would hurry up and tell us something."

Gina nodded. "Me, too."

Dr. Springfellow entered the room with a hopeful expression on his face. "Mr. Bryson," he said, "you must be living right."

"What do you mean, Doctor?"

"The preliminary X-rays showed a crack in your daughter's skull and a massive blood clot on the brain. But when we Xrayed again shortly before the surgery, we found nothing but a mild concussion. So we don't have to operate after all."

"Are you saying she's out of danger?"

"Let's say I think she will be, shortly."

"Thank God!"

"Normally I don't believe in miracles," Dr. Springfellow continued, "but when I see something like this, I wonder. Did we make a mistake with the first X-ray, or was a miracle involved here?"

"When can I see Amanda?" Steve asked.

"Right now if you'd like. But I want to keep her overnight at the least."

Steve took a moment to digest all he'd seen and heard. An instant before he was convinced Amanda's good prognosis came about as the result of prayer. Now he wasn't so sure. The doctors probably made a mistake with the first X-ray. Logically what else could it be?

Later he drove back to the castle. Gina sat beside him in the front seat of his town car, and he wondered what she might be thinking. Dr. Springfellow had assured them Amanda would recover, but Gina didn't appear convinced. Neither was Steve. But what parent wouldn't be concerned after a riding mishap like Amanda's?

Gina had said she received a text from Polly's mother after she arrived at the hospital, giving Polly's account of the accident. Steve got a similar text message. Polly claimed Amanda only rode Cricket for a short time. Then they returned to the horse barn because Amanda wanted to ride Hitler.

According to Polly Hitler was trouble as soon as Amanda mounted him, but they were some distance from the castle when he started pitching. Amanda fell off and hit her head on the trunk of a tree. Polly got off her horse to see if she could help, and both horses ran away.

Steve didn't want to discuss what happened with Gina or anyone. He wasn't perfect, he made mistakes, and this time,

Gina was right. She warned Steve Amanda might try something like this. He should have listened, but he didn't want to think about that now. His only child was in the hospital.

Gina looked over at Steve. "Penny for your thoughts"

Her grin touched him. A slow smile formed in his heart. "Thanks for asking, but I don't have any cash on hand right now. I do have credit cards though." He sent her a grin. "Unless of course you take IOU's."

Gina giggled. Steve grinned because he loved to see her laugh.

"Are you still going back to New York in the morning?" she asked. "Or should I say *this* morning?"

"I have to go eventually. But I think I'll put it off for a few more days. I want to make sure Amanda is as healthy as Dr. Springfellow claims she is."

Gina grew silent, and Steve thought he knew why. "I'm sorry I didn't choose the doctor you wanted, Gina. Frankly Larker gives me the creeps."

"Do all so-called Bible thumpers give you the creeps?"

"Who are you talking about?"

"I think you know exactly who I'm talking about," she said.

"As I told you before, you sound like my mother."

AMANDA'S HEALTH IMPROVED QUICKLY. She left the hospital on Sunday and was soon well enough to continue her studies. Steve left for New York on Wednesday morning.

By Wednesday afternoon Gina was prepared and ready for Amanda's next tutoring sessions, especially the one on how early Americans washed, starched, and ironed their clothes with an antique flatiron. She'd scheduled the flatiron lesson for Friday. She'd put off that class long enough.

For now Gina planned to go into the laboratory—one way or another. She had to know what was going on in there no matter who tried to stop her. But first she hurried to the kitchen to check on everyone's whereabouts.

She studied her watch to make sure it still worked; it did. Netty would be in the kitchen. Gretel was in the washroom. Gretel often did the wash at three o'clock on Wednesday afternoon. Amanda had gone for a swim. This was the perfect time for Gina to put on her detective hat and explore the tower, but getting behind the locked door wouldn't be easy.

Gina stood in the doorway searching for something to say that would enable her to accomplish her mission. Netty was at the stove stirring a metal pot with a big spoon.

"Netty."

Netty jerked around like a frightened mouse.

Gina manufactured her sweetest smile. "I didn't mean to scare you, but I need your help."

"My help?"

"Yes. I need to go to the secret room in the tower, and I want you to help me because it's the right thing to do."

"It is?"

"Absolutely. Now I want you to get the keys to all the rooms in the tower and bring them to me. Do you know where your mother keeps them?"

"She wears them on her belt except when she's sleeping. At times they jingle, but people seldom notice them."

"Is there any way you could persuade her to give them to us?"

"Mama would want to know why we want them."

"Tell her Dr. Hollister needs them, and it's very important. I think your mother likes me. I think she'll do as I ask."

It worked. She and Netty were climbing the stairs in minutes. Then they were inside the laboratory, the forbidden room. Gina expected to see a chemistry lab with bubbling liquids encased in glass globes and chalkboards filled with long equations only a mathematician could understand. What she found were colorful oil paintings, dozens of them, and expertly done as well.

"These paintings are wonderful," Gina said to Netty. "Who's the artist?"

"Mr. Bryson. And we should leave as soon as possible. We shouldn't be here. Mama needs her keys back. She has to go down to the storeroom for supplies."

"Give me another minute or two. Then we'll go. "

Some of the paintings were landscapes. Others were portraits. Each was signed *Steve B.* Was Steve's part in the mad scientist scenario merely a figment of Gina's imagination?

One of the paintings was covered by a blue cloth, and she wanted to see it. But to uncover it would be intrusive. Nevertheless she *had* to see the painting.

Gina reached for the cloth.

"Please don't remove the cloth, Doctor," Netty said with deep emotion. "It would be wrong for one of us to do that."

"I know, Netty, but I have to. Please try to understand."

Gina pulled back the cloth. A little girl stared back at her. The child in the portrait had reddish-brown curls, and amber lights surrounded her like a kind of glow. The little girl looked younger than Amanda and nothing like her. Yet it was clear to Gina the child was real and important to Steve. No artist could paint a portrait like this one unless the model was someone he cared for deeply.

Maybe this was a painting of Myra when she was a little girl. Myra had changed her hair color about every week or two, so the original color could have been reddish. *Does Steve still love Myra?* The thought penetrated Gina's heart, and a flash of jealousy branded her mind like a hot flatiron. *Flatiron? Where did that come from?*

She glanced at Netty. "Do you know the name of the child in the painting?" Gina asked.

"No, ma'am."

Gina covered the painting with the blue cloth again. "Okay, Netty. I'm ready to go now."

They left the room and locked the door behind them.

AMANDA SPENT Thursday night at Polly's. From the way Amanda dragged around on Friday morning after returning to the castle, they'd had a late night. Gina was prepared for the lesson she was calling "Ironing in Earlier Days." But it could have merely been titled *Ironing* because people seldom ironed clothes anymore.

Gina gathered the flatiron, the box of starch she'd purchased at a survival store, and the gold cotton skirt she'd also bought there for this very lesson. Clothes weren't made of all cotton material much anymore. But cotton was the perfect cloth for this particular lesson.

She'd warned Netty and Gretel she'd be conducting Amanda's tutoring session in the kitchen. Amanda was seated at the kitchen table, looking sleepy and about as excited as an overfed dog after wolfing down five hamburger patties. Gina began to hum in hopes of keeping Amanda awake.

A wood or coal-burning stove would be best, but for this particular lesson, the electric stove in the kitchen would have to do. She put the starch in a big pot of water and let it boil.

"It'll take a while to bring the starch to a boil," Gina explained. "And then we must let it cool off before dipping the skirt in it. It'll give you time to complete the history lesson we talked about."

Amanda nodded, looking sleepier than ever. She got out her workbook and opened it. Whether or not Amanda read a single word was yet to be learned.

"After that we'll need to hang the skirt on a clothesline to dry," Gina instructed. "And when it's dry, guess what we'll do with it then?"

"Throw it in the trash and set fire to it," Amanda said.

Gina had to laugh. She couldn't stop herself despite the hint of sarcasm in Amanda's unsuitable remark. Teachers and college professors were told not to let their guards down, but Gina was not your average instructor. Gina wasn't average, period.

Amanda's cell phone rang.

"Don't answer it," Gina warned. "You're supposed to turn off your phone during class."

"But I think it's Daddy." Amanda reached for her phone. "He said he might call."

Gina tried not to show emotion. She looked away, frowning. "All right, go on. Answer the phone."

"Hello, Daddy," Amanda said into the cell phone. "Yes, I'm feeling fine." She paused. "Dr. Hollister is fine, too. But I'm in class right now." There was another long hesitation. Then Amanda pulled the phone away from her ear. "Daddy wants to know what we're doing in class today. What should I say?"

Gina's heart did an internal nose dive. "Tell him what he wants to know, of course." She thought of hot coals with herself sitting on them as Amanda explained the lesson to Steve.

Amanda glanced back at Gina again. "Daddy wants to know what you call this lesson."

"Tell him it's a history lesson on everyday life in early America."

Amanda repeated what Gina had said.

"Now Daddy wants to know what this lesson has to do with reading and spelling."

"Tell him I said you have to know how to read before you can read directions." Gina held in a smile. "In order to write down directions, you must be able to spell. Ironing clothes the old-fashioned way requires instructions and directions, especially lessons connected to a flatiron."

After a short delay Amanda said, "Daddy would like to learn more about the proper use of flatirons. He didn't like the way you used them in the past."

Gina laughed, probably loud enough for him to hear on his end. "Tell your father I said there are a lot of ways to use a flatiron. Today I'm teaching you one of those ways. Also tell him you have to go now. It's time to dip the skirt into the hot starch."

"I think Daddy must have heard you, Dr. Hollister. He's laughing."

"Tell him I said laughter is good for the soul. But you must hang up now, Amanda. We have a lesson to finish."

Gina dipped the cotton skirt in the pot of hot starch. They'd need to wait until the starch cooled before she could wring out the wet garment and hang it up to dry. It could take a while. Maybe if she put the hot starch, pot and all, in the refrigerator, she could shorten the process. It wouldn't be the way early Americans did it, but it would certainly save a lot of time.

On Wednesday morning Gina had an early breakfast and planned her day. At the same time she couldn't get memories of the paintings in the laboratory out of her mind, especially the one of the child. The little girl in the painting was adorable. If it turned out her name was Myra, okay, Gina could handle it. Myra Bryson was Amanda's mother and should be honored for motherhood if for nothing else.

Polly's parents went out Tuesday night, and Polly spent the night at the castle with Amanda. Gina knew the girls had plans for later on that morning, plans that didn't include Bible study, but that was exactly where they were headed. Otto was already notified and would be driving them to the two-story house where the service would be held. Dr. Larker was the scheduled speaker, and Gina didn't want to miss it.

As soon as they arrived, Amanda said, "Polly and I don't want to sit close to the front."

"Why?" Gina frowned. "So y'all can do a little whispering while Dr. Larker's speaking? Not going to happen. We're taking chairs as close to the front as we can get."

Gina grabbed Amanda's hand. Then she took Polly by the hand, half dragging the girls forward in the direction of the pulpit.

Gina relaxed against the back of her chair. She knew the lesson was going to be on forgiveness. It was a popular topic right now, and she could hardly wait to learn why Caleb Cantu called this particular lesson special.

At last Dr. Larker stood behind the podium.

"Isn't that the doctor that helped Amanda after she fell?" Polly whispered.

"Yes." Gina sent the girls a shushing gesture. "That's him."

"Welcome," he said. "And for those who don't know, I'm Dr. Larker. I'm giving the morning lesson." He cleared his throat. "Today will be a little different from what you might be accustomed to hearing. Please turn with me in your Bibles to the Old Testament and then to the Book of Numbers."

He paused. "In the Bible numbers are important. I'm not talking only about the Book of Numbers, though it is certainly important. Today we'll talk about the numbers two and three." He paused as if about to say something worth remembering. "Adam and Eve were two. Father, Son, and Holy Spirit are three. Matthew eighteen, verse twenty says, 'For where two or three are gathered together in my name, there am I in the midst of them.'

"I thought a lot about this scripture verse, and it finally came to me." Dr. Larker moved closer to the pulpit. "When the Lord is in you, you are no longer one but two. And when we pray with a spouse or friend in the name of Jesus, two people are not praying but three. When we're in Christ Jesus, we are never alone," he said. "Whether you're widowed or never married, God and you still make two. And remember you must be born again." He hesitated. "Let that sink in."

I might never marry, Gina thought. It was a possibility she didn't want to consider. *Nevertheless the Lord and I make two. Why didn't I know this a long time ago? The Lord and I make two!*

The lesson was new and fresh and, for her, inspiring. She knew she'd never forget it. But the lesson wasn't on forgiveness as she expected. The rest of the morning message was a blur. Slowly she digested what she'd heard.

Dr. Larker cleared this throat again, much louder this time, as the time drew near for the lesson to end. Gina sat a little straighter, focusing her attention on what was being said.

"Next Wednesday's sermon will be on tithing."

Tithing? Gina shook her head. What about forgiveness?

She noticed a stack of small cards in a sack attached to the back of the chair in front of her. She took one of the cards to see what it said.

The top of the card read, "Give us suggestions for future sermons." Without giving it much thought, Gina wrote "forgiveness" on the suggestion card and put the card and the pencil back where she found them. She needed to forgive a lot of people, including Steve. She'd think more about it but at another time.

Dr. Larker held his Bible with both hands. "Before the singing begins, I want to urge you to attend our Bible study group tonight. Our topic will be forgiveness."

Forgiveness? Gina grinned. Her suggestion was selected, and she'd barely finished posting her request.

AFTER THE SERVICE Gina drove the girls to Polly's house. Gina had liked Polly's mother when they finally met after the accident and was eager to see her again. The warmth shining in Anna Newton's eyes had reminded Gina of her friend, Nicole.

As soon as they arrived at the Newtons' home, the girls raced inside and slammed the door shut behind them. Gina stood on the front porch and rang the bell. When the door opened the smell of bread baking captured her senses. Mrs. Newton stepped forward and invited Gina to come inside.

At their first meeting Gina had felt acceptance in the company of Polly's pretty mother. Today the older woman's blue eyes sent out a different message as the girls sat side by side on the brown couch, whispering. Gina and Mrs. Newton engaged in small talk until the girls finally left the room.

"Polly forgot and left her phone at home when she went and spent last night at the Bryson mansion with Amanda," the older woman said. "Her father and I checked her caller ID to see if she missed any important calls and found several calls to a number in Boulder. Polly doesn't know anyone in Boulder, and neither do we."

Gina tensed. *Paulo attends college in Boulder.*

"We called the number," Anna went on. "At first nobody answered, but we finally learned the calls came from an apartment near the university."

Gina tried to think of something helpful to say. "Do you know who was being called?"

"Yes," the older woman said. "I'm afraid we do."

Gina knew, too, without being told.

Mrs. Newton shook her head. "A college boy returned our call and left a message."

"For Amanda?" Gina asked.

"Yes. I wrote down all we know about this, including the young man's contact information." She handed Gina a sheet of white paper. "We wanted you to have it."

"Thank you, Anna. I'm so sorry about ... about everything." Gina dropped the note in her purse. "I'm sure Mr. Bryson will regret this, too, when he learns about it."

"We especially regret it. Mr. Bryson is my husband's boss." Anna Newton gazed downward as if she didn't want to look Gina in the eye. "We don't want our Polly associating with college boys. She's only fourteen."

"I understand completely. Mr. Bryson doesn't want Amanda associating with college boys either."

Anna Newton still looked away. "I don't know how to put this, but the girls went riding on dangerous horses. They could have been killed. Now this. We can't allow Polly to visit with Amanda anymore, nor can Amanda come here."

What? Gina turned, facing Mrs. Newton. She didn't want to believe what she'd heard. "I see what you mean," she said at last. "But—"

"It's nothing personal," Mrs. Newton said, cutting off her protest. "I hope you and Mr. Bryson will understand."

Gina stood. "Of course." She wondered if she should stay a while longer or simply leave.

"I am sorry," Anna Newton said. "Polly likes Amanda. I know she'll miss her."

"Amanda will miss Polly, too." Gina offered Polly's mother her hand. "I must find Amanda and go. And you'll never know how sorry I am about this."

"Children can be a problem sometimes, especially a child who's lost her mother."

"That's very true."

"Perhaps when Amanda's father remarries, things will be different." Anna smiled. "From what I've seen of Steve Bryson, someone like you would be perfect for him."

"Me?" Gina pressed her hand to her chest. "Why I'm only Amanda's tutor, Mrs. Newton. Nothing more." She turned to leave.

"I tutored Mr. Newton's younger sisters before we married."

Gina stopped and glanced back at Anna, questioning what the woman had meant.

Anna's smile held a hint of amusement. "Now you know," she said.

Mrs. Newton's meaning couldn't have been clearer. Gina blushed. Did her demeanor or facial expressions expose her true feelings for Steve Bryson? The possibility embarrassed her, but the news about Amanda shook her to the core.

She must get in touch with Steve immediately. This business with Amanda had gone far enough. And Gina didn't want to wait until he returned from New York to tell him the news either. She should have let him know Amanda called Paulo as soon as it happened. But she'd wanted to believe her when Amanda promised never to phone him again. In hindsight she should have listened to her head instead of her heart.

GINA OPENED the front door of the Newton home and stepped onto a long porch, stretching across the front of the rustic, one-story ranch-style house. Polly leaned against one of the cedar support posts.

"Where's Amanda?" Gina asked. "I need to find her so we can go."

Polly's answer was matter-of-fact. "She ran away."

Gina felt her eyes widen and her heart race. "Ran away? When?"

"A few minutes ago." Polly motioned toward the country road in front of the house.

Gina bit her bottom lip. "Did you and Amanda have a fight or something?"

A look of sadness dwelled in Polly's eyes. She shook her head. "No."

"Did you see where she went?" Gina reached out and patted Polly on the shoulder.

"No. I chased after her, but then I tripped and fell. She was gone by the time I got to the front porch. And now I'm staying right here, hoping she'll come back."

"Are you all right?"

"Yes. I wasn't hurt."

"Good. Do you know why Amanda would run off like that?" Gina's throat tightened. "Think, Polly. There must be a reason."

"Our cook saw us on the back porch talking and said Amanda was in big trouble. It must be why she left."

"Can you remember what else the cook said?"

"She said Mama was mad at Amanda for phoning college boys. That's when Amanda ran around to the front on the house. I told her to stop, but she wouldn't."

"And then what happened?"

She shrugged. "I followed her around to the front of the house like I told you. I hope you find her, Dr. Hollister. Amanda sure looked scared."

"Don't worry. We'll find her." Gina gave Polly another gentle pat on the shoulder. "She can't have gone far." Gina opened her purse and fumbled for her cell phone but was unable to find it. "Polly, may I borrow your phone? I need to call Mr. Bryson's guards. I must have left my phone at the mansion."

Polly sent Gina a helpless, puzzled look. Then Gina remembered. Mrs. Newton not only had Polly's phone, she'd checked it.

Steve returned to his New York hotel around three on that same Wednesday afternoon to relax before dressing for the dinner that night. An important client would be at the party. Steve couldn't miss the function or be late without a good excuse. However he couldn't resist checking the main desk before going up to his room.

"Any messages?" he asked.

"As a matter of fact, you have one, sir." The desk clerk handed Steve an envelope. "A Gina Hollister texted the hotel, looking for you. She couldn't get hold of you on your cell phone. The text message she sent is in the envelope."

He read the message in the elevator on his way up to his room.

"Tell Mr. Bryson I tried texting him and calling him by phone without success. Please tell him to contact me immediately. This is important. Gina Hollister"

Steve's heart took a dive. Amanda must have had a relapse or another accident. Steve hurried to his room, planning the text he would send Gina as he went. He should have known his daughter's swift recovery after being pitched off Hitler was too good to be true.

When Gina didn't return any of his text messages or calls, he tried the landline. It rang and rang. At last Netty picked up.

"Amanda and Miss Gina aren't here, sir," she said. "They must still be in town. And I wasn't told about any emergency."

Steve froze. Something urgent must have occurred in town. He had no choice but to miss the meeting scheduled during the dinner hour and fly back to Colorado immediately.

GINA AND OTTO found Amanda in a church not far from Polly's home. At the castle later and seated at her desk in the sitting room next to her bedroom, Gina glanced at the clock. 8:30 p.m. After an early supper she'd given Amanda a long reading assignment, then sent her to her room to work on it. Now Gina was in the process of writing down what happened at the Newton home earlier to provide Steve the information as soon as possible.

A wave of melancholy covered her like a blanket as Gina continued to compose the letter. For weeks she'd known what had to come next. She must quit her job and fly back to Texas. *Now is the time. Too much has happened to put it off any longer.*

She reached for the phone and touched in Aunt Sarah's number in Oklahoma. Aunt Sarah was a retired classroom teacher, and she was looking for a temporary job to supplement her monthly teacher retirement income. Gina was sure she'd be more than happy to take Gina's place as Amanda's tutor for the rest of the summer.

"Then you'll do it?" Gina asked after explaining the situation.

"Yes, absolutely."

"Praise the Lord! Now Aunt Sarah, what I want you to do is fly to Durango as soon as possible. I need you here by Monday morning. Can you make it?"

"I don't see why not. Assuming I can get a flight, I'll be there as soon as possible."

"Perfect."

When Gina could no longer hear her aunt's sweet voice, a wave of deeper sadness swept over her. She climbed the stairs to the tower room. She wanted to see the painting of the bluebonnets one more time, as well as the portrait of the little girl.

At last she arrived at the small entry hall. She longed to enter the room where all Steve's paintings were kept, but the door would be locked. At least the tower room where the bluebonnet painting hung was always available.

Night shadows darkened the tower room. She switched on an overhead light and hurried over to the painting. She'd never examined it closely. Now she would. Steve had said the artist was somebody named Jones, and he had other paintings by that artist. In the corner she noticed the title for the first time: "Bluebonnet Bride."

Many might find the title of the painting strange since only flowers, stems, and leaves appeared in the painting, and no bride at all, but it made perfect sense to Gina. The painting represented a field of bluebonnets where flowers for bridal bouquets were selected. A tear moistened the edge of her eye because Gina knew she'd never be a bride.

She snapped a picture of the painting and headed for the entry hall. After all Steve had said he sort of bought the painting in honor of Gina. In the entry she gazed at the door to the other room again. The door was always locked, but she turned the doorknob anyway—just in case. It opened. Gina was stunned.

The first thing she saw was the painting of the child. But where was the blue cloth? And why wasn't the door locked? It was almost as if the door had been left open deliberately, as if Steve wanted her to see the painting again.

Would it be wrong to take a picture of this painting?

Gina didn't want to think so. Somehow she was convinced that in this case it would be oh so right. She snapped the picture and stood there a little longer, studying the portrait. At last she left the room.

She drifted back down the winding stairs only to go down another flight and another. She'd reached the entry hall leading to the family entrance to the mansion. The heavy front doors burst open, and Steve hurried inside.

"What happened?" Steve demanded. "Are you and Amanda all right?"

Gina frowned, puzzled. "We're fine."

"Fine? Then why did you call me back here? I came all the way from New York on a week night and missed an important meeting with a client."

"I didn't ask you to fly back here. I asked you to phone me."

"Then why didn't you answer my call or call me back?"

"I texted you from a store in town," she said. "My cell phone was here at the castle."

He didn't say a word, but standing there with his hands on his hips and a hard look in his eyes, he didn't have to speak. His body did it for him. "What's all this about?" He released a deep breath of air. "No don't answer. Let's go to my office first. We can talk there."

Gina followed Steve to his office. He offered her a chair, and she sat down. He remained standing. "Amanda was visiting in the Newton home when a serious problem came up," she explained. "That's when Amanda ran away."

"Ran away?"

"Yes. It took Otto and me forever to find her hiding in a church."

"A church!" He sent a harder look. "What was she doing there, thumping Bibles?"

"All I know is she told me once a church was a good place to hide." Gina suddenly felt weak, glad she was sitting down.

Steve collapsed onto an easy chair. "Now let's get this straight. You sent me an urgent message, right?"

"Yes."

"So what's going on?"

"I never intended for you to miss your meeting over this," Gina explained. "But Amanda has gotten out of hand."

"You sent me a text to tell me my daughter got out of hand? Why didn't you wait until I got home? I mean it's not exactly news, is it?"

"There's been a new development. I didn't know how you'd want me to handle it."

"You're completely in charge. You can handle things as you see fit. I thought a PhD would know that."

The muscles in Gina's throat tightened again. His insinuations infuriated her. But she'd learned to hold in her emotions years ago. She turned in her chair to face him, trying to calm down. "Amanda isn't welcome in the Newton home anymore," she said.

His eyes narrowed. "What?" Steve rose from his chair, towering over her. Hands in the air he paced back and forth. "Would you mind telling me what you're talking about?"

"Amanda used Polly's cell phone to call Paulo Ponte in Boulder, that college boy she met at the swimming pool in Colorado Springs."

Steve shook his head with more than a hint of disgust. "I leave for a few days, and my household goes up in smoke. I thought Amanda had forgotten the boy." Steve rubbed the back of his neck as if completely unaware he was doing it. "I don't know what could have gotten into her."

"I'm sorry, Mr. Bryson." Gina looked up at him from her chair. "I know you're worried about your daughter. So am I. I should have told you this before, but Amanda phoned Paulo at least once when we first arrived at the castle."

"Phoned him? You should have told me this the day it happened, *Doctor* Hollister."

"I know. But Amanda made me promise I wouldn't. She said if I didn't tell you, she'd never call Paulo again."

"And you believed her?" Steve's jaw tightened. "I think I'll fly to Boulder and give Paulo a piece of my mind."

"Why not phone him instead? I happen to have his telephone number in my purse."

"Maybe I will." Steve sat back down in his chair, pressing the palm of his right hand to his forehead as if he had a fever or a terrible headache.

"I haven't mentioned any of this to Amanda," she said.

"And why not?"

"She was upset when we found her in the church. I thought this was something you'd want to do." She glanced back at him. "You're her father."

He glared at her. "I hold you responsible for all of this. You should have kept a closer eye on my daughter." He pointed a finger at Gina. "You were hired to look after her."

Anger welled inside her, steadily growing. She covered her pounding heart with one hand to keep it from jumping out of her chest. "I was hired to tutor your daughter, Mr. Bryson."

If she didn't do something, the fury inside was bound to erupt and spew out like an out-of-control volcano. She counted to ten, then twenty, then thirty; she swallowed slowly and cleared her throat.

"I can understand how you must feel," she added, feigning an air of composure. "But you had no right to point your finger at me."

He dropped his hands and shook his head. "Okay. I'm sorry."

She'd never seen Steve like this. She wondered if something else bothered him, something that had nothing to do with his daughter or leaving New York. "I'm doing the best job I can. But don't worry. I'm resigning my position right now."

"I never suggested you resign," he said in a calmer voice. "If I fly back to New York immediately, I'll have missed the opportunity to speak with my client. I think it's only fair you help me out."

"What do you mean?"

"Tomorrow night my client and I are invited to a dinner party at a hotel in town. Mr. Foster was kind enough to meet me there so we can continue our discussion. On the following morning he and I will be flying out to the meeting in Brussels."

"What does any of this have to do with me?" Gina asked.

"I want you to go to the dinner party with me—as my date."

She took a deep breath. "Mr. Bryson, how many times must I tell you? I don't date my employers." She slowly let out the air, waiting to see how he would respond.

"Those rules of yours again, huh?"

"Not all my rules are unchangeable. I plan to change the part about me keeping this job."

Steve sent her a hard look. "What are you driving at?"

Gina was looking down at her cell phone. When she looked up she wasn't smiling. "I told you. Maybe you weren't listening. I'm handing in my resignation starting immediately."

"You can't mean that, Gina. I have to fly to Brussels. Who will look after my daughter?"

"I've thought of that," she said. "My aunt from Oklahoma City has agreed to come here and take my place until you can find someone else. She's a retired classroom teacher who teaches the old-fashioned way. I think you and Aunt Sarah should get along perfectly. She's packing now and should be here tomorrow or the day after."

"What about the rent-to-own agreement you signed?"

"I don't need it after all. I won't go into all the details now, but I've made other arrangements."

He glanced away. "I see." His voice dripped outrage. "I could haul you to court for breaking your contract."

"But you'd never do something like that, would you?"

"I haven't decided yet." He clenched and unclenched his fists. "Why don't we go to the green room and talk about this rationally? It's peaceful there."

"Whatever you say."

STEVE WAS COUNTING on closing a deal to sell oil mud to a company in Brussels, and he still hoped to do it, but it wasn't as important anymore. *Gina is what's important,* he reminded his brain. Steve wanted her to stay in Colorado. As they headed down the hall, he noticed Gina managed to keep up with his long stride, step for step. *If only our minds were in step.* Her body language said she was far from him; it wouldn't be easy to talk her out of leaving. And why did he have the urge to put his arms around her?

He'd married Myra because he had to. He'd be marrying Gina because he— *Marrying Gina? From what planet did that thought originate?* For weeks Steve had tried to delete the word "marriage" from his vocabulary. Yet there it was again. He willingly admitted he wanted Gina in his life. Maybe he even loved her. But marriage?

Okay, he loved her. But that was as far as he was willing to go with this romance thing. Marriage was bad news the first time. He was convinced it would be the second time, too.

Of course Gina was nothing like Myra. Gina was a loving person, a loyal friend, and ... and a Bible thumper. *Bible thumper. Now there's the main problem.* Gina had never preached to him, but she would sooner or later. It was merely a matter of time.

Steve wanted to take Gina's hand and hold it as they continued toward the green room. They'd made the first turn down a long hall when childhood memories of sermons and Bible study groups jumped out from nowhere.

He also recalled how he felt when he drove by the two-story house on the outskirts of Durango where Gina attended services. He remembered lights coming from inside, calling out to him. Obviously they were studying the Bible. Strangely enough he'd wanted to be a part of it.

A lump filled his throat. Why after all these years did he still want to go back to a God who wasn't there when he needed Him most? A picture of Baylee formed in his mind. Steve pinched the bridge of his nose, hoping a sudden headache and all disturbing memories would disappear.

He shook his head. Baylee was always just beneath the surface of his mind. How many times must he remind himself? *She's gone and never coming back.* Memories of Baylee he'd tried to forget had returned, and it was becoming harder and harder to push them away. Was he still running from God?

Gina deserved to know why he was so opposed to Christianity. But how could he explain a loss of faith to someone like Gina Hollister? He'd intended to tell her about the backsliding, the doubts, everything. Now he'd lost his nerve and didn't know when he'd be able to retrieve it again.

Why did people he loved always die or disappear in spite of all he did to stop it from happening? And why did he keep driving by the house where services are held? Did he expect God to come over to the car and invite him inside?

GINA SMELLED coffee the instant Steve opened the door to the green room. Memories flooded her of the day she searched his office for a possible hidden stairway. Now she knew every inch of Steve's office and the green room, too. He deposited her on a brown couch then moved over to a serving table. A silver coffee service sat in the middle of an elaborate electric warming tray.

"Coffee?" he asked.

"No thank you." She wanted coffee, but sometimes it put her nerves on edge. And she needed to keep her guard up.

He poured himself a cup and sat on the couch beside her. The aroma of his coffee mingled with her desire to take a cup and leave the room.

"I don't want you to go, Gina," he said.

"I realize that."

"Is there anything I can do to get you to change your mind?"

"I've made my decision."

He took a sip and set his cup on the table in front of them. "I'd agree to any salary arrangements you want, if you'd only promise to stay."

"Surely by now you know this isn't about money."

"You're talking about God," he said, "aren't you?"

"Yes," she said softly, "among other things."

"Gina."

She loved the way he said her name and the deep sound of his voice. As they talked he kept gazing at her mouth. Then he maneuvered closer to her on the couch. She knew he intended to kiss her. Gina swallowed. If she didn't do something fast she'd be in his arms

She stood. "I think I'll have a cup of coffee now," she said.

Steve nodded. "I could have Gretel bring in a fresh pot."

"I'm sure it won't be necessary."

He followed her to the serving table.

Her fingers trembled as she remembered the overturned pitcher of ice water at his hotel in Colorado Springs and hoping to prevent a similar accident. She picked up the heavy silver coffee pot easily enough. Holding on to it was another matter. Her hands trembled more than she would have thought possible. The pot wobbled in one hand, and she reached out with the other to steady it.

"Let me help you," he said before she touched it with her left hand.

He took the steaming pot from her and set it back on the table.

"Thank you." She tried to stop the smile forming on her lips and in her heart but was unsuccessful. "Another minute and I might have dropped the coffee pot on this lovely gold rug."

"It wouldn't have mattered if you had." He poured her a cup. "This old relic my mother calls a rug should have been replaced years ago."

He handed her the coffee, looking as if he would like to kiss her. This could not continue. She took her cup of coffee and moved to the fireplace. Steve was right behind her. Trapped in a web of emotions, she placed the cup on the mantle. He hadn't moved an inch. With the stone fireplace at her back, a sudden cold chilled her.

"You mentioned your mom." She tried to remain calm. "Does she come here often?"

"As often as she can, especially during the winter season." He stood directly in front of her. "Surely you know you mean a great deal to me," he said barely above a whisper. "And I want you to stay."

"Your mother must ski then," Gina said, ignoring his comment.

He leaned toward her, propping one arm on the mantle beside her head. "I'm not going to let you go, Gina."

"I suppose for someone your mother's age, skiing can be a little ..." Her heart hammered against her ribs. "Can be dangerous."

"Yes," he said tenderly, "it certainly can."

He'd moved closer when she said "dangerous." The word described him perfectly. He brushed her cheek with his fingertips.

The door opened, and Netty burst into the room. From the look on her face, something was terribly wrong.

"Oh, Mr. Bryson," Netty exclaimed, "I'm *so* glad you're home!"

"What's wrong, Netty?"

"It's your daughter."

"Amanda? Something's wrong with Amanda?"

Netty sniffed. "Mama and I are worried sick. Here. Read this!" Netty handed him a sheet of paper. "This just came in on the fax machine."

As he read the fax, his eyes widened.

"What does it say?" Gina exclaimed.

"Amanda's missing. Otto thinks she was kidnapped. We must go immediately!"

"AMANDA IS HIDING SOMEWHERE!" Gina insisted. "As I told you earlier, she once said a church is the best place to hide. Nobody ever looks for someone in a church, she said. And Otto and I found her hiding in a church. Remember?"

"I remember. Get to the point."

"She could be there or ..." Gina hesitated then touched her forehead with the back of her hand as if a light had gone on inside her brain. "I think I know where Amanda is."

"Where?" he demanded. "If you know something, *anything*, tell me!"

"I think she ran off somewhere to meet Paulo Ponte."

"Paulo Ponte?" He frowned as if the word "doubt" were written all over his face. "Merely because she phoned Paulo doesn't mean she'd run away with him."

If only she could somehow persuade Steve to consider the possibility that Amanda was going to Paulo.

"Come on," he said in a loud voice. "We need to get going."

They raced to Steve's van. As soon as they climbed inside, he switched on the motor, his cell phone, and the speaker. The timer on the dash said 9:39.

"Security!" he said. "My daughter is missing. She could be kidnapped. Find her!"

Then he called the authorities in town and made other calls, too. Gina's head swam, watching as Steve took charge of the situation. She had no idea he knew so many people in state and local government. If she'd ever wondered if he was a tycoon, she had her answer.

Gina was glad Steve was a take-charge kind of guy, but she wasn't able to get a word in. Was Steve running in the wrong direction? If there was ever so much as a brief lull in his rapid telephone conversations, she meant to tell him exactly what she thought.

"Steve." She cleared her throat. "May I suggest that—?"

He held the receiver away from his ear and gave her a shushing gesture.

She tried again. "Please. I have a different slant on all this. Why won't you listen?"

"In a minute," he said with a dismissive air. "I'm talking to one of my security guards. It might be important."

He returned his attention to the call. "Now let me get this straight. Amanda said she had permission to spend the night with one of her friends in town."

Permission? I didn't given Amanda permission to sleep over with any of her friends but Polly. And Polly certainly can't be the friend he's referring to. Until Netty came in with the news, Gina had thought Amanda was in her room, doing the homework she'd assigned. In hindsight she should have checked to make sure.

"Barbie," Steve said. "Is that the name you said, Otto?"

Gina froze. Amanda never mentioned a Barbie.

"So," Steve continued, "about half an hour after Amanda arrived at a house in Durango, a blonde-haired girl and a boy left the house in a blue car. But Amanda never left the house as far as you know. Is that correct?"

There was a short pause. Then Steve shouted, "Of course she was with the boy. Did it ever enter your head Amanda might have been wearing a blonde wig?"

Blonde wig? Gina frowned. *What if Amanda's the one in the wig and Paulo was with her?*

"Ask him to describe the girl and the boy," Gina demanded.

Steve rolled his eyes. "Doctor, will you please stop interrupting?"

He had no intentions of getting back to her soon, so she'd spend the time deciding what to do next. It was a long drive from the castle to Steve's private office in town.

Aunt Sarah called. *Thanks goodness.* Gina sent up a prayer of thanks. Her aunt had managed to book a flight to Durango and would be on the plane within the hour. Gina wanted to tell Steve the news, but he probably wouldn't listen.

They finally arrived, and Gina went straight to one of the offices used by Steve's employees so she could make phone calls without being interrupted. If she hoped to reach Paulo Ponte before Amanda did, she must call him without delay.

Thank goodness Polly's mom gave me Paulo's contact information before I left the Newton home. Gina had no idea why she trusted Paulo, but somehow she did. The desk clerk at the hotel said he was a fine young man, but that wasn't the only reason. Sometimes she just had to go with her instincts.

She touched in the number. The telephone rang and rang. It soon became clear that Paulo wasn't going to answer. She would leave a message.

"Paulo." She cleared her throat. "This is Dr. Gina Hollister, calling on behalf of Amanda's father, Steve Bryson. We need to speak to you. Reply to this message using this number as soon a possible."

Gina trembled. Where was Paulo? Why wasn't he answering? And where was Amanda? Was she safe?

It was time to try something else. She texted Paulo with shaky fingers. Then she waited. Ten minutes later she called him again. This time Paulo answered, and she told him what happened.

"Amanda's on her way to see me," he said with a charming

Italian accent. "She's probably at the airport in Durango right now. She'll fly to Denver first and then on to Boulder."

"But how is that possible? Amanda has no money for a ticket."

"I would never expect her to pay for her own ticket," Paulo said. "I took care of that for her."

I should have known. "Thank you, Paulo. You've been a big help. But did you know Amanda is only fourteen years old?"

After a lengthy pause he said, "Is Amanda really only fourteen?"

Gina could hear the doubt in his voice. "Yes."

"I thought she was a lot older."

"I hoped that was the case. I'm glad to hear it is."

Gina ended the call and hurried back to Steve's private office, thinking perhaps she understood why Amanda liked Paulo. He was a very appealing young man but much too old for Amanda Bryson.

Steve still had his phone tied up. Then Otto and another bodyguard came in and started talking loudly on their phones. Unless she could outshout them, it was unlikely she'd be able to get Steve's attention.

All right, when all else fails, let the shouting begin. But before she could raise her voice, Steve hung up his phone and turned back to Gina. "Now what was it you wanted to say?"

"I know where Amanda is."

Steve's look was incredulous. "What?"

"I talked to Paulo, and she's at the airport right here in Durango."

"Keep on those phones," Steve said to his men. "We're on our way to the airport. I'll be contacting you from there." As he opened the glass door for Gina, Steve eyed her suspiciously. "This better not be a wild-goose chase."

"It isn't. Paulo said Amanda was flying to Denver tonight and then on to Boulder. If we hurry we can reach her before her plane takes off."

"Boulder, huh?" He got in his car, reached for his cell phone, and selected a number. "This is Bryson. Contact the airport. Tell them to hold all flights to Denver until I get there. I think my daughter might be onboard. Tell them she's a runaway and a minor."

Gina hadn't always cared for people with take-charge attitudes because they tended to be bullies. Now she found take-chargers awesome. Come to think of it, she found Steve awesome. *If only things were different.*

After they found Amanda and made arrangements for Steve to pick up Aunt Sarah, Gina would say her goodbyes and stay at the airport until she booked a flight back to Texas. Netty could ship her belongings to her later.

A sudden sadness and an inner chill swept over her. It was hard to leave, but it was better to make a clean break than drag it out any longer. If she stayed the entire two months, she'd never be able to go.

At the airport they found Amanda alone in a waiting area, wearing a blonde wig.

"Amanda," Gina cried as they ran up to her, "are you all right?"

Amanda didn't reply, but she seemed almost relieved when Steve and Gina sat down beside her. "I'm so embarrassed and ashamed." Amanda jerked off the wig, throwing it on the floor near her feet, then turned away as if she didn't want to look anybody in the face. "Paulo sent me this text message." She handed Gina her cell phone.

Gina pulled a handkerchief from her purse and gave it to Amanda. "Here, honey. You need this. And I'm going to read the message aloud." She cleared her throat as a delaying tactic because she had no idea what the message might contain.

"You lied to me, Amanda," she read. "You told me you were eighteen. But I found out you are only fourteen. Don't come to Boulder. I never want to see you again. Paulo."

Gina finished reading and gave Amanda a hug.

"Paulo doesn't love me anymore," the girl sobbed. "Nobody does."

"I love you, Baby," Steve said.

"Oh, Daddy, I love you, too."

Steve took his daughter in his arms. It was the family moment Gina had prayed for since they arrived in Colorado.

"I'm sorry. All this is my fault," Amanda said between sobs. "I shouldn't have run away. I shouldn't have ridden Hitler or called Paulo. I shouldn't have done a lot of things. Can you forgive me?"

"Sure, Baby." Still holding her Steve patted the back of her head. "Everything will be all right. But I would like to know who you left the castle with."

Amanda went on. "I met a boy this morning when Dr. Hollister took Polly and me to a Bible study at a house way out in the country," Amanda explained, her sobs subsiding. "After the service ended Dr. Hollister went to the restroom. We were waiting for her in the entry hall near the front door when Roger, a boy Polly knew, came up and started talking to us."

She dabbed her eyes with Gina's handkerchief. "Roger's so cute, and he asked me for my phone number, so I gave it to him. Then he gave me his number. Later Polly said I shouldn't have given him my number because he was on the wild side, but I called him anyway from my room at the castle when I should have been working on the reading assignment Dr. Hollister gave me."

Amanda went on. "We talked a long time. He's very creative, and he has a car. He mapped out plans for how to get me out of the castle without anyone knowing. He even gave me the wig. I won't tell all of his plans now, but they sure worked." Tears rolled down both her cheeks. "I'm so sorry, Daddy." She sobbed softly. "Honest I am."

Steve hugged his daughter again. "It's all right, sweetheart. We'll get through this together."

As Steve and Amanda sat there at the airport hugging each other, Gina slipped away to book a flight to Texas. Fortunately for her, there was a cancellation, meaning she'd be flying to

Austin in less than two hours. With a much too heavy heart, Gina went back to Steve and Amanda to say goodbye.

"Where have you been?" Steve was seated on a bench with Amanda, but he got up when she approached. "We were worried about you."

"I'm fine. I went to get a ticket." She held out a piece of paper. "Here's the information for Aunt Sarah's flight so you can pick her up in the morning. I'm flying back to Austin tonight."

"Gina." Steve took her in his arms and held her close. "Please don't go."

Amanda got up then and joined in on the hug. Enveloped in their embrace Gina almost felt like a member of the family.

"I'm sorry for what I did, Dr. Hollister," Amanda said. "Please stay. I'll be good. I promise."

"I ...I can't. But it has nothing to do with you, Amanda."

"Then it just leaves me," Steve said.

Gina faltered, but she wouldn't look at him. His deep voice was compelling enough, but seeing his face would make saying goodbye nearly impossible.

"I need to explain," Gina said, "why I feel so strongly about my views on education."

"That doesn't matter now," Steve said gently.

"Yes it does matter," Gina said with deep emotion. "I knew what would work for Amanda because I'm ...I'm exactly like her."

"What are you talking about?" he asked.

"I have a learning problem almost identical to Amanda's, and I've been hiding it for years."

"But why?"

"I don't know. Maybe I was ashamed of being who I am, but I'm not anymore. The good news is, with God's help I've managed to overcome my problem most of the time."

"You're very brave," he said softly.

She sniffed as she felt hot tears pricking her eyes. Steve was so kind, so gentle. She loved him. But he'd reminded her of someone from the moment they first met: her father, Phil Arnold, and then the mad scientist. She was as silly and gullible and naive as she'd always been, regardless of the PhD. Yet Steve had accepted her for the woman she was, calling her charming and intelligent.

I don't want to go. And I knew Steve a long time ago. I know I did. If only I could remember where and when. She dismissed the troubling thought, turned to Amanda, and managed to produce a fleeting smile. "You'll overcome your problems, too, Amanda," Gina said, "like I did. And remember …never give up."

"I won't."

"I know you won't." Gina glanced toward the loading area. "I have to go."

"We'll go back with you," Steve said.

"No, you need to go to Brussels. It's what you do, and Amanda needs to go back to the castle. My aunt will be arriving here by plane in the morning at nine, and she'll take my place as Amanda's teacher for as long as you need her. Gretel and Netty are there for Amanda now."

"If you go," Steve said tenderly, "I'll have to go after you."

"It would be a waste of time." Gina peered at Steve and Amanda for what she supposed would be the last time. "Until tonight I never realized how much you two love each other. And it's so good to see it."

"Don't do this," Steve said.

"I must. And Steve …" Gina swallowed. "God has a special plan for your life. It's up to you to find out what it is."

She'd never felt so alone as when she returned to the waiting area, ticket to Austin in hand, and sat down to wait for her flight to be announced. She needed to think. With over an hour to wait until the jet took off, she had plenty of time.

It was almost midnight. Gina found a seat by a window. In minutes the jet would take off. Today would become Thursday morning. The day began at the castle, followed by the worship service. The conversation with Polly's mother came next, and then all the other events, making this the longest Wednesday of her entire life.

Gina wasn't always successful, but she wasn't a quitter either. Besides two good things had happened. They found Amanda, and Gina had a seat by a window. Flying made her nervous—always had and probably always would. So what could she do to fight against this menace? Keep trying and never give up.

The Bible called Scripture verses swords. "The Sword of the Spirit" meant Bible verses could and perhaps should be used as weapons against despair and spiritual darkness. Her current enemy was discouragement. Gina was no expert when it came to memorizing Scriptures, but she knew a few Bible verses by heart. The Lord's Prayer indicated God tested mankind: *Forgive us our sins, for we forgive everyone who does us wrong. And do not bring us to hard testing.*

Hard testing?

She'd stared out the window on her side for what seemed a very long time. Pictures formed in her mind as memories flooded her brain. Gina had thought she was done with flashbacks. Apparently not. She ducked her head, trying to focus on something else. It didn't seem to work.

All at once she was in her fifth-grade class in Glory Corners, the little town in southern Oklahoma where her maternal grandmother lived and where she and her mother had lived after the divorce. Gina never made a single friend during the three years they lived there. She shut her eyes, hoping the memories would go away. But there was one time, one good memory, when a young man was kind to her once. She never knew his name. She'd simply called him "the substitute teacher."

Gina was a nickname. Her real name was Virginia, Virginia Hollister. Just about everybody in Glory Corners called her

Virginia, including the college student who substituted for the regular teacher during P.E. one day. The first thing he did was give the class instructions on how the playground time was to be handled. Gina barely looked at him when he passed on those instructions. Why should she? He was a teacher. Teachers hated her.

It was bad enough she was unable to read well, spell, or answer questions in class most of the time. The real horror came during physical education class when team captains chose team members because Gina was always chosen last.

"Your teacher, Mrs. Gray, said Emma Garcia and Harry Jones are your team captains for today," the substitute teacher had said. "Will Emma and Harry please step forward?"

They did, and then he said. "Emma, you may choose first."

"Yes, sir. And I choose ..." She giggled. "I choose ...Virginia."

"Virginia?" someone said.

Everybody laughed. Gina ducked her head, wishing she could hide under the nearest bush.

"I mean Suzy," Emma corrected.

Gina happened to glance at the substitute teacher, and he sent her a look so filled with kindness and understanding she felt warm inside, regardless of what had just happened. Then he glared at Emma. "Emma, what you said just now was downright mean."

"I'm sorry. I meant to say Suzy. Guess I forgot."

"I don't think you forgot at all. I think you did it deliberately. So Virginia, step forward please."

Gina's heart had become a hard lump in the middle of her chest. Somehow she'd managed to do as he said, but on shaky legs.

"You will be one of our team leaders today instead of Emma." The substitute teacher turned to the other team leader. "Harry, step forward, and wipe that grin off your face."

Gina hadn't wanted to be a team leader. In her mind she was terrible in sports and wasn't sure she knew all the rules of the game they were about to play. She'd turned to the substitute teacher, shaking her head vigorously so he'd know she didn't want the job he offered.

His answer was a genuine smile. Then he walked over and took her hand in his, leading her forward. "Don't be afraid," he'd whispered. "You're going to be the best team leader this class ever had."

His grin lingered in her mind, and for the first time, Gina remembered he had dimples. *Dimples?*

The flashback ended. Her thoughts didn't. Was she imagining things, or did she see Steve in the teacher's grin? No. The substitute teacher wasn't Steve. It would be too ironic, and Gina didn't believe in irony. Nevertheless the instant she saw Steve for the first time in the parking lot, she knew he looked familiar. He reminded her of someone.

She also knew she didn't trust him. Myra made sure of it. Though his late wife planted the seeds of doubt in her heart, Gina was the one who watered those seeds. Why did it take so long for her to come to terms with a simple fact? She'd called Steve names like "womanizer" and "Gingerbread Man." She'd accused him of backing a mad scientist financially or actually being a mad scientist, and all without proof. Now she had a hunch Steve was the sub-teacher who came to her rescue when she was in the fifth grade.

If Steve was indeed the young man from her past, he'd never stopped rescuing her. Was the take-charge Steve Bryson she knew now the substitute teacher she knew then? And why did she have to discover this now, when it was too late?

GINA MET Nicole for lunch on Tuesday at an Austin mall. Her friend must have sensed Gina didn't want to talk about Steve because she never mentioned him by name, though she might as well have.

"Maybe it's all for the best," Nicole said after they started eating. Her meaning couldn't have been clearer.

"So you and Robert are getting married, huh?" Gina meant to change the topic of their conversation. "Congratulations."

"Thanks," Nicole said. "And remember I want you as my maid of honor."

"I'm counting on it."

"Oh, Gina," Nicole said, "I don't know how to put this without coming right out and saying it."

"Then come right out and say it. You always do eventually."

"Robert and I accepted teaching jobs at a college in Florida."

Gina caught her breath. "What?"

"I hate to chicken out on the learning center deal at the last minute like this, but the center was always more your dream than mine anyway."

Nicole was spontaneous and full of surprises, but this one took the prize.

Gina thought it would have been nice if Nicole had prepared her for this. She swallowed then took a deep breath, trying not to overreact. She lifted her glass and took a swallow of ice water. Why complain? Nicole's decision was already made. Moreover Gina knew she hadn't been completely honest with Nicole by never mentioning she inherited money from her aunt. Now she would.

"Please say you're glad for us," Nicole said.

Gina wiggled her nose teasingly. "You're glad for us."

Nicole laughed. "Oh, Gina, thanks for understanding."

Later they stood between their cars in the parking lot. Gina reached out both arms and hugged Nicole. "Promise me we'll phone each other at least once a week, okay?"

"You got it," Nicole said.

"And we'll write often, hear? I'll need the details about the wedding," Gina reminded her. "I especially want all the details on my bridesmaid dress, and as soon as possible."

Nicole nodded, wiping her eyes. "I'll miss you, Gina."

"I'm gonna miss you, too."

"And, Gina, if we ever have a daughter, I'm going to name her after you no matter what Robert says."

Gina waved until Nicole was out of sight.

THREE WEEKS later Gina flew from Austin to a little town in Florida called Refuge Lake to attend Nicole's wedding. Her bridesmaid dress was yellow. It fit perfectly, and she thought of nothing but Steve the entire time she was in Florida, wishing he were there with her. She returned to her mother's house in Austin around noon the day after the wedding.

Gina spent the next two days cleaning house and packing for the move to Hill River. Construction on the learning center would begin in three weeks, and Steve was still on her mind. *Why do I think about him all the time?* She fought an ongoing desire to text or call him. Once she considered contacting the airport to check flight connections between Texas and Colorado.

I have to stop doing this! Steve is yesterday. My future is now. If only her heart would believe that and behave accordingly.

As Steve drove down the freeway, he couldn't get Gina out of his mind. He flipped on the radio and heard a man say, "Brothers and sisters, I have a special message for you today." Steve hesitated before changing to something else but couldn't figure out why.

As he hesitated the man went on. "Don't change to another channel. My name is Pastor Rick Becon. And what I have to say was designed just for you." He grew silent for a moment. "Is there somebody you need to forgive? Is there a bunch of folks you need to forgive? Is God in your life? Think about it."

"Mother," Steve said aloud. "I'm no Bible thumper, but I need to forgive my mother. And I ...I need God in my life."

"If you don't repent and be born again," the radio pastor warned, "you'll spend all of eternity in hell. Choose God, and live forever."

What is this born-again stuff all about?

"The Old Testament Book of Genesis tells about Adam and Eve," the preacher explained. "They were the first two people God ever created, but they sinned, causing them to lose the closeness they once had with God the Father.

"God had given them a beautiful place to live called the

Garden of Eden. The garden contained every kind of tree you can think of, and they were allowed to eat from the trees in the garden—all but one. If they ate fruit from the Tree of the Knowledge of Good and Evil, they would surely die.

"Well," the pastor said, "as you probably know, the devil, called Satan, tempted them to eat the forbidden fruit, and they did. As sinners Adam and Eve were kicked out of the garden. All their descendants were sinners too because they were *born* of Adam and Eve." He'd emphasized the word born. "We must forgive; we must repent. It's why we must be *born again.*"

Steve thought about the sermon for the rest of the day. He also thought about it on his way to, from, and during his business trip to New York. He was thinking about it again on the first Wednesday night after he returned to Colorado from New York. But he had no idea why he drove by the two-story house belonging to Caleb and Bonny Cantu, then parked his car down the block a ways. He'd picked up Gina at Caleb's big old frame house several times, but this time he'd come just because he felt drawn to it.

He also felt stupid, sitting there in his car in the dark like some kind of criminal. If that wasn't bad enough, he wanted to go inside.

Steve doubted his true mission in life was to make a lot of money. He'd thought it was to help kids, and he was doing that. But something was missing. He thought of the painting in the tower room, the one of his late sister, Baylee.

Why did she have to die? She was just a kid, and so smart, too. The other kids were always jealous of Baylee. Would he ever forget the horrible day when Baylee and Steve were in elementary school? He didn't want to think about it, not again. But the memory rolled on anyway.

Steve was two years older than his sister, and after school one day, he was on his way to the parking lot to meet Mom when he saw Baylee, surrounded by three of the meanest kids he knew.

They were calling Baylee names. "Teacher's Pet" was one of the nicer names, and they were all laughing. Baylee was crying.

Steve should have done something to help her. He shut his eyes briefly. *Why didn't I?* He blinked again. He had just stood there watching, afraid to open his mouth. But if he could go back in time and rescue her from those bullies, he would. He shook his head, bemoaning his failure. A few days later Baylee got a fever, and then ...

He didn't want to remember the sad day his sister died. In addition to those terrible memories, one question continued to flood him. Why didn't he help Baylee when he had the chance? Then thoughts of the kid he *did* help entered his mind, the one who looked so much like Baylee.

She was being bullied, too, and it happened when he was a college freshman at a junior college in Oklahoma. As a sort of last resort, Steve was hired to substitute for the physical education teacher at an elementary school but only for one day.

Now what was the name of the kid he helped? Virginia. Yes, Virginia. Virginia Hollister. As in Gina Hollister? *No. That's ridiculous!* Her name was Virginia, not Gina. And yet ...

It was several minutes before he was able to get the possibility out of his mind. Then three words filled his brain: *forgiveness* and *born again.* He reached for his cell phone, touching in his mother's number. He needed to forgive his mom.

"Hello," his mother said in the confident, no-nonsense voice he knew so well.

"Mom, this is Steve." He shook his head. Why did he say what he just said? Steve had been an only child since his sister died. Who else would be calling her mom?

"Oh, Stevie," his mother put in. "So glad you called. Where are you? What country, I mean?"

"I'm calling from Colorado in the good old USA."

"I hope you're getting enough rest. I know how busy you are."

"Don't make excuses for me, Mom. I'm sorry for not calling sooner—and for a lot of things."

"Oh, I understand," she said, "because—"

He interrupted. "Mom, let me talk this time. Okay?"

"Okay. Sure, Son."

"I've got a lot of things to say before I lose my nerve." He paused to give his mother time to respond, but all he heard was silence. "I've always loved you and Dad. Still do."

"I know," she said so softly he could barely hear.

"But after Dad died, all my goals in life disappeared. I felt cheated. I didn't expect to like doing things the Bryson way, but turns out I did. Still a part of me also wanted to be the other Steve." He hesitated. Steve knew what he wanted to say but didn't know how to say it.

"Stevie, are you still on the line?"

"Yes, Mom, I'm here, and what I'm about to say might hurt you a little. But you hurt me bad when you made me quit school after Dad died. I didn't let on, but I got mad at you for that."

"Mad at me?"

"Yes. But I'm not angry anymore. Can you forgive me?"

"Of course I can. I'm a mother. Don't you know mothers love their children no matter what?"

"I never recovered from Baylee's death," he said slowly. "I should have helped her more when I had the chance. Those bullies in her class hurt her. I just stood there, letting it happen. Now when I see a bully hurting a kid, I want to hit them." He glanced down at his watch. "I have to go now, Mom. I'll call you again very soon."

"Promise?"

"Promise."

He was turning off the phone when he heard a tap on his car window on the driver's side. Steve jerked around. Had God showed up to invite him inside?

It was Caleb who appeared beside his car. Steve rolled down the window.

Caleb grinned. "Won't you come in and have coffee with us?"

"Thanks, but I can't." End of conversation as far as Steve was concerned. He'd hoped Caleb would go back inside, but he kept standing there. Then memories of an earlier time rushed into Steve's mind.

Caleb and Steve were college roommates, best friends back in college. They played on the same basketball team. Caleb tried to get Steve to attend church with him, but he wouldn't. He never had much faith to begin with, and his faith left completely after the divorce. He'd been cold to Caleb ever since. So why did Caleb leave the door to their relationship open? Did he expect them to become friends again some day?

Steve looked back at Caleb. He was still standing by his car and hadn't moved a muscle.

"Do you mind if I get in the car so we can talk a minute?" Caleb asked.

Steve tensed. *Here it comes.* Like Gina, Caleb had never tried to preach to Steve, but he would—sooner or later. It was the way Bible thumpers operated.

"Sure," Steve finally said. "Go ahead and get in."

Caleb went around and climbed in the passenger seat.

"So," Steve shrugged, "what's up?"

"I was wondering if you might be interested in playing on an independent basketball team as a relief player—when you're in town, of course."

Steve was taken off guard. He hadn't expected basketball.

In the glow of the streetlight, Caleb's boyish smile caused him to look a lot younger. He'd hardly aged a day since their freshman year in college, and Caleb had something, all right. The question was, did Steve want it, too?

"Well," Caleb said, "what do you think?"

"About what?"

"Basketball. One of our players moved to another state recently, and you're an excellent forward."

"What team are we talking about?" Steve asked.

"The Whitesocks."

"And are the Whitesocks affiliated with a church?"

"Nope." Caleb slapped down his hands on his knees. "It's a bunch of guys who like to play basketball. And we need an extra player."

"Where do you practice?" Steve asked.

Caleb grinned. "We practice at the gym down the street from where I live, but we have our business meetings here at the house. We couldn't find any other place to meet."

"How many members of your church are on your team?"

"One," Caleb said. "Me."

"And that's it?"

"That's it."

Steve had to admit playing basketball again did sound like fun, and he could use a little physical exercise. He knew he'd probably regret it, but he had the urge to say yes.

"Want in?" Caleb asked.

"Let me think about it for a while and check my schedule. I'll give you a call next week, okay?"

"Okay." Caleb offered Steve his hand. "I've gotta run, but the offer for coffee's still on."

"Maybe another time."

Steve continued to sit in his car until Caleb went inside.

Basketball. It sounded like something he'd like to do. But if he wanted to see Gina again, he wouldn't find her in Colorado. He'd have to return to the Lone Star State.

STEVE COULDN'T GET basketball out of his mind. It was the last thing he thought about before going to sleep, and the first thing to enter his mind the next morning. He hadn't planned to text

Caleb, but he found himself doing so before having his first cup of coffee. Thirty minutes later he'd become a relief player, promising to meet Caleb at his home to discuss upcoming game schedules and more.

Two hours later Steve knocked on Caleb's front door. He checked his watch, waiting for the door to open. It was ten a.m. on Tuesday.

Caleb opened the door. "Steve." He smiled. "Come right in."

A wave of regret covered Steve like a dark blanket. What was he doing here?

The big living room Gina talked about was straight ahead. The entry door was behind him. He was about to turn around and leave when Caleb gestured toward a door to their right.

"We can meet in here. It's a little room where mothers with small children sit during our services. I call it the cry room."

Cry room? Now Steve knew for sure he shouldn't be here. Regardless he went into the little room and sat down beside Caleb, and all they talked about was basketball.

Around noon Steve's tummy reminded him it was time to eat. "Caleb," he said, "how about if I take you to lunch? I know how much you like Italian food, and I know a great Italian restaurant."

"I'd love to, and thanks for asking. But I watch a certain program on television every Tuesday at noon, and I try never to miss."

Steve checked his watch again. "How long is this program?"

"Half an hour."

Steve knew the program was probably religious, and he couldn't believe he had the desire to watch it. "How about if I stay and watch the show with you, and then we can go eat Italian food?"

Caleb nodded. "Sounds good to me."

GINA HADN'T SEEN MUCH of her mother since Mom moved to San Antonio. However they had talked on the phone almost daily. Mom was trying to convince Gina to attend the Hollister family reunion at Hill River. Gina finally agreed, wondering why her mother wanted to go to the reunion in the first place.

It's not as if Mom's still a Hollister, even though she did keep calling herself Lucille Hollister after the divorce. Gina still hadn't met the man in her mother's life, didn't know so much as his name, but Mom vowed to introduce them before the reunion.

STEVE SAT beside Caleb in his private sitting room, trying to relax, trying not to worry about what might be coming next on the television screen. A pastor stepped up to the podium.

"Hello," he said to the television audience. "I'm Pastor Joe Slone. Ready from some strong teaching?"

Everybody in the audience clapped, including Caleb. Steve questioned why he was still sitting there. And yet he didn't want to leave.

"Imagine a long sheet of paper," Pastor Slone said. "And on the top right of the sheet, write the word *eternity*." He nodded. "Yes, I said eternity. And under the word eternity, put a dot."

The pastor waited as if people were actually doing as he asked them to do in the physical realm.

"Now on the top left of your imaginary sheet of paper, write your name." He hesitated. "I'll give you a moment to do it. By the way your name here represents your time on earth." He paused again. "Okay. Now put a dot under your name."

Imagine this, imagine that. What was this guy doing, playing mind games?

"Now at the top right of your imaginary sheet of paper, put your imaginary pens on the dot below the word eternity." He grew silent again. "Ready? Okay. From the dot draw a line to the bottom of the page." He waited a moment before speaking again. "The line you just drew doesn't end at the bottom of the page. It continues to our sun and keeps going, out of our solar system, out of our galaxy. And even then it doesn't stop moving. It never stops!"

His pause was longer than any of the previous ones. Steve wondered if he ever intended to speak again.

"Look back at the top of the page," the pastor finally said. "You have your name and the word eternity. Our lives on earth are smaller than the smallest speck. Yet eternity is forever. Where do you want spend eternity—in heaven with God the Father ...or that other place?"

He closed his eyes. Steve though he might be praying.

"I have one more thing to say," Pastor Slone explained, "and here it is." His eyes opened. "Adam and Eve sinned in the Garden of Eden, and we are all their descendants. All of us are *born* of Adam and Eve. But now we must be born from above. We must be *born again*."

Steve was moved. He didn't know what just happened, but he knew it was important.

Later on the drive home, he couldn't remember Caleb turning off the television or what they ate for lunch. But he remembered the long sheet of imaginary paper and what he learned from the pastor behind the podium.

ON A SATURDAY MORNING in early September, Gina put on a sleeveless blue dress and drove to San Antonio. A letter from Steve came on Friday, but she'd promised herself she wouldn't open it.

She arrived in San Antonio shortly before ten. Her mother had already prepared picnic lunches for three. *Three? Is Mother's dream man planning to attend the Hollister family reunion?*

"We can leave as soon as he arrives," her mother said.

"Do you realize I still don't know who *he* is?"

A loud knock caused her mother to practically jump out of her chair. "That must be him."

Gina noted a flash of panic in her mother's eyes when she said those words. "Let me get it." She rose from the couch. "I'm dying to see this guy." She opened the door and felt her eyes widen. "Daddy, what are you doing here?"

His quick smile was edged in doubt. "I was …I was invited."

Gina glanced back at her mother, and the truth hit her. "Daddy's Mr. Wonderful?"

Lucille Hollister nodded, dropping her eyes momentarily as a flush popped out on her cheeks.

Tip Hollister went over and stood at Lucille's side, circling her with his arms.

"I'm sorry, Gina," her mother said. "I should have told you about this ages ago."

"You certainly should have." Gina slammed the front door and marched into the kitchen.

"Gina, wait," her father called after her.

She dipped her thumb and forefinger into the fruit salad, pulled out a fresh grape, and popped it into her mouth. Juice ran down her lower lip. She wiped it away, first with her tongue and then with the back of her hand.

Her back to the doorway, she pictured her father coming up behind her. Then his big hands seized her shoulders from behind.

"I love you, Gina. And I love your mother, too. I always have."

Ignoring him Gina fished for another grape.

"I mean it, honey."

"And I love your father," her mother tacked on as she came up to join them.

"How sweet." Gina whirled around and glared at her father. "But who's going to comfort Mom when you take off again?"

A look of regret covered his face "I should never have left in the first place. I was miserable."

"You say it now, but actions speak louder than words."

"I deserved that," he said softly.

"Like most young couples," Lucille put in, "we both had false expectations when we were first married. I thought your father was Prince Charming."

"I thought your mother was Cinderella," her dad added. "I've been going to a counselor at your mother's church in San Antonio, Gina, and I've learned the hard way nobody's perfect, least of all me." He winked at Lucille. "I love your mother ... exactly the way she is."

"Ditto to what he said," Lucille added.

"So now you want to waltz back into our lives like nothing happened?" Gina asked.

"I'd like to come back all right," he said softly. "But it's up to you, Gina."

"What do I have to do with it?"

"Your mother and I want us to be a family again, but if it can't happen, I'll disappear."

The flash of pain in her father's eyes jarred something hard in the center of her being. A sort of chain reaction resulted, a reaction Gina seemed to have no control over. But she knew it came from God. The cold part of her heart melted ever so slightly, as an inner strength and a spirit of forgiveness swept through her. Her daddy's doubtful smile turned tender, and he reached for her.

In one swooping instant of restoration, the three of them began to cry and hug each other.

"I'm sorry."

All three voices blended together. Gina had no idea who said it first.

*T*hirty minutes later Gina was back in the car and on her way to Hill River, Texas. Her father's pickup was one car behind her. When had Daddy switched from fancy cars to pickup trucks? *He really has changed.* Earlier when they stopped to fuel both vehicles, she'd seen her mother snuggle close to her father in the front seat of his truck. At last they were a couple again. And the three of them were a family.

After another thoughtful moment Gina turned on the car radio. "Ever burned your finger or maybe your entire hand?" the guy on the radio asked. "Did you like the experience? If your answer is yes, you're gonna love hell."

Gina giggled.

"I'm J. F. Fenson, Pastor of Wildwood Church, here to warn you. If you don't want to burn in hell, you better *repent* of all your sins while the door to salvation is still open, forgive *everybody*, and get right with God. The door *will* close. But who knows when?"

Repent and forgive. A coincidence? She shook her head. No. This message came from the Kingdom of God, and she knew she needed to follow up on it.

SHORTLY AFTER THE NOON MEAL, Gina left her parents at the family reunion and got back in her car. She drove to the nearby building site on Bluebonnet Hill where the learning center would be located and got out of the car.

Since childhood she'd put all her efforts into making herself acceptable to others, trying harder and harder, and in many ways, she was successful. Nobody would call Dr. Hollister slow or downright retarded, but she knew self-esteem wasn't all she needed.

She'd forgiven her father and everybody else she could think of, including Amanda's grandmother, Lola Ford. But she still had one more person to forgive. She grew still for a moment, considering.

How could she forgive the silly young girl people called stupid? How could she forgive Gina Hollister?

Gina was her worse critic. It would be hard to forgive herself, harder than forgiving any of the others. She would need time to reach that mountain and deal with the issue—someday. All at once she sensed an urging deep inside, a desire to leave *someday* and walk into the now. Tomorrow might never come. Gina strolled up the hill to its highest point.

Good-bye, self-doubt; good-bye, flashbacks; good-bye, chains of dyslexia. It was time to forgive Gina Hollister for not being like everybody else. Besides she didn't want to be like everyone else anymore. She wanted to be like Jesus.

LATER GINA SAT under a tree at the top of the hill. Her thoughts returned to her parents. *Mom and Dad are getting remarried. What a blessing! Evidently love means romantic endings for some people, just not for everybody, and that's okay. Everything is okay. Now.*

The magic with Steve began right here on Bluebonnet Hill. She knew she'd never forget it, and she hadn't. Gina gazed at the cool, soothing water. Come spring the hill would be a sea of wildflowers. She wished Steve and Amanda could be here to see it. She shook her head. *It's not gonna happen.*

She and Steve were complete opposites. But so were her parents. Her mother and father now readily admitted their differences caused misunderstandings. But hadn't those same dissimilarities served as glue, keeping their love alive in spite of all the problems?

Gina wanted a husband who shared her faith. Steve could never be such a man. Yet she yearned for so much more now. She stood to her feet, determined to get on with her life.

Wait a minute. Was that Steve's van pulling up and parking next to her Buick at the bottom of the hill? She couldn't believe her eyes. He was climbing up the hill straight for her. Was she dreaming?

As he got closer she saw he had a big grin on his face and was carrying a large sack of some kind.

"What are you doing here?" she asked. She'd sounded abrupt and immediately regretted it. She forced a smile. "Hi, Steve."

"Hi, yourself."

"Are you here to buy the big lot next to mine? I remember you liked it, and it's still for sale as far as I know."

"No. I bought that lot several weeks ago. I came back to Texas to see you, Gina. How will you build the center without the rent-to-own agreement I gave you?"

"I ...I don't need it. I inherited a bundle from Aunt Rose."

"I thought your aunt died soon after we arrived in Colorado. Was there a delay in the reading of the will?"

"There was no delay. I knew I was her heir right after the funeral." She sent him an imploring glance. "I never meant to deceive you. I should have explained all this when it first happened. Can you forgive me?"

He cocked his head to one side. "You betcha. I'm into forgiveness myself now, big time."

I'm into forgiveness. What did he mean? What was he saying? She lifted her head and gazed up at him. "How did you know where to find me?"

"I wouldn't have if you hadn't shown me around the day we floated down the river in inner tubes. I stopped by the reunion. Your parents told me."

Steve sat down under her tree, and she joined him. He put his arm around her. "Netty told me she took you to my secret room in the tower, and you saw the painting of the little girl."

"Yes. And the portrait was beautiful," she said. "You're a wonderful artist. Is Myra the little girl in the painting?"

"No. Two little girls inspired the painting. One of them was named Virginia, the kid I helped when I was in college."

"Virginia? Really? Did you know my real name is Virginia? Gina's a nickname."

"I didn't at first, but I do now. I took another look at those contracts you signed, especially the rent-to-own agreement."

Gina gasped, overwhelmed by what he said. "Are you saying I'm the kid you've been talking about? I thought the kid was a boy."

He shook his head. "The child I helped was a young girl who reminded me of my sister."

"I didn't know you had a sister."

He glanced away. "She died in childhood."

A lump of sympathy hit her in the heart. "I'm so sorry."

Steve nodded. "Thank you." He didn't speak for a moment, but the hint of sadness in his eyes spoke volumes. "I was attending a junior college in Oklahoma when I met you for the first time. I was the substitute teacher at your elementary school but for only one day, and when I saw you being mistreated by your classmates, I had to step in and help.

"I missed the opportunity of helping my sister shortly before she died of a fever," he said. "Her name was Baylee. It was because of Baylee I turned the castle into a home for orphan children. I'd never helped anyone until I helped you. Helping you changed my life, gave me a second chance to do what's right."

"And your sister is the little girl in the painting?"

"Yes."

"This is amazing." She wanted to know more, but maybe now wasn't the time. "I was sure I knew you on the day we met in the parking lot, but I couldn't remember how or when. I kept trying to make a connection. I made all kinds of outlandish claims as to who you were. All wrong, of course."

She sighed. "I've made terrible mistakes," she went on. "I'm so sorry. Still I would never have guessed you were once my substitute P.E. teacher when I was in the fifth grade. But I should have known when those dimples of yours jumped out at me."

"You're not the only one who makes mistakes, Gina. I've made plenty. I guess you could say we're a couple of imperfect people like everyone else." He sent her a soul-searching gaze. "After you left I took another look at my life. And you were right about a lot of things."

"Are you saying Steve Bryson can be wrong?"

He grinned. "Yeah. That's what I'm saying."

"Shocking."

They both laughed.

"Take those colored overlays and games, for instance. They're not half bad. I mean they certainly work for Amanda. I loved the history lesson of yours—learned a couple of things, too, like the proper use of flatirons. By the way Amanda is waiting for you at her grandmother's house in Austin and dying to see you."

"I hoped you'd say that." She mentally hugged herself. "I can't believe all this."

"Believe it," he said, "because it's true. Your honesty in telling about your own learning problems and how you overcame them motivated Amanda beyond my wildest dreams. Now she plans to become a PhD someday and work with children, as you do. And she's already had two sessions with Dr. Larker."

"You're kidding."

"Nix, as Gretel would say. I'm serious."

"You?"

"I can be serious when I want to be."

Gina looked down at the plastic bag he was holding. She was itching to see inside, but she would never suggest he waste time opening it when there were so many serious things she wanted to discuss. For starters she wanted to say, "I love you, Steve." But a quick check on reality deemed the option unlikely.

He reached into the sack then and pulled out a loaf cake of some kind wrapped in clear plastic. One end of the wrapper was partly open. The scent of fresh gingerbread sweetened the air. Her mouth watered. Gingerbread castles and the knights who defended them played on the stage of her mind.

Steve broke the cake down the middle and handed Gina half of it. He took a bite. "I love the taste of gingerbread."

"Of course you do." Gina giggled. "It's why I called you the Gingerbread Man."

Steve laughed. "Thanks a lot," he said. "You know my life has never been better than at this moment. And I finally know what the special plan for my life is."

"You ...you do?" Gina asked.

"Yep." He winked. "Did you get the letter I sent you?"

Gina was already blushing when guilt overwhelmed her. She looked down. "I got the letter, but I haven't opened it yet."

"If you had you'd know why I'm here." Steve opened the bag again and removed an ordinary-looking wooden pipe, the kind tobacco smokers used. "You see I think it's time we got together, don't you?"

"What does any of this have to do with anything?" she asked. "And if you expect me to smoke that pipe, you're living in la-la land."

The laughter dancing in his eyes warmed his entire face. "I

thought we'd spend our honeymoon in Europe, if it's all right with you."

Europe? Honeymoon? Did I miss something? Or did he just ask me to be his wife?

She should have read the letter.

STEVE STUDIED GINA FOR A MOMENT. He'd know what to say if this was a business meeting. But how does a guy reveal what's on his heart to a Christian woman like Gina? He'd know what to do if the problem were merely her dyslexia. She was plenty smart. But she never read the letter. *If she had it sure would make telling about the recent changes in my life easier.* Gina knew nothing about the miracle, and he had no idea how to explain it.

"I wish you'd let me in on your little well-kept secret," Gina said. "I had no idea I meant anything to you."

"I would have told you, but you flew back to Texas before I could get the words out. But after you left I realized I can't live without you."

"Did you say what I think you said?"

"Yes," he said. "But I have a business to run. I want to marry you as soon as possible."

"Hold it, Steve. This train is moving way too fast for me. We need to slow down, stop the engine, and give this train time to change tracks. Those business partners of yours, waiting to drive through with a business deal, can wait."

"We don't need to wait. Bricot International owns a jet plane —several, in fact."

"So you can fly off into the sunset whenever you want?"

"Yes, but I'll want you right there in the plane with me, sitting beside me every time I leave."

He must have touched her heart in some way because tears were gathering at the edges of her eyes.

"I love you, Gina. I'm asking you to marry me. I'd like to hear your answer."

"I ...I can't."

"Can't? You mean you don't love me?"

"Yes, Steve, I love you. But I can never marry you. I'm a Bible thumper, remember? You're not."

Tears trickled down both her cheeks. He pulled a handkerchief from his pocket and handed it to her.

"And I thump harder now than when you met me in the parking lot." She sniffed. "I could never marry a man who doesn't share my faith in God."

"Well, you're looking at one of those Bible thumpers, right now."

She gasped. "Are you saying you share my faith?"

"Yes, and I'm about as devout as they get."

"Oh, Steve, this is like a beautiful—"

"Dream?"

"Yes." She wiped her eyes with his white handkerchief.

"I was a backslider, Gina, running from God, blaming Him for all my mistakes, failures, and yes, my sins. I was a genuine prodigal son." He shook his head. "I don't know. Maybe I was also what some call a lukewarm Christian because I only attended church services every once in a while. But I'm not that man anymore."

"Are you saying you're born again?"

"Absolutely." He grinned. "Care for a better explanation?"

"Yes! I'd love it, especially coming from you."

"How do you explain something like this?" He shrugged. "I don't even know how to start. All I know is God entered my life, and I'm a different person now. A kind of understanding covered me like a warm blanket, and I had the desire to repent of all my sins, forgive others, and turn my life over to the Lord. And I asked Him to come into my life and stay there forever like the guy I heard on television said to do. Does this mean I'm born again?"

Gina nodded, wiping her eyes again. "Oh, Steve, thank you for telling me this. It makes all the difference." She handed the handkerchief back. Then she took the pipe and the two pieces of gingerbread and put them back in the sack. She smiled. "God has given me the desires of my heart."

"Me, too." He still didn't know what was going on in that mind of hers, but he knew he loved her and always would. Nothing else mattered. "Will you marry me and let me take you to Germany on our honeymoon so we can visit German castles?" he asked. Without giving her time to answer, he said, "We'll need to make a stop in Belgium first, since I have another business meeting to take care of in Brussels. And speaking of castles we'll still have an apartment in the castle where all those kids I was telling you about will be living. Are these plans okay?"

"That's a definite yes," she said.

He wiped his brow with a flair for the dramatic.

"Oh, Steve, how could I have doubted you when you are so clearly my knight in shining armor?"

"So how 'bout if we get Amanda, your parents, and my mom, and we all fly back to Colorado in the corporate jet? We could squeeze in Nicole and Robert, too. And of course we'll also want Caleb and Bonny Cantu, Dr. Larker, and my household staff at the wedding." He grinned. "We could get married at the two-story house you like so much."

"I want to marry you, Steve, but not in Colorado. I'm a Texas girl. I've always dreamed of being a Bluebonnet Bride. I want us to marry here on Bluebonnet Hill in the spring when the wildflowers are in bloom."

"Spring?" Steve felt his eyebrows lift a notch. "I want us to get married now. I know you'll want a beautiful wedding, and I have connections. I can get you the best wedding out there in a week, two at the most."

He sent her the sweetest look he could muster. "I want us to marry as soon as possible, and husbands and wives must learn to compromise, right?" He winked with teasing overtones. "I heard somewhere compromise is a good tactic when seeking peace."

"So you were listening after all."

"I always listen to you," he said. "And if you can't become a Bluebonnet Bride, how about becoming a Bluebonnet Mom?"

"Steve!" Gina blushed. "What are you saying?"

"I'm making a gentlemanly offer of marriage, meaning we get married now in say … Austin. You build your center, including a nice apartment large enough for us and all the children we might one day have, right here on Bluebonnet Hill. And if we need to expand, the lot I bought should cover it. Then all future family reunions could be held on Bluebonnet Hill.

"Oh," he added, "that reminds me. Remember the piece of furniture you liked at the hotel in Colorado Springs, the one you call a hutch? Well, it's yours now." He hesitated. "What do you think? Is *this* a plan you can live with?"

"It's perfect. But I still have one more question to ask before this is a done deal."

He rolled his eyes in a comical way and then grinned. "Okay. Let's hear it."

She cleared her throat. "Did you ever at any time in your life consider becoming a mad scientist?"

"Nope." Steve laughed out loud. "I can honestly say I never did. But I'm sure mad about you."

Then he kissed her, and somehow he knew their love would last a lifetime.

"All fear is gone," Gina said. "God is our Savior, Lord, and King, and you're the keeper of my heart."

Steve nodded. "And now for the wedding."

Two weeks later, wearing a white lacy wedding gown, Gina stood beside Steve under an arch covered in bluebonnets. All their loved ones were there. Tycoons like Steve made the impossible possible, and they had already said their wedding vows. Dr. Larker pronounced them man and wife, and Steve didn't seem to mind at all.

Miracles happened. Who but someone like Steve knew bluebonnets could be flown in from indoor nurseries from around the world for celebrations like this in mid September, or that someone like Amanda's grandmother could change for the good? Gina almost fell out of her chair when Steve informed her Mrs. Ford insisted they have their backyard wedding at her lovely home in Austin.

The sweet scent of roses in Texas yellow blended with the brilliant blue of the imported wildflowers. Amanda and Nicole wore blue bonnets like the one Gina bought at the antique shop in Hill River. They were holding small bouquets of yellow roses, and their dresses were in a lighter shade of blue.

Gina held a bouquet of bluebonnets. Caleb and Drake Rather, wearing dark blue suits, stood up for Steve on the opposite side of the arch. How it all came together in two weeks was another miracle.

Dr. Larker cleared his throat. "You may kiss the bride."

Gina gazed at Amanda, wondering what she might say or do. She glanced at Steve, and he was studying Amanda's face, too.

Are we forgiven? she asked silently.

Her worries lasted only a moment. Amanda smiled, and all Gina's silent questions were answered ...with love and acceptance. Joy bubbled up from deep inside her heart. She and Amanda were not merely friends again but daughter and stepmother.

Steve took Gina in his arms and kissed her, and love overflowed between them, perhaps spilling over into the hearts of all the guests. And Gina knew she, Steve, and Amanda would see wildflowers again in the spring on Bluebonnet Hill. Bluebonnets would cover the pastures then and would be found hidden between the rocks and down by the river. She was already a Bluebonnet Bride. Come spring maybe she would also be a Bluebonnet Mom-to-be.

Steve kissed her again. Then she knew for sure.

ABOUT THE AUTHOR

Molly Noble Bull has published with Zondervan, Love Inspired, Barbour Publishing, and others. *Sanctuary*, her long historical, won the 2008 Gayle Wilson Award in the inspirational category and tied for first place in a second national contest for published authors that year. Later, the publisher went out of business, and Hartline Literary published *Sanctuary* under a new title, *The Secret Place*. Molly's Gothic historical, *Gatehaven*, won the Grand Prize in the 2013 Creation House Fiction Writing Contest. *When the Cowboy Rides Away* won the 2016 Texas Association of Authors contest in the Christian western category. Barbour Publishing published *The Secret Admirer Romance Collection* on May 1, 2017, and Molly's novella in that collection is titled "Too Many Secrets." *Cinderella Texas* and *The Secret Place* were published by Hartline's White Glove Publishing.

Learn more about Molly by visiting her website, www.mollynoblebull.com. You can follow Molly at Amazon here: http://bit.ly/mollynoblebull.

When the Cowboy Rides Away

Western Romance

Maggie Gallagher, twenty-one, runs the Gallagher Ranch in South Texas and has raised her little sister and orphaned nephew since her parents and older sister died. No wonder she can't find time for romance!

When the Cowboy Rides Away opens two years after Maggie loses her family members. Out for a ride with her sister, she discovers Alex Lancaster, a handsome cowboy, shot and seriously wounded, on her land. Kind-hearted and a Christian, Maggie nurses him back to health despite all her other chores.

How could she know that Alex has a secret that could break her heart?

Blue Plate Special

by Award-winning Author Susan Page Davis

Book One of the True Blue Mysteries Series

Campbell McBride drives to her father's house in Murray, Kentucky, dreading telling him she's lost her job as an English professor. Her father, private investigator Bill McBride, isn't there or at his office in town. His brash young employee, Nick Emerson, says Bill hasn't come in this morning, but he did call the night before with news that he had a new case.

When her dad doesn't show up by late afternoon, Campbell and Nick decide to follow up on a phone number he'd jotted on a memo sheet. They learn who last spoke to her father, but they also find a dead body.

The next day, Campbell files a missing persons report. When Bill's car is found, locked and empty in a secluded spot, she and Nick must get past their differences and work together to find him.

Books Afloat

Columbia River Undercurrents - Book One

Historical Romance

Blaming herself for her childhood role in the Oklahoma farm truck accident that cost her grandfather's life, Anne Mettles is determined to make her life count. She wants to do it all–captain her library boat and resist Japanese attacks to keep America safe. But failing her pilot's exam requires her to bring others onboard.

Will she go it alone? Or will she team with the unlikely but (mostly) lovable characters? One is a saboteur, one an unlikely hero, and one, she discovers, is the man of her dreams.

Stay up-to-date on your favorite books and authors with our free e-newsletters.

ScriveningsPress.com

www.ingramcontent.com/pod-product-compliance
Lightning Source LLC
Chambersburg PA
CBHW070627100726
47907CB00007B/1890